PENGUIN ⬤ CLASSICS

THÉRÈSE RAQUIN

ÉMILE ZOLA, born in Paris in 1840, was brought up in Aix-en-Provence in an atmosphere of struggling poverty after the death of his father in 1847. He was educated at the Collège Bourbon at Aix and then at the Lycée Saint-Louis in Paris. After failing the *baccalauréat* twice and then taking menial clerical employment, he joined the newly founded publishing house Hachette in 1862 and quickly rose to become head of publicity. Having published his first novel in 1865 he left Hachette the following year to become a full-time journalist and writer. *Thérèse Raquin* appeared in 1867 and caused a scandal, to which he responded with his famous Preface to the novel's second edition in 1868 in which he laid claim to being a 'Naturalist'. That same year he began work on a series of novels intended to trace scientifically the effects of heredity and environment in one family: *Les Rougon-Macquart*. This great cycle eventually contained twenty novels, which appeared between 1871 and 1893. In 1877 the seventh of these, *L'Assommoir* (*The Drinking Den*), a study of alcoholism in working-class Paris, brought him abiding wealth and fame. On completion of the Rougon-Macquart series he began a new cycle of novels, *Les Trois Villes: Lourdes, Rome, Paris* (1894–8), a violent attack on the Church of Rome, which led to another cycle, *Les Quatre Évangiles*. While his later writing was less successful, he remained a celebrated figure on account of the Dreyfus case, in which his powerful interventions played an important part in redressing a heinous miscarriage of justice. His marriage in 1870 had remained childless, but his happy, public relationship in later life with Jeanne Rozerot, initially one of his domestic servants, brought him a son and a daughter. He died in mysterious circumstances in 1902, the victim of an accident or murder.

ROBIN BUSS is a writer and translator who works as a freelance journalist and as television critic for *The Times Educational Supplement*. He studied at the University of Paris, where he took a degree and doctorate in French literature. He is part-author of the article 'French Literature' in *Encyclopaedia Britannica* and has published critical studies of works by Vigny and Cocteau, and three books on European cinema, *The French through Their Films* (1988), *Italian Films* (1989) and *French Film Noir* (1994). He has translated a number of other volumes for Penguin, including Émile Zola's *L'Assommoir* and *Au Bonheur des Dames*.

ÉMILE ZOLA

Thérèse Raquin

*Translated with an Introduction
by* ROBIN BUSS

PENGUIN BOOKS

PENGUIN BOOKS

Published by the Penguin Group
Penguin Books Ltd, 80 Strand, London WC2R ORL, England
Penguin Group (USA) Inc., 375 Hudson Street, New York, New York 10014, USA
Penguin Books Australia Ltd, 250 Camberwell Road, Camberwell, Victoria 3124, Australia
Penguin Books Canada Ltd, 10 Alcorn Avenue, Toronto, Ontario, Canada M4V 3B2
Penguin Books India (P) Ltd, 11, Community Centre, Panchsheel Park, New Delhi – 110 017, India
Penguin Books (NZ) Ltd, Cnr Rosedale and Airborne Roads, Albany, Auckland, New Zealand
Penguin Books (South Africa) (Pty) Ltd, 24 Sturdee Avenue, Rosebank 2196, South Africa

Penguin Books Ltd, Registered Offices: 80 Strand, London WC2R ORL, England

www.penguin.com

First published 1867
This translation first published 2004

033

Translation and editorial matter copyright © Robin Buss, 2004
All rights reserved

The moral right of the translator has been asserted

Set in 10.25/12.25 pt PostScript Adobe Sabon
Typeset by Rowland Phototypesetting Ltd, Bury St Edmunds, Suffolk
Printed and bound in Great Britain by Clays Ltd, Elcograf S.p.A.

ISBN-13: 978-0-140-44944-0

www.greenpenguin.co.uk

Contents

Chronology

1840 2 April Émile Zola born in Paris, the son of an Italian engineer, Francesco Zola, and of Françoise-Emilie Aubert.

1843 The family moves to Aix-en-Provence, which will become the town of 'Plassans' in the Rougon-Macquart novels.

1847 Francesco Zola dies, leaving the family nearly destitute.

1848 The rule of King Louis-Philippe (the July Monarchy, which came to power in 1830) is overthrown and the Second Republic declared. Zola starts school. Karl Marx publishes *Manifesto of the Communist Party*.

1851 The Republic is dissolved after the *coup d'état* of Louis-Napoleon Bonaparte, who in the following year proclaims himself emperor as Napoleon III. Start of the Second Empire, the period that will provide the background for Zola's novels in the Rougon-Macquart cycle.

1852 Zola is enrolled at the Collège Bourbon, in Aix, where he starts a close friendship with the painter Paul Cézanne.

1858 The family moves back to Paris and Zola is sent to the Lycée Saint-Louis. His school career is undistinguished and he twice fails the *baccalauréat*.

1860 The start of a period of hardship as Zola tries to scrape a living by various kinds of work, while engaging in his first serious literary endeavours, mainly as a poet. These years saw the height of the rebuilding programme undertaken by Baron Haussmann, Prefect of Paris from 1853 to 1869, which is indirectly reflected in several of Zola's novels, including *Thérèse Raquin*.

1862 Zola joins the publisher Hachette, and in a few months becomes the firm's head of publicity.

1863 Makes his début as a journalist.

1864 Zola's first literary work, the collection of short stories, *Contes à Ninon*, appears.

1865 Publishes his first novel, *La Confession de Claude*. Meets his future wife, Gabrielle-Alexandrine Meley; they marry in 1870.

1866 Leaves Hachette. From now on, he lives by his writing.

1867 Publication of *Thérèse Raquin*, the story of how a lower-middle class woman and her lover kill her husband, but are afterwards consumed by guilt. In the Preface to the second edition (1868), Zola declares that he belongs to the literary school of 'Naturalism'.

1868-9 Zola develops the outline of his great novel-cycle, *Les Rougon-Macquart*, which he subtitles 'The Natural and Social History of a Family under the Second Empire'. It is founded on the latest theories of heredity. He signs a contract for the work with the publisher Lacroix.

1870 The outbreak of the Franco-Prussian War leads in September to the fall of the Second Empire. Napoleon III and Empress Eugénie go into exile in England and the Third Republic is declared. Paris is besieged by Prussian forces. *La Fortune des Rougon* starts to appear in serial form.

1871 Publication in book form of *La Fortune des Rougon*, the first novel in the Rougon-Macquart cycle. After the armistice with Prussia, a popular uprising in March threatens the overthrow of the government of Adolphe Thiers, which flees to Versailles. The radical Paris Commune takes power until its bloody repression by Thiers in May; the events would have great importance for the Socialist Left. Zola was shocked both by the anarchy of the Commune and by the savagery with which it was repressed.

1872 Publication of *La Curée*, the second of the Rougon-Macquart novels. Part of it had appeared in serialized form (September–November 1871), but publication had been suspended by the censorship authorities.

1873 Publication of *Le Ventre de Paris*, the third of the cycle, set in and around the market of Les Halles.

1874 Publication of *La Conquête de Plassans*.

1875 Publication of *La Faute de l'Abbé Mouret*.

1876 *Son Excellence Eugène Rougon* follows the career of a minister under the Second Empire. Later in the same year, the seventh of the Rougon-Macquart novels, *L'Assommoir* (*The Drinking Den*), begins to appear in serial form and immediately causes a sensation with its grim depiction of the ravages of alcoholism and life in the Parisian slums.

1877 *L'Assommoir* is published in book form and becomes a bestseller. Zola's fortune is made and he is recognized as the leading figure in the Naturalist movement.

1878 Zola follows the harsh realism of *L'Assommoir* with a gentler tale of domestic life, *Une page d'amour*. Buys a house at Médan.

1879 *Nana* appears in serial form, before publication in book form in the following year. The story of a high-class prostitute, the novel was to attract further scandal to Zola's name.

1880 Publication of *Les Soirées de Médan*, an anthology of short stories by Zola and some of his Naturalist 'disciples', including Maupassant. Zola expounds the theory of Naturalism in *Le Roman expérimental*. In May, Zola's literary mentor, the writer Gustave Flaubert, dies; in October, Zola loses his much-loved mother. A period of depression follows and he suspends writing the Rougon-Macquart for a year.

1882 Zola's next book, *Pot-Bouille*, centres on an apartment house and the character of the bourgeois seducer, Octave Mouret. The novel analyses the hypocrisy of the respectable middle class.

1883 Mouret reappears in *Au Bonheur des Dames*, which studies the phenomenon of the department store.

1884 *La Joie de vivre*. Towards the end of the year, *Germinal* starts to appear in serial form and is published in book form the next year. Set in a northern French mining community, this powerful novel is Zola's most politically committed fictional work.

1886 *L'Œuvre* provides a revealing insight into Parisian artistic and literary life, as well as a reflection of contemporary aesthetic debates, drawing on Zola's friendship with many leading painters and writers. However, Cézanne reacts badly to Zola's portrait of him in the novel, and ends their friendship.

1887 *La Terre*, a brutally frank portrayal of peasant life, causes a fresh uproar and leads to a crisis in the Naturalist movement when five 'disciples' of Zola sign a manifesto against the novel.

1888 Publication of *Le Rêve*. Zola begins his liaison with Jeanne Rozerot, the mistress with whom he will have two children.

1890 *La Bête humaine*, the story of a pathological killer, is set against the background of the railways. Though not the best novel in the cycle, it is to be one of the most popular.

1891 *L'Argent* examines the world of the Stock Exchange.

1892 *La Débâcle* analyses the French defeat in the Franco-Prussian War and the end of the Second Empire.

1893 The final novel in the cycle, *Le Docteur Pascal*, develops the theories of heredity which have guided *Les Rougon-Macquart*.

1894 With *Lourdes*, Zola starts a trilogy of novels, to be completed by *Rome* (1896) and *Paris* (1898), about a priest who turns away from Catholicism towards a more humanitarian creed. In December, a Jewish officer in the French Army, Captain Alfred Dreyfus, is found guilty of spying for Germany and sentenced to life imprisonment in the penal colony on Devil's Island, off the coast of French Guiana.

1897 New evidence in the case suggests that Dreyfus's conviction was a gross miscarriage of justice, inspired by anti-Semitism. Zola publishes three articles in *Le Figaro* demanding a retrial.

1898 Zola's open letter, *J'Accuse*, in support of Dreyfus, addressed to Félix Faure, President of the Republic, is published in *L'Aurore* (13 January). It proves a turning-point, making the case a litmus test in French politics: for years to come, being pro- or anti-Dreyfusard will be a major component of a French person's ideological profile (with the nationalist Right leading the campaign against Dreyfus). Zola is tried for libel and sentenced to a year's imprisonment and a fine of 3,000 francs. In July, waiting for a retrial (granted on a technicality), he leaves for London, where he spends a year in exile.

1899 Zola begins a series of four novels, *Les Quatre Évangiles*, which would remain uncompleted at his death. They mark his transition from Naturalism to a more idealistic and utopian view of the world.

1902 29 September Zola is asphyxiated by the fumes from the blocked chimney of his bedroom stove, perhaps by accident, perhaps (as is still widely believed) assassinated by anti-Dreyfusards. On 5 October his funeral in Paris is witnessed by a crowd of 50,000. His remains were transferred to the Panthéon in 1908.

Introduction

*(New readers are advised that this Introduction makes
the details of the plot explicit.)*

Thérèse Raquin is the only one of Émile Zola's works outside
his novel-cycle *Les Rougon-Macquart* and his polemic *J'Accuse*
that is widely read. Indeed, with a few individual works from
that twenty-volume cycle, it represents the height of his achieve-
ment as a novelist. Published in 1867, when Zola was only
twenty-seven, it was not his first work of fiction, but it is the
book that established his reputation as one of the outstanding
novelists of the younger generation. Denounced by the critic of
Le Figaro as 'putrid', 'a pool of filth and blood',[1] it achieved a
notoriety that would pursue Zola throughout his life and, at the
same time, established the 'experimental' method that he would
apply in the twenty volumes of *Les Rougon-Macquart*. We can
say, with his biographer Henri Mitterand, that 'Zola's career as
a novelist only really begins with *Thérèse Raquin*.'[2]

The novel does, however, differ from the later works in some
important respects. *Les Rougon-Macquart* was a hugely ambitious project, designed (according to its subtitle) to constitute
'The Natural and Social History of a Family under the Second
Empire'.[3] The individual volumes in the cycle centre on a particular aspect of life in that period: provincial and national
politics (*La Fortune des Rougon, Son Excellence Eugène Rougon*); the Parisian working class (*Le Ventre de Paris, L'Assommoir*); the industrial working class (*Germinal*); the peasantry
(*La Terre*); and so on. Entering into these different milieux is
part of the pleasure of reading Zola, and he supported the
fictional narrative with extensive documentary research – into
life in a large department store, for example, when writing *Au
Bonheur des Dames*, or among workers on the railway, for *La*

Bête humaine. Behind the chief protagonists in all these novels, one is aware of a host of minor figures and, beyond them, of the crowd: the crowd in the Parisian streets and markets, the shoppers in the department store, the miners, politicians, priests, soldiers, stockbrokers, workers and peasants who populate the background of the picture.

This is not the case in *Thérèse Raquin*. Here is a tale of adultery, murder and madness, set mainly in a single location and with a cast of four leading characters and four minor ones (five, if we count the cat, François). Only during the scenes on the river (Chapters XI and XII) and in the Morgue (Chapter XIII) does one have any sense of other people moving around in the background; only very exceptionally does the writer introduce another character with a speaking part, like the painter who makes a fleeting appearance in Chapter XXV. For the rest of the time, he concentrates our attention on Thérèse, Camille, Laurent and Madame Raquin, with occasional appearances by the group of guests who visit them every Thursday: Grivet, the Michauds, father and son, the son's wife, Suzanne; and, of course, by the cat. In the forefront of this picture is Thérèse, the half-Arab orphan who is abandoned by her father to be brought up by her aunt, the haberdasher, Madame Raquin. Thérèse has to compete for her aunt's affections with her cousin, Madame Raquin's sickly son, Camille. It is an uneven struggle. Camille gets all the attention, while Thérèse learns to hold in her frustration and resentment, her natural energy and health smothered by the possessive mother and feeble son. When the time comes, she accepts marriage to Camille for want of anything better and prepares for a life of endless Thursday evenings playing dominoes in the company of Madame Raquin's friends: the former policeman, Michaud, and his son, and the railway clerk, Grivet. The stage is set for a tragedy that will be set off by the arrival of Camille's friend Laurent, a sturdy lad, self-indulgent and unscrupulous, who releases the full force of Thérèse's passionate nature – under the watchful eye of François, the cat.

The novel is intentionally claustrophobic. *Thérèse Raquin* is a chamber piece, a melodrama, a horror story about two murderers who descend into madness, haunted by the shade of their victim and observed eventually by a paralysed woman, who cannot move or speak, but has to listen and watch as they disintegrate in front of her. We are meant to share her feeling of powerlessness and revulsion. We are fascinated spectators of what happens to Thérèse and Laurent, alongside the stricken Madame Raquin – and the equally mute and eloquent cat.

The significance of the cat can be overestimated. After all, the beast does little in the book except what cats do in real life. It hangs around and watches quietly, as its human owners get on with their lives. But Laurent, in his folly, attributes to the cat supernatural powers of understanding and judgement: when he and Thérèse start their affair, the cat seems to be watching them with disapproval; after the murder, it seems to know what has happened to Camille. Perhaps we make a mistake similar to Laurent's when we think that the cat plays a significant role in the novel. Perhaps the animal is purely for decoration, but few critics would think so. They have often compared François to the cat in Manet's painting *Olympia* (exhibited in 1865). From here, they have gone on to see him as a symbol of female sexuality, a 'familiar' or demon, and (like Laurent) as the reincarnation of the dead Camille.[4] He could be any or all of these things. A modern psychoanalyst might even wish to read something into the fact that the cat has the same name as Zola's father, François (Francesco), who died when Zola was barely seven years old. But the attention critics have paid to François the cat comes more from a desire to link Zola's novel to Manet's painting, because of what one knows to be Manet's role in Zola's intellectual life at the time: 'We will see Olympia's cat in Thérèse Raquin's bedroom,' says Henri Mitterand.[5] The presence of this knowing cat in Manet's painting and in Zola's novel provides a peg on which to hang the assertion of the artist's importance to the novelist's work.

However, this focus on the cat implies some immediate connection, as though one were suggesting that Zola might have seen Manet's painting in the Salon of 1865 and thought: 'Ah! I can use that cat!' This may, indeed, have been the case, but in itself the transfer of the cat to the novel is purely trivial, whereas we know that, in fact, the study of Manet and other painters was of crucial importance to Zola's thought and to his development as a writer. Rather than influences, in the narrow sense, it is better to think in terms of the aesthetic climate in which Zola was working, at a formative moment in his life and a time of great intellectual excitement. The constituents of that environment can be summed up under the heading of four names: Paris; Édouard Manet; Honoré de Balzac; and Claude Bernard.

Paris is where Émile Zola was born, the son of a civil engineer; but when he was three years old the family moved south, to Aix-en-Provence, because his father was to work on building what is now called the Canal Zola. Then, in April 1847, the father, François Zola, died suddenly of pneumonia, caught apparently during a coach journey to Marseille. Émile and his mother stayed on in Aix, where from 1852 he boarded at the Collège Bourbon. One of his fellow pupils and close friends (among a collection of otherwise rather unsympathetic schoolmates) was the painter Paul Cézanne.

François Zola had left a complicated financial legacy, and his wife, Emilie, was to spend many years in an unsuccessful battle to retrieve a share of the capital of the canal company from François's main backer, the politician Jules Migeon. It was in order to further this suit that she eventually settled in Paris, leaving her son at school and, in the holidays, with his grandparents in Aix. Then, in February 1858, after the death of her own mother, Emilie called on Émile to join her. At the age of seventeen he returned to the capital to finish his studies at the Lycée Saint-Louis.

The young Zola must have felt a great sense of excitement and new horizons at this return to Paris from the provinces, though for many years his life in the capital was to be hard. Emilie failed to obtain any money from her lawsuit and her husband's estate. Émile fell ill and left the *lycée* without passing his *baccalauréat*, and for two years he was obliged to earn a living by taking menial clerical jobs, until he joined the dispatch department of the publishing firm Hachette in March 1862. At the same time, he was reading and writing voraciously. He even considered becoming one of the many writers employed by the prolific Alexandre Dumas, but when he made inquiries, he found that Dumas was not recruiting ghosts for the moment.

At the same time, during these years of penury, he was discovering Paris. He was a keen *flâneur* (if one can be keen about strolling) and wandered around the city in the heyday of the Second Empire, at a time when it was being transformed by the efforts of Baron Haussmann. Haussmann, Prefect of Paris, was responsible for the major programme of rebuilding between 1853 and 1869, which destroyed many remnants of the medieval city, putting in their place the broad avenues of the grand boulevards and other characteristic features of modern Paris. Many other buildings, including most of those mentioned in *Thérèse Raquin*, were being pulled down and rebuilt at the time. This city in transition forms the background to many of Zola's novels in *Les Rougon-Macquart*.

The city has a less obvious, but still important, role in this earlier novel. The Paris of *Thérèse Raquin* is not the Paris of high society, finance, politics or business. Nor is it precisely the working-class Paris of *L'Assommoir* (*The Drinking Den*). Its characters all come from the lower-middle classes: junior civil servants, officials, clerks and shopkeepers. The city in which they live is not the glamorous Paris of the boulevards, the Opéra and the tourist sights (though they may walk along the Champs-Élysées on a Sunday); theirs is the Paris of dingy backstreets and dank, ill-lit premises; of railway offices; of the Morgue.

Above all, it is the Paris of the Seine. The river is constantly present. It passes only a few steps from the Passage du Pont-Neuf, where Thérèse and Mme Raquin live; they have moved here from the little Norman town of Vernon, which also lies on the Seine, about fifty-five kilometres downriver from Paris. Laurent comes from the village of Jeufosse, built around an island in the river, between Vernon and Mantes-la-Jolie. Camille and Laurent work for the Orléans Railway Company, which had its headquarters in the Gare d'Orléans, right beside the Quai d'Austerlitz (it is now known as the Gare d'Austerlitz).

Camille is drowned at Saint-Ouen, on that wide meander of the Seine to the north-west of Paris, and his body ends up in the Morgue, on the Quai de l'Archevêché, on the tip of the Île de la Cité. Of this novel, if of any, it could be said that a river runs through it.

The Seine, however, is not just any watercourse; it is the main artery of Paris. The city, like all large cities during the nineteenth century, had come to be seen not only as a place of culture and civilized society, or even as a place of opportunity (the role that Balzac eventually gives it in *Le Père Goriot*), but also increasingly as a site of poverty, misery, loneliness, alienation, crime, vice and degradation. The young Zola had experienced the excitement of arriving in Paris as an ambitious young poet with the future ahead of him, but he had also experienced disappointment and poverty. He had known the bohemian Paris where he had his first sexual experience and lived with his first mistress. He had seen the filth and cold of the city, witnessed what it could do to those who failed, and sensed the terrible realities hidden in its meaner streets. This, too, was exciting, the stuff of literature, whether in the poems of Baudelaire or the popular novels of Eugène Sue.

The river in *Thérèse Raquin* has several faces, but they are mainly sinister or, at least, negative ones. At Vernon, Mme Raquin has a garden that goes right down to the Seine where Thérèse likes to lie in the grass, thinking of nothing; but even here she fantasizes that the river is about to rise up and engulf her. Camille enjoys strolling beside the river on his way to and from work, watching it flow and, like Thérèse, has no thoughts in his head; but the river is not to be lucky for him. After the murder, Laurent sees dreadful visions in the Seine at night, though he later finds a moment of peace strolling along the *quais*, momentarily forgetting his crime . . .

The river, linking the places and people in the book, has a symbolic function, as do so many inanimate objects in Zola's work. One can also read it as a mythical place, the river Lethe, river of oblivion and death; or see it as a figure for the unconscious, for dark desires and for the terrors of the mind. Zola himself, like Laurent, lived for a while in the Rue Saint-Victor, a few minutes' walk from the *quais*, he worked briefly for the Compagnie des Docks, he spent summer afternoons lazing on the water at Vitry. He must often have walked along the banks of the Seine, especially at times when he was unemployed, staring into the river, as his characters do in *Thérèse Raquin*.

The Seine, as it flowed through the peaceful landscape of northern France, had an increasing appeal for writers and artists. Among the latter, the trend was towards subjects taken from everyday life, landscapes painted (or at least sketched) in the open and scenes of simple people engaged in ordinary activities: the peasants of Jean-François Millet's *L'Angélus* (1859), for example. Millet spent much of his life in the Norman riverside village of Barbizon, which gave its name to a school of painting dedicated to the countryside and the open air.

Zola had come to Paris from Aix with instructions from his school friend Paul Cézanne to report back on the art scene in the capital, and this he did, giving an account of the Salon of 1859, the biennial exhibition sponsored by the Académie des Beaux-Arts and the official showcase for new work in the visual arts. Already, the Salon was starting to reflect conflicts between different trends, and it was turned into a battleground with the arrival of the Impressionists in the 1860s, though the seeds of these upheavals were sown in 1859, when works submitted by Manet and Whistler were rejected by the Académie.

In 1861, a painting by Pissarro was also rejected by the Salon committee, and protests from the younger painters grew. The emperor, Napoleon III, demanded that for the following exhibition, in 1863, the painters who had been rejected by the Académie should be allowed to exhibit their works in another part of the Palais de l'Industrie, in what became known as the Salon des Refusés. It was at the first of these that Édouard Manet exhibited his pastoral scene *Le Déjeuner sur l'herbe*, which showed two young students, fully clothed in modern dress, apparently enjoying a picnic beside a naked woman, with another bathing in the river behind them. The Empress Eugénie was shocked by this canvas and it caused a scandal.

Zola wrote a passionate defence of *Le Déjeuner sur l'herbe* and Manet's other outrageous painting, *Olympia* (the one with the cat). As Robert Lethbridge argues, Zola may have seen Manet's notoriety as a means to establish his own name, even though Manet himself may have had doubts about 'such blatant exercises in publicity'.[6] He would become an acquaintance of Manet, of Pissarro and of other writers and painters. In late 1867, Zola sat for a portrait by Manet, which was exhibited in the Salon in 1868. He would later record the artistic life of the 1860s and the struggle of the Impressionists in one of the novels of *Les Rougon-Macquart*, *L'Œuvre* (1886). Outside literature, painting was the art that interested him most. He often referred to Manet as a 'Naturalist' painter, using the word to associate the new, anti-Romantic movement in art with his own practice in literature.

This connection with the world of the plastic arts is reflected in various ways and at different levels in *Thérèse Raquin*. The most overt link is the character of Laurent, a young peasant who has come up to Paris and wants to be an artist, not because he is driven by any particular urge to paint, but because he thinks that a painter's life will be 'a jolly business, not too tiring', and allow him to 'smoke and lark around all day long' (Chapter V). Zola's description of Laurent's paintings, in particular the portrait of Camille, shows how futile this approach is, and this gives the writer an opportunity to describe what painting should not be: Laurent's technique is 'stiff, dry, like a parody of the primitive masters', he is hesitant and he paints 'with the tips of the brushes . . . making short, tight hatching strokes, as he might when using a pencil' (Chapter VI). Ironically, it is only in a state of nervous collapse following Camille's murder that Laurent discovers a real talent for painting – evidence of Zola's belief in the relation between neurosis and artistic creation.

Particular paintings may have directly inspired some of the scenes in the novel: *Le Déjeuner sur l'herbe* could well have been in Zola's mind as he described Thérèse, Laurent and Camille in Saint-Ouen finding a shady spot with a carpet of green where the 'fallen leaves lay on the ground in a reddish layer', while the 'tree trunks were standing upright, numberless, like clusters of Gothic columns, and the branches dipped right down to their foreheads, so that their only horizon was the bronze vault of dying leaves and the black-and-white shafts of the aspens and oaks', making 'a melancholy pit in the silence and cool of a narrow clearing' (Chapter XI). And the image of the dead girl whom Laurent sees in the Morgue, her 'fresh, plump body ... paling with very delicate variations of tint ... half smiling, her head slightly to one side, offering her bosom in a provocative manner' with 'a black stripe on her neck, like a necklace of shadow' (Chapter XIII), was probably suggested by Manet's Olympia, who has a black velvet choker round her neck. In each case, though, if Zola has borrowed from Manet, he has transposed the meaning of the work, giving it a more sinister significance that fits his purpose in the novel.

In any case, it is not necessary to find such direct correspondences between particular paintings and passages in the novel to be aware of the influence of painting on the author. Contemporary critics talked about the 'painterly' qualities of his writing. His descriptions are carefully composed, with a strong sense of colour. In *Thérèse Raquin*, in fact, he uses a palette of dark colours and half-tones to convey a strong sense of chiaroscuro. The adjectives 'yellow' and 'yellowish' occur with particular frequency, as do 'greenish', 'bluish', etc., in settings that are dark, dingy and gloomy. Apart from which, Zola's mind was so imbued with ideas about painting that they influence his whole aesthetic: he wanted to do in literature what painters do on canvas: to represent the reality of nature without mere imitation of nature, discovering its poetic truth and the individual essence of the person creating the work.

Thérèse Raquin was not Zola's first published work; it came after a rather long literary apprenticeship and an extended reflection on the nature of literature and the tasks of the writer. His first book, which appeared in 1864, was a collection of Provençal stories, the *Contes à Ninon*. In the following year, he published the semi-autobiographical *La Confession de Claude*, and this was followed in 1866 by the short novel *Le Vœu d'une morte*, a story of love and devotion. He even wrote a serial novel in the manner of Eugène Sue, *Les Mystères de Marseille*, which he later dismissed as merely a pot-boiler (though Henri Mitterand and others have found it interesting and pointed out how much time and effort Zola devoted to the work). He was a prolific journalist, a literary and art critic, and the author of an important manifesto, 'Two Definitions of the Modern Novel', a paper which he sent to the Congrès scientifique de France, held in Aix-en-Provence in December 1866.

He was also reading a good deal, going to the theatre, visiting exhibitions, talking to a widening circle of friends – all of which helped to define what he saw as the current situation of literature and the writer's task. Zola had read with interest the exiled Victor Hugo's essay on literary genius, *William Shakespeare* (1864). The 1860s saw a continuing reaction against Romanticism in literature, with the publication in 1866 of the first volume of *Le Parnasse contemporain*, an anthology of poetry including work by Paul Verlaine, Leconte de Lisle and Stéphane Mallarmé: Zola was to make fun of these Parnassians a couple of years later in an article for *L'Événement illustré*; he was no longer greatly interested in poetry, despite his schoolboy efforts at writing verse.

His chief concern was the novel, a form that carried less prestige than poetry, but had a much wider appeal to an increasingly literate public. If it was to establish and retain its status as a major literary form, it would have to demonstrate that it was not merely frivolous entertainment, but a literary art, offering at the same time a means to analyse human psychology and human society. The historical novel, popular in the earlier years of the century, had revealed new possibilities for the genre as an analytical tool, and Balzac had shown how fiction could use an imaginative construct to explore the workings of society in the novels of *La Comédie humaine*.

Zola greatly admired Balzac, whom he discovered only in the mid 1860s: he praised in particular Balzac's ability 'to see both the inside and the outside of contemporary society'.[7] Eventually, *Les Rougon-Macquart* would be an enterprise comparable to Balzac's, doing for the Second Empire what *La Comédie humaine* had done for the Restoration: the opening of *Thérèse Raquin*, carefully situating the coming action with its description of the Passage du Pont-Neuf, has a decidedly 'Balzacian' feel, recalling the scene-setting first pages of novels such as *Le Père Goriot* and *César Birotteau*. The aim is to establish a realistic environment in which the characters can develop, both as individuals and as representatives of their class and time.

The break with the fantastic story-telling of the Romantics and, at the same time, with the popular novel of adventure and melodrama, was most decisively made by the novelist whom Zola would come to admire most among his contemporaries: Gustave Flaubert. Flaubert's *Madame Bovary* had been published in book form in 1857, but was already the subject of a prosecution for obscenity and blasphemy when it appeared as a serial in the previous year (charges on which Flaubert was acquitted). Zola would soon be able to sympathize with Flaubert's predicament – and also to appreciate how useful a sensational controversy could be for the sales of a novel and the fame of its author. Throughout his life, he was happy to attract controversy and to exploit his reputation for scandal.

Zola came late to Flaubert's masterpiece, as he had done to Balzac, not reading *Madame Bovary* until the mid 1860s; but it made an enormous impression. The story of the adulterous doctor's wife, who dreams of romance and commits suicide after an unhappy love affair, was important to him on many counts, including as an analysis of the tedium of contemporary provincial society and as an exercise in style. Flaubert's method was as far removed as one could imagine from that of prolific popular novelists such as Alexandre Dumas or Eugène Sue: he honed every word, he wrote and rewrote tirelessly, he had an almost religious veneration for his art and he aimed as far as possible to remove the artist from his work. The writer was to be a recorder of reality who shrank from nothing: the description of Emma Bovary's death from poisoning makes no concessions to the sensibilities of the susceptible reader; nor does it, on the other hand, indulge in the horror for its own sake. The writer merely observes and refuses to turn away. Flaubert, for Zola, was 'the pioneer of the century, the painter and philosopher of our modern world'.[8]

Flaubert's immediate imitators included the brothers Edmond

and Jules Goncourt, now remembered chiefly as the authors of a literary journal. In 1864, they published their fifth novel, *Germinie Lacerteux*, the story of a servant girl's descent into alcoholism, degradation and hysteria. The writers' brief Preface – 'the public likes false novels, this is a true one' – became a manifesto of Naturalism. They began by proclaiming that, in a democratic age, the 'lower orders' deserved to be the subject of a novel, and that the novel, as a genre, was now 'the great, serious, passionate and vital form of literary study and social inquiry', having taken upon itself 'the studies and duties of science'. The Goncourts were aware of the influence of their method and subject matter on Zola, their younger contemporary, whom they referred to in a rather proprietorial manner as 'our admirer and our pupil'.[9]

Even when literary and artistic Romanticism was at its height in France, in the 1820s and 1830s, there had been critics who saw it as a futile reaction against an age that was becoming increasingly scientific and utilitarian. 'The idea of beauty presided over the civilization of Antiquity; modern society is increasingly dominated by those of truth, justice and utility,' one wrote in the *Revue encyclopédique* in 1828,[10] and this argument helped to explain the social alienation of the Byronic outsider. Zola was to use a similar contrast between the novel in Antiquity ('a pleasant lie, a tissue of wonderful adventures') and the modern novel, adapted to the 'scientific and methodical tendencies of the modern world'.[11] Balzac, in his Preface to the *Comédie humaine*, had put forward the idea of the novelist as a kind of natural scientist, classifying society in much the same way as Buffon[12] had classified the natural world: 'there will always be social species as there are zoological species'.

The image that Zola uses most frequently is not the Balzacian one of the Naturalist, but that of the surgeon. In the Preface to the second edition of *Thérèse Raquin*,[13] in which he defends the novel against its critics, he writes of having performed 'on two living bodies the analytical work that surgeons carry out on dead ones'; and he sees himself as 'a mere analyst, who may have turned his attention to human corruption, but in the same way as a doctor becomes absorbed in an operating theatre'. The writer, he insists, is describing, analysing, representing with the detachment of an artist looking at his nude model or a doctor examining a patient.

It is not surprising, therefore, that he finds the ultimate philosophical underpinning of what he is doing not in art or literature, but in science. The title of his theoretical work *Le Roman expérimental* (1880) should not be read in what would almost certainly be its modern meaning, referring to fiction that experiments with literary form. What Zola means is the novel *as experiment*, in the scientific sense, adopting a title that deliberately echoes the doctor and scientist Claude Bernard's *Introduction à l'étude de la médecine expérimentale* (1865) and *La Science expérimentale* (1878). The first of these was among the works that most influenced Zola's intellectual development in the years leading up to the writing of *Thérèse Raquin*, with its description of the application of scientific method to medicine and the need for systematic observation and verification.

The underpinning of Bernard's ideas came from the Positivist philosophy of Auguste Comte, whose *Cours de philosophie positive* had been published between 1830 and 1842. With the anti-Romantic critics of the 1830s, Comte believed that humankind had entered a stage of development dominated by positive, scientific understanding, which could be applied not only to the natural world, but also to society; it was to be based on observation of material phenomena and on experience, rejecting theoretical or metaphysical propositions that could not be verified by experiment or observation.

Comte's philosophy was to influence Zola particularly through the writings of the critic and historian Hippolyte Taine, whom he may first have encountered thanks to one of his teachers at the *lycée*, Pierre-Émile Levasseur,[14] and he would certainly have encountered Taine later, after he started to work for the publisher Hachette, Taine being one of their authors. It was through Taine that he came to appreciate Balzac, and he would pay tribute to the critic in a long article in *La Revue contemporaine* (15 February 1866), later saying of Taine that 'he is, in our age, the highest manifestation of our curiosities, or of our need to analyse, of our desire to reduce everything to the pure mechanism of the mathematical sciences'.[15]

Taine's literary and historical criticism was based on a Positivist approach that saw writers, like other historical figures, as the product of 'race, milieu, moment'. But if the task of the critic is to study the work of writers who are shaped by their heredity and their environment, why should the writer not treat the characters in fiction in the same way? They, too, can be treated as the product of a particular race, milieu and historical moment. The novel, instead of being a mere fantasy, will become a laboratory in which the novelist carries out his experiment, a scientific instrument for the analysis of individuals and society.

Of course, Zola was writing in the days before Freud and psychoanalysis; theories of human psychology contained elements that we would nowadays find odd. In particular, doctors still believed in the idea of 'temperament', which derived from the medieval concept of 'humours'. According to the Larousse dictionary of 1875, human temperaments could be divided up into bilious, sanguine, nervous and lymphatic, with an additional category, phlegmatic (a combination of lymphatic and bilious). The nervous and sanguine temperaments were to be considered more or less normal, while the bilious and lymphatic were weaker and pathological.[16]

The Larousse dictionary shows that there had been some development in the concept since the Middle Ages. For a start, the melancholic temperament had been discarded, and the temperaments were no longer considered to be so closely related to particular organs of the body or to the four elements, earth, air, fire and water. Nor were they thought of as innate: a person's temperament could alter according to circumstances, so there were cases of 'mixed' temperaments and many individuals were unclassifiable. But the basic theory – that humans could be divided into psychological types according to certain physiological criteria – was still accepted, not least by Zola. 'In *Thérèse Raquin* I set out to study temperament, not character,' he wrote in the Preface to the second edition, meaning by this that he wanted to show how human beings of a particular disposition react when placed in a given set of circumstances. And throughout the novel he refers to the sanguine temperament of Laurent and the nervous temperament of Thérèse, these two temperaments being opposite and complementary. Laurent is earthy, driven by his animal needs, while Thérèse is nervous, changeable, hysterical; and each of the main protagonists in the novel has physical characteristics that correspond to the traditional descriptions of his or her particular temperament: Laurent's ruddy cheeks, Thérèse's pale face and the lymphatic Camille's blond hair.[17] What Zola aims to do here is exactly what he attributed to the Goncourts in his review of *Germinie Lacerteux*: putting 'a certain temperament in contact with certain facts and certain beings'.[18] And the Goncourts themselves had written in their diary: 'Since Balzac, the novel has had nothing in common with what our fathers understood by "novel". The present-day novel is made with *documents* described or noted down from nature, just as history is made out of written documents.'[19] The 'milieu' and the 'moment' were ready for Zola's first serious attempt to apply his theories in *Thérèse Raquin*.

In December 1866, Zola published a short story in *Le Figaro* under the ironic title 'Un mariage d'amour' ('A Love Match'). This tells how a young man, Michel, marries a 'thin, nervous' girl, Suzanne, who is 'neither ugly, nor beautiful'. For three years they live together in harmony, until Suzanne starts to fall passionately in love with one of her husband's friends, Jacques. Tacitly, the two lovers get the idea of killing Michel.

One day, all three of them set out for a day on the river at Corbeil. After ordering dinner, they hire a boat and, when it is hidden behind the tall trees on an island, Jacques starts a fight with Michel, who bites him on the cheek. After a short struggle, he pushes Michel overboard, then capsizes the boat. Michel is drowned, the two lovers are rescued and no one suspects murder.

Every day, Jacques goes to the Morgue. When at last he recognizes Michel's body, he feels a shudder of horror, though up to then the thought of the crime has left him unmoved. Hoping to drive away his fears, he marries Suzanne, but the couple find that their passion for one another has cooled and they are haunted by the spectre of Michel. In fact, they come to hate one another, each accusing the other of being responsible for the crime. The scar on Jacques's face is a permanent reminder of the killing and horrifies Suzanne whenever she sees it.

Finally, their suffering becomes intolerable and each of them decides to get rid of the sole witness to their crime. Finding each other preparing poison, they realize what is happening, burst into tears and take the poison themselves, dying in each other's arms. 'Their confession was found on a table, and it was after reading that grim document that I was able to write the story of this love match.'

It is clear that the outlines of Zola's future novel are in this story, which occupies four pages in the Petits Classiques Larousse edition of *Thérèse Raquin*, where it is reproduced in full.

Though the final sentence of 'Un mariage d'amour' makes it sound like a news story, the inspiration for the plot came from a novel by Adolphe Belot and Ernest Daudet, *La Vénus de Gordes*, which Zola had received from the publisher in his capacity as a book reviewer. This was the melodramatic story of a love affair in the Lubéron, in which a woman and her lover try to poison, then shoot her husband, a crime for which they are imprisoned, the woman eventually dying of yellow fever in the penal colony of Cayenne. There is a long way from this to 'Un mariage d'amour', and further still to *Thérèse Raquin*.

Zola started working on his first major novel early in 1867. In fact, he was engaged on two books: *Thérèse Raquin*, which he wrote in the mornings; and *Les Mystères de Marseille*, which occupied his afternoons. He was quite clear in his mind that *Thérèse Raquin* was the more important of the two. He had proposed it in February to Arsène Houssaye for the periodical *La Revue du XIXe siècle*, as a development in six parts of 'Un mariage d'amour'; but by the time the novel was written, in June 1867, *La Revue du XIXe siècle* had folded, so it was transferred to *L'Artiste* (another publication of Arsène Houssaye and his son, Henri), where it appeared, under the same title as the short story, *Un mariage d'amour*, in three parts from August to October, with a few cuts, which the Houssayes had asked for to spare their readers' sensibilities. In November

1867, the novel appeared in book form under its final title.

'The work is very dramatic, very poignant, and I am counting on a horror success,' Zola wrote in a letter of 13 September 1867.[20] Those who reviewed the novel on its first appearance (like Louis Ulbach, quoted earlier) saw Zola's intention, though they did not always share his estimate of the novel's qualities: 'a tormented work', 'medical dissections', 'crude colours', 'brutality', 'mire, blood and bestial love', were some of the terms used to describe Zola's work,[21] which was generally ascribed to the genre of the horror novel. The horror element, in this psychological study, is indicated by Zola's vocabulary. One drawback is the relative poverty of the vocabulary which Zola has at his disposal to describe the psychological state of the three main protagonists (Thérèse, Laurent, Mme Raquin) from Chapter XXII onwards. It is a vocabulary mainly drawn from the language of sensational fiction: 'sinister', 'horrible', 'base', 'monstrous', 'fear', 'repulsion', 'anguish' and 'terror' recur over and over. Characters are 'mad with terror and despair' and suffer 'crises of terror and agony' which make them stammer and stutter as they speak. In their agitation, they dream of 'tranquil happiness' and 'simple affection', yet they are condemned to suffer 'torments' and 'agonies'.

In one respect, in particular, the language fails him: he is obliged to speak of 'remorse' in relation to Laurent and Thérèse; yet, as an atheist engaged in an essentially materialistic project, he has been at pains to insist that what the two murderers feel has nothing to do with the Christian idea of conscience: it is a purely nervous and physiological reaction. When Thérèse does pray for forgiveness (Chapter XXIX), Zola makes it clear that her 'dramas of repentance' are acted out for the sole benefit of Mme Raquin, and that they are calculating, selfish and hypocritical – all the more so since this play-acting imposes 'the most unspeakable agony' on her aunt. But, despite this, it is hard for the reader not to interpret her feelings of remorse and those of Laurent as indications of guilt brought about by a sense of sin. Regardless of where the remorse comes from, most readers now see this as a very moral tale.

*

Despite having sometimes been obliged to have recourse to the language of melodrama, *Thérèse Raquin* is a novel of considerable power, which it owes partly to its compression, its structure and the simplicity of its plot. It has the urgency and inevitability of a classical tragedy. It stands, too, as a bridge between the Gothic novel and the modern psychological thriller, using the vocabulary of sensationalist horror in an earnest attempt to get inside the minds of the perpetrators of a crime and to study the repercussions of their act. One should be careful about taking too literally Zola's own claims for his method in writing the novel: there is something slightly disingenuous about his protestations, in the Preface to the second edition, that he is doing nothing more than a doctor examining a patient or a painter studying a model. In any case, however much Zola claimed throughout his career that his enterprise was essentially scientific, he never believed that the novelist was engaged in a purely mechanical exercise, any more than he thought that an artist like Manet was simply reproducing reality. The proof is here in this novel, in the character of Laurent. If the artist's work is just to recount what he sees, then how is it that Laurent, who does not have the talent to do this at the start of the book, acquires it as a result of the nervous strain to which he is subjected by the murder? From the start, Zola had a high concept of the writer's individual contribution to the work and to the art that he brings to it. The careful structure of this novel, its complex links to the art and literature of its age, and its network of symbolic references – not least those represented by that enigmatic presence, François, the cat – make it far more than an outdated exercise in psychological analysis, and justify its enduring popularity in Zola's work.

NOTES

1. It has been suggested that the critic in question, Louis Ulbach, writing as 'Ferragus', may have colluded with Zola in order to create a sensation around the novel. See Armand Lanoux, *Bonjour, Monsieur Zola* (Paris: Hachette, 1962).

2. Henri Mitterand, *Zola. I. Sous le regard d'Olympia, 1840–1871* (Paris: Fayard, 1999), p. 572.

3. The Second Empire: the period of rule by the Emperor Napoleon III (1852–70).

4. See, for example, the three pages that François-Marie Mourad devotes to the cat, François, in his annotated edition of *Thérèse Raquin* (see Further Reading); and Robert Lethbridge's article, where he says that 'the cat … although at first sight of minor importance, is one of a network of symbols at the heart of the narrative' (see Further Reading, p. 291).

5. Mitterand, *Zola. I.*, p. 433. The link between the novel and Manet's painting is a key theme in Mitterand's biography: for the cat, see also the reference to *Olympia* on p. 507; and, for the more general links, see the chapter 'Thérèse et *Olympia*', pp. 566–600.

6. Lethbridge, see Further Reading, p. 280.

7. Quoted by Mitterand, *Zola. I.*, p. 441.

8. From Zola's work of 1881, *Les Romanciers naturalistes* (quoted by Mitterand, ibid., p. 665).

9. Edmond and Jules Goncourt, *Journal. Mémoires de la vie littéraire* (Paris: Fasquelle, Flammarion, 1956), vol. 2, p. 474.

10. *Revue encyclopédique*, vol. XXXIX (1828), p. 117.

11. In his 'Two Definitions of the Modern Novel' (quoted by Mitterand, *Zola. I.*, p. 513).

12. See Chapter III, notes 2 and 4.

13. See pp. 3–8.

14. See Mitterand, *Zola. I.*, pp. 163–5.

15. In *Mes haines* (2nd ed., Paris: Charpentier, 1879, p. 231).

16. See *Grand dictionnaire universel du XIXe siècle* (Paris: Larousse, 1875), article 'Tempérament', p. 1578.

17. See Mitterand's Introduction to the 1970 Garnier-Flammarion edition of *Thérèse Raquin*, where he gives a table showing all the characteristics of these three, Thérèse, Laurent and Camille, according to the temperament of each.

18. In *Le Salut public de Lyon* (February 1865).

19. Edmond and Jules Goncourt, *Journal*, vol. 2, p. 96. This entry for 24 October 1864 was made at the time when the Goncourts were writing *Germinie Lacerteux*.

20. Émile Zola, *Correspondance*, ed. B. H. Bakker (Montreal: University of Montreal Press, 1978), vol. I, p. 523.

21. Quoted by Russell Cousins, *Zola: Thérèse Raquin* (London: Grant and Cutler, 1992), p. 12.

Further Reading

Nin M. Athanassoglu-Kallmyer, *Cezanne and Provence: The Painter in his Culture*, (Chicago: University of Chicago Press, 2003)

Brown, Frederick, *Zola. A Life* (New York: Macmillan, 1995)

Hemmings, F. W. J., *The Life and Times of Émile Zola* (London: Paul Elek, 1977)

Lapp, John C., *Zola before the 'Rougon-Macquart'* (Toronto: University of Toronto Press, 1964)

Schumacher, Claude, *Zola. Thérèse Raquin* (Glasgow: University of Glasgow Press, 1990)

Wilson, Angus, *Émile Zola. An Introductory Study of His Novels* (London: Secker and Warburg, 1952)

Two studies of *Thérèse Raquin* (with quotations in French):

Cousins, Russell, *Zola. Thérèse Raquin* (London: Grant and Cutler, 1992)

Lethbridge, Robert, 'Zola, Manet and *Thérèse Raquin*' in *French Studies*, XXXIV, no. 3 (July, 1980), pp. 278–99

Critical Edition (French):

Émile Zola, *Thérèse Raquin*, ed. François-Marie Mourad (Paris: Petits Classiques Larousse, 2002)

Note on Adaptation and Translation

The relatively simple narrative of *Thérèse Raquin*, and the fact that it is set almost entirely in one location, soon made Zola consider an adaptation for the theatre. He had written a melodrama from *Les Mystères de Marseille*, so it was natural for him to think of adapting his other novel of the time for the stage. His play from *Thérèse Raquin* eventually opened at the Théâtre de la Renaissance in Paris on 11 July 1873, where it ran for only nine performances (though it was occasionally revived later).

A more elaborate stage adaptation was made by Marcelle Maurette in 1947, and another by Raymond Rouleau in 1981. The last of these is generally considered the most successful and most faithful to Zola's presumed intentions, though it is also furthest from the plot of the novel: Rouleau gives Camille overtly homosexual leanings, for example, and makes Suzanne a victim of sexual abuse.

There have also been several versions for the cinema, the best-known being Jacques Feyder's (now lost) 1928 silent version, a Franco-German co-production, stylistically influenced by German expressionist cinema; and Marcel Carné's film of 1953, with Simone Signoret and Raf Vallone, which was a success on first release, though it departs considerably from the novel. For example, Carné introduces the character of a sailor who tries to blackmail Thérèse and Laurent after the murder, and he reworks the plot in various other ways to make it more plausible for a twentieth-century audience.

The first English translation of *Thérèse Raquin* that I can find was one by John Stirling published in America in 1881. It was not until the Irish novelist George Moore negotiated the translation rights in 1884 with the publisher Henry Vizetelly (and his son, Ernest, who did the translations) that Zola's work began to appear in England. The Vizetellys brought out their first translation of *Thérèse Raquin* in 1886 and there have been several other versions since then. As its source, the present translation uses Henri Mitterand's edition for Garnier-Flammarion (1970), which reproduces the text of the 1868 edition, together with Zola's Preface to the second edition of that same year.

Two previous translators, Leonard Tancock (who did the version for Penguin Classics published in 1962, which the present translation replaces), and Andrew Rothwell (whose version for Oxford World Classics appeared in 1992), point to certain characteristics of Zola's novel which make it 'an awkward work to translate' (Rothwell) and set 'peculiar problems' (Tancock) for the translator. One of these is Zola's tendency to refer repeatedly to characters by certain set phrases: 'the old haberdasher' (for Mme Raquin); 'the drowned man' (for Camille); 'the retired police commissioner' (for Michaud). Both translators consider these to be, in Tancock's words, 'impossibly clumsy locutions' and have chosen to rephrase them. I find these repetitions less bothersome than my predecessors appear to have done, and on the whole, when Zola refers to Michaud as 'the retired police commissioner', I do the same.

In fact, I am slightly surprised at these previous translators' uneasiness about Zola's style. As well as their problem with clumsy locutions, both Tancock and Rothwell feel that Zola 'fails to graduate his climaxes' (Tancock), 'so that subsequent intensification can only be achieved by accumulation and repetition' (Rothwell). Both of them have felt it was not part of the translator's job to correct 'such pervasive stylistic features', but to retain them with regret. I accept that, as I point out in my Introduction, there is a problem in the limited vocabulary at Zola's disposal to describe the mental state of the two main characters, but this is a feature of the text, and not a difficulty for the translator.

Finally, Rothwell also says that he has made 'some alterations to the tense-sequences in certain passages' and points to Zola's frequent use of the imperfect tense, and that 'it has proved necessary on occasion to decide between frequentative and narrative uses of the French imperfect tense, a distinction which Zola deliberately blurs in order to convey the monotony of the life led by the Raquin household, but which can lead to apparent temporal contradictions in English'.

In fact, Zola's use of the imperfect is one of the characteristic features of his style. As Anne Judge and F. G. Headley say in their *Reference Grammar of Modern French*:[1] 'Flaubert and then, to a far greater extent, Zola are said to have "given the imperfect artistic overtones" which it never had before', using it to place 'the reader in the middle of the action . . .' And the 'artistic overtones' may be 'artistic' in the narrow sense as well as in the general one. Grévisse,[2] talking about the same 'narrative' use of the imperfect, notes that it is sometimes called the 'picturesque' imperfect and quotes Brunetière's 'well-chosen description [when he says]: "it is a painter's technique . . . The imperfect, here, serves to prolong the duration of the action being described by the verb, and in a sense immobilizes it before the reader's eyes" ' – which seems particularly significant in the case of Zola, given his interest in applying the techniques of painting to writing.

It is not possible to follow Zola's choice of tenses precisely when translating into English, but in translating *Thérèse Raquin* I have been constantly aware of Zola's use of verb tenses and have tried to find an appropriate English equivalent. I hope overall that I have managed to convey something of Zola's style, even if his repetitions, superlatives, accumulations and imperfect tenses may occasionally strike the English reader as odd. Having said that, my overriding aim has been to produce a readable and accurate translation that will respect the qualities of a remarkable novel and bring it to a new generation of English readers.

NOTES

1. A. Judge and F. G. Headley, *A Reference Grammar of Modern French* (London: Edward Arnold, 1983), p. 107.
2. Maurice Grévisse, *Le Bon Usage*, revised by André Goosse (Paris: Duculot, 1986), p. 1291.

THÉRÈSE RAQUIN

Preface to the Second Edition (1868)

I naïvely thought that this novel could do without a Preface. Being accustomed to speak my mind out loud and to stress the least detail in what I write, I hoped that I might be understood and judged without having to explain myself further. It seems that I was wrong.

The critics greeted this book with anger and indignation. Some virtuous folk, in no less virtuous newspapers, puckered their faces in disgust as they picked it up with the tongs to throw it on the fire. Even the little literary papers – those same literary papers that every evening report the gossip from bedrooms and private dining rooms – held their noses and spoke of stinking filth. I have no complaint to make about this reception; on the contrary, I am charmed to discover that my colleagues have the sensitive feelings of young ladies. It is quite evident that my book belongs to my critics and that they may find it repulsive without giving me any cause for protest. What I do mind, however, is that not one of the prudish journalists who have blushed as they read *Thérèse Raquin* seems to me to have understood the novel. If they had understood it, perhaps they would have blushed even more, but at least I should now be enjoying the private satisfaction of seeing that they were disgusted for the right reason. Nothing is more irritating than to hear honest writers protest about depravity when one is quite certain that they make these noises without knowing what they are protesting about.

It is necessary, therefore, for me to present my work to these critics myself. I shall do so in a few lines, simply in order to avoid any misunderstanding in the future.

In *Thérèse Raquin* I set out to study temperament, not character.[1] That sums up the whole book. I chose protagonists who were supremely dominated by their nerves and their blood, deprived of free will and drawn into every action of their lives by the predetermined lot of their flesh. Thérèse and Laurent are human animals, nothing more. In these animals, I have tried to follow step by step the silent operation of desires, the urgings of instinct and the cerebral disorders consequent on a nervous crisis. The love between my two heroes is the satisfaction of a need; the murder that they commit is the outcome of their adultery, an outcome that they accept as wolves accept the killing of a sheep; and finally what I have been compelled to call their 'remorse',[2] consists in a simple organic disruption, a revolt of the nervous system when it has been stretched to breaking-point. I freely admit that the soul is entirely absent, which is as I wanted it.

The reader will have started, I hope, to understand that my aim has been above all scientific. When I created my two protagonists, Thérèse and Laurent, I chose to set myself certain problems and to solve them. Thus I tried to explain the strange union that can take place between two different temperaments, showing the profound disturbance of a sanguine nature when it comes into contact with a nervous one. Those who read the novel carefully will see that each chapter is the study of a curious case of physiology. In a word, I wanted only one thing: given a powerful man and a dissatisfied woman, to search out the beast in them, and nothing but the beast, plunge them into a violent drama and meticulously note the feelings and actions of these two beings. I have merely performed on two living bodies the analytical work that surgeons carry out on dead ones.

One must admit that it is hard, having completed such a task and still entirely devoted to the serious pleasures of the search for truth, to hear people accuse you of having no other end except that of describing obscene pictures. I am in the same position as one of those painters of nudes who work untouched by a hint of desire, and who are quite astonished when a critic announces that he is scandalized by the living flesh in their paintings. While I was writing *Thérèse Raquin*, I forgot everybody and lost myself in a precise, minute reproduction of life, giving myself up entirely to an analysis of the working of the human animal; and I can assure you that there was nothing immoral for me in the cruel love of Thérèse and Laurent, nothing that could arouse evil desires. The humanity of the models disappeared as it does in the eyes of an artist who has a naked woman lounging in front of him and who considers only how to put that woman on his canvas in all the truth of her form and colour. So I was greatly astonished when I heard my book described as a pool of mud and gore, a drain, a foul sewer, and heaven knows what else. I know the little games that critics play; I've done the same myself. But I must admit, I was a little disconcerted by this single-minded hostility. What! Was there not just one of my colleagues prepared to explain my book, let alone defend it? In the chorus of voices proclaiming: 'The author of *Thérèse Raquin* is a wretched hysteric who enjoys exhibiting pornography,' I waited in vain for a single voice to reply: 'No, this writer is a mere analyst, who may have turned his attention to human corruption, but in the same way as a doctor becomes absorbed in an operating theatre.'

Notice that I am not at all asking for the sympathy of the press towards a book that, apparently, revolts its delicate senses. I do not hope for so much. I am merely astonished that my fellow writers have turned me into a kind of literary sewage worker, even though their experienced eyes should detect an author's intentions within ten pages; and I am content merely to beg them humbly to be so kind in future as to see me as I am and to discuss me for what I am.

Even so, it would have been easy for them to understand *Thérèse Raquin*, to consider it from a viewpoint of observation and analysis and to show me my true faults, without picking up a handful of mud and throwing it in my face, in the name of morality. It would have demanded a little intelligence and a few general notions of real criticism. In the scientific field, the accusation of immorality proves absolutely nothing. I do not know if my novel is immoral; I admit that I have never concerned myself with making it more or less chaste. What I do know is that I never for a moment thought I was putting in the filth that moral individuals find there. I wrote every scene, even the most passionate ones, with the pure curiosity of a scientist. And I defy any of my critics to find a single page that is really licentious or written for the readers of those little pink volumes, those indiscretions of the boudoir and the back stage,[3] which are published in editions of ten thousand at a time and warmly recommended by the same newspapers that were so sickened by the truths in *Thérèse Raquin*.

So, a few insults, a lot of silliness: that is all I have read up to now about my work. I am stating it here calmly, as I would to a friend who asked me privately what I thought of the attitudes of critics towards me. A highly talented writer, to whom I was complaining about the lack of sympathy that I enjoy, replied with this profound observation: 'You have one huge failing which will close every door to you: you cannot talk for two minutes to a halfwit without letting him know that he is one.' This cannot be helped. I realize that I am harming myself with the critics by accusing them of lacking in intelligence, yet I cannot prevent myself from showing the contempt that I feel for their narrow outlook and the judgements that they hand down blindly, without any system behind them. Of course, I am referring to everyday criticism, which applies all the literary prejudices of fools and is unable to adopt the broadly human outlook that a human work needs if it is to be understood. Never have I seen such ineptitude. The few blows that minor critics have thrown at me in connection with *Thérèse Raquin* have, as always, landed on thin air. Their aim is essentially misdirected: they applaud the pirouetting of some over-painted actress and then bewail the immorality of a physiological study, understanding nothing, not wanting to understand anything, and constantly hitting out whenever their idiocy panics and tells them to hit out. It is infuriating to be beaten for a crime that one did not commit. At times, I regret not having written obscenities; I feel that I should be happier getting a beating that I deserve, amid this hail of blows stupidly landing on my head, like tiles from a roof, without my knowing why.

In our times, there are only two or three men who can read, understand and judge a book.[4] I accept criticism from them, certain that they would not speak until they had discovered my intentions and assessed the results of my efforts. They would be very careful not to mention those great empty words: 'morality' and 'literary modesty'. They would recognize my right, at a time when we enjoy freedom in art, to choose my subjects wherever I please, asking me only for works that are conscientious, and knowing that only stupidity harms the dignity of literature. They would surely not be surprised by the scientific analysis that I tried to apply in *Thérèse Raquin*. They would recognize it as the modern method and the universal research tool that our century uses so passionately to lay bare the secrets of the future. Whatever their conclusions, they would accept my point of departure: the study of temperament and of the profound modifications of an organism through the influence of environment and circumstances. I would be faced with true judges, with men honestly searching for truth, without puerility or false modesty, who do not feel that they must appear to be sickened by the sight of naked, living anatomical specimens. A sincere study purifies everything, as fire does. Of course, my work would be very humble in the presence of this tribunal that I have imagined: I should call down on it all the severity of those critics and wish it to come away from them blackened with crossings-out. But at least I should have the great joy of having been criticized for what I tried to do, not for something that I did not do.

Even now, it seems to me that I can hear the judgement of such great critics, whose methodical and Naturalist criticism has revived the sciences, history and literature. '*Thérèse Raquin* is the study of too exceptional a case; the drama of modern life is more adaptable than this, less enveloped in horror and madness. Such cases are to be shifted to the background of a novel.[5] A wish to lose none of his observations encouraged the author to foreground every detail, so giving still more tension and harshness to the whole. Apart from that, the style does not have the simplicity required by an analytical novel. In short, for the writer now to make a good novel, he will have to see society from a broader perspective, paint it in its many and various guises, and above all adopt a clear, natural written style.'

I have tried to reply in twenty lines to attacks that are annoying because of their naïve bad faith, and I notice that I have started to discourse with myself, as always happens when I keep a pen in my hand for too long. I will stop, knowing that readers do not like this. If I had the will and the time to write a manifesto, I might perhaps have tried to defend what one journalist, speaking of *Thérèse Raquin*, called 'putrid literature'.[6] But, then, what's the use? The group of Naturalist writers to which I have the honour to belong has enough courage and energy to produce strong works that carry their own defence in them. One must have all the bias and blindness of a particular type of critic to oblige a novelist to write a Preface. Since, out of love for clarity, I have committed the sin of writing one, I ask pardon of intelligent folk who can see clearly without having someone light a lamp for them in broad daylight.

Émile Zola

15 April 1868

At the end of the Rue Guénégaud, if you follow it away from the river, you find the Passage du Pont-Neuf, a sort of dark, narrow corridor linking the Rue Mazarine to the Rue de Seine.[1] This passageway is, at most, thirty paces long and two wide, paved with yellowish, worn stones which have come loose and constantly give off an acrid dampness. The glass roof, sloping at a right angle, is black with grime.

On fair summer days when the sun burns down heavily on the streets, a whitish light penetrates the dirty panes of glass and lurks miserably about the arcade. On foul winter days, on a foggy morning, the glass roof casts only shadows over the slimy paving: mean, soiled shadows.

Built into the left wall are dark, low, flattened shops which exhale the dank air of cellars. There are secondhand booksellers, toyshops and paper merchants whose displays sleep dimly in the shades, grey with dust. The little square panes of the shop windows cast strange, greenish reflections on the goods inside. Behind them, the shops are full of darkness, gloomy holes in which weird figures move around.

On the right, along the whole length of the passageway, there is a wall, against which the shopkeepers opposite have set up narrow cupboards; nameless objects, goods forgotten for twenty years, lie there on narrow shelves painted a repellent shade of brown. A woman selling costume jewellery does business from one of the cupboards, offering rings at fifteen sous,[2] delicately placed on a bed of blue velvet at the bottom of a mahogany box.

Above the glass roof, the wall extends, black, crudely rendered, as though stricken with leprosy and crisscrossed with scars.

This Passage du Pont-Neuf is not a place for strolling. People use it to avoid making a detour, to gain a few minutes. Down it walk busy folk whose only thought is to march briskly straight ahead. You see apprentices in their aprons, seamstresses delivering their finished work, and men and women with parcels under their arms. You also see old men lurking in the dreary light of the glass roof, and gangs of little children who come running here after school to kick up a row, banging their clogs on the pavement. The crisp, hurried sound of footsteps on stone rings out all day long with irritating irregularity. No one speaks, no one stops; all these people are speeding past on their business, walking quickly along with downcast eyes, without sparing a single glance for the displays of goods. The shopkeepers look suspiciously at any passer-by who by a miracle happens to pause in front of their windows.

In the evening, the arcade is lit by three gaslights enclosed in heavy, square lanterns. These hang down from the glass roof, on which they cast patches of yellowish light, spreading pale circles of luminescence around them that shimmer and appear to vanish from time to time. The passageway looks as though it might really be a hiding-place for cutthroats; great shadows spread across the paving and damp draughts blow in from the street; it has the appearance of an underground gallery dimly lit by three funerary lanterns. The shopkeepers make do with nothing more than the meagre illumination that the gas lamps cast on their windows. Inside the shops, they merely set up a lamp with a shade on a corner of the counter, which allows passers-by to detect what is lurking at the back of these holes where darkness inhabits even in daytime. Along the dingy line of windows, that of a paper merchant shines out: the yellow flames of two shale-oil lamps burn into the blackness. And, on the opposite side, a candle stuck into the glass mantle of an oil lamp puts glimmering stars in the box of costume jewellery. The woman who owns the shop is dozing at the back of her cupboard, with her hands wrapped in a shawl.

A few years ago, facing this jewellers', there was a shop with bottle-green woodwork oozing humidity from every crack. The sign was a long narrow plank with the word *Haberdashery* in black; and, on one of the glass panes in the door, was a woman's name in red letters: *Thérèse Raquin*. Window displays on either side reached far back into the shop, lined with blue paper.

In daylight, all that the eye could see was these windows, in a soft chiaroscuro.

On one side, there were a few articles of clothing: fluted tulle bonnets at two or three francs apiece; muslin sleeves and collars; and woollens, stockings, socks and braces. Each item, yellow with age, hung pitifully from a wire hook, so that the window, from top to bottom, was full of whitish rags that took on a mournful appearance in the transparent gloom. The brand-new bonnets shone whiter, making bald patches against the blue paper lining the window, while the coloured stockings, hanging from a rail, struck dark notes against the pale, dim emptiness of the muslin.

On the other side, behind a narrower window, were piled large skeins of green wool, black buttons sewn on to white cards, boxes of every size and colour, hairnets with steel drops stretched across circles of bluish paper, fans of knitting needles, tapestry patterns and reels of ribbon – a pile of dull, washed-out objects that had doubtless been reposing in this same spot for five or six years. All the colours had faded to a dirty grey in this cupboard rotten with dust and damp.

Around midday, in summer, when the sun's rays burned down redly on the squares and streets around, you could make out the serious, pale face of a young woman behind the bonnets in the other window. Her profile stood out dimly against the blackness of the shop. A long, narrow, sharp nose reached down from the short, low forehead; her lips were two slender lines of pale pink; and her short but strong chin was attached to the neck by a supple, plump curve. You could not see her body, which was shrouded in gloom; only the profile of the face was visible, dull white, with a wide-open, black eye pierced in it, seeming to be crushed under the weight of a thick, dark mass of hair. There it stayed for hours on end, calm and motionless, between two bonnets on which the damp rails had left two lines of rust.

In the evening, when the lamp was lit, you could see the inside of the shop. It was longer across than it was deep. At one end, there was a little counter, while at the other a spiral staircase led up to the rooms on the first floor. Against the walls stood display cases, cupboards and lines of green boxes; four chairs and a table completed the furniture. The room seemed naked and cold; the merchandise was packed up and squeezed into corners, instead of lying around here and there with its cheerful mixture of colours.

Normally, there were two women sitting behind the counter: the young woman with the serious face and an old one who would smile as she dozed. The latter was about sixty, with a placid, chubby face that turned pale under the light of the lamp. A large tabby cat would crouch at one end of the counter, watching her as she slept.

Further on, sitting on a chair, a man of some thirty years would be reading or chatting to the young woman in a low voice. He was small, puny and listless in manner, with a thin beard and his face covered in freckles: he looked like a sickly, spoiled child.

Shortly before ten o'clock, the old woman would wake up. They shut the shop and the whole family went upstairs to bed. The tabby purred as it followed its masters, rubbing its head against each banister as it went.

Upstairs, the house consisted of three rooms. The staircase opened into a dining room that also served as a sitting room. On the left was a porcelain stove in an alcove, with a sideboard opposite. Then there were chairs along the walls and a round table, fully open, occupying the middle. At the back, behind a glazed partition, was a dark kitchen. There were two bedrooms, one on either side of this living room.

The old woman, after kissing her son and daughter-in-law, would retire to her room. The cat slept on a chair in the kitchen. The couple went into their own room; this had a second door, leading to a staircase, which opened into the arcade through a dark, narrow alleyway.

The husband, constantly shivering with fever, would go to bed, while the young woman opened the window to close the shutters. She used to stay there for a few minutes, facing the great black wall with its crude rendering, which rose up and extended beyond the glass roof of the gallery. She would cast a vague glance at this wall and silently go to bed in her turn, with an air of contemptuous indifference.

II

Mme Raquin was a former haberdasher from Vernon.[1] For nearly twenty-five years, she had lived in a small shop in that town. A few years after the death of her husband, she had grown tired of it all and sold off the business. Her savings, together with the money from this sale, gave her a capital of forty thousand francs, which she invested, so that it brought in an income of two thousand a year. This would be easily enough for her. She lived a reclusive life, knowing nothing of the agonizing joys and sorrows of this world. She had created an existence of peace and happiness for herself.

For four hundred francs, she rented a little house with a garden running down to the Seine. It was a secluded, private residence that faintly suggested a convent; a narrow path led to this retreat, which was set in the midst of wide meadows. The windows of the house overlooked the river and the empty slopes on the far bank. The good lady, who was now over fifty, buried herself in this solitude and enjoyed days of tranquillity with her son, Camille, and her niece, Thérèse.

Camille was then twenty years old. His mother still spoiled him like a little boy. She loved him because she had fought to keep him alive during a long childhood full of suffering. One after the other, the child had had every fever and every kind of sickness imaginable. For fifteen years, Mme Raquin kept up the struggle against these dreadful illnesses that came one after another to wrench her child away from her. She conquered each one in turn through her patience, her care and her devotion.

When he had grown up and been saved from death, Camille was still trembling from the repeated shocks that had struck him. His growth had been arrested and he remained small and stunted. The movements of his spindly arms and legs were slow and wearisome. His mother loved him all the more for the weakness that bowed him down. She looked with triumphant tenderness on his poor, pale little face and remembered that she had given life to him more than ten times.

In the occasional periods of respite from his suffering, the child attended classes at a commercial school in Vernon. There he learned spelling and arithmetic. His education did not go beyond the four rules of adding, subtraction, multiplication and division, and a very basic knowledge of grammar. Later on, he took lessons in writing and doing accounts. Mme Raquin became very nervous when anyone advised her to send her boy off to boarding school; she knew that he would die if he was away from her, and said that the books would kill him. Camille remained in his ignorance and this ignorance was like an additional weakness in him.

At eighteen, with nothing to do and bored to death in the atmosphere of tender care with which his mother encased him, he took a post as clerk in a cloth merchant's. He earned sixty francs a month. He had the sort of unquiet spirit that made it unbearable to him to remain idle. He felt calmer, his health was better, when he was doing this mindless task, this clerical job that kept him bent all day over the invoices, over those vast lines of figures, each one of which he spelled out patiently. In the evening, worn out, his head empty, he had a sense of profound enjoyment in the exhaustion that overtook him. He had to row with his mother before she would allow him to enter the cloth merchant's; she wanted to keep him always beside her, tucked up in a blanket, far from the hazards of life. The young man put his foot down. He demanded work as other children demand toys, not out of any sense of obligation, but by an instinctive, natural need. His mother's tenderness and devotion had given him a vicious streak of egotism; he thought that he loved who-ever felt sorry for him and caressed him, though in reality he lived apart, buried in himself, caring only for his own well-being and seeking by every possible means to multiply his own plea-sure. When he got sick of Mme Raquin's loving kindness, he threw himself with delight into a mindless occupation that kept him away from her herbal teas and her potions. Then, in the evening, when he got back from the office, he ran down to the banks of the Seine with his cousin Thérèse.

Thérèse was then eighteen years old. One day, sixteen years earlier, when Mme Raquin was still a haberdasher, her brother,

Captain Degans, brought a little girl to her in his arms. He was back from Algeria.[2]

'Here's a child; you're its aunt,' he told her, with a smile. 'Her mother is dead . . . I don't know what to do with her. I'm letting you have her.'

The haberdasher took the child, smiled at her and kissed her ruddy cheeks. Degans stayed at Vernon for three days. His sister hardly asked him any questions about the girl that he was giving her. She had a vague notion that the dear little thing had been born in Oran and that her mother was a native woman of great beauty. An hour before he left, the captain handed over a birth certificate in which Thérèse was recognized by him as his child and bore his name. He left and they never saw him again. A few years later, he was killed in Africa.

Thérèse grew up sleeping in the same bed as Camille and wrapped in the warm tenderness of her aunt. She had an iron constitution and was treated like a sickly child, sharing her cousin's medicine and kept in the warm atmosphere of the sick boy's room. She stayed for hours crouching in front of the fire, lost in thought, staring straight into the flames without blinking. This convalescent life that was imposed on her drove her back into herself. She became accustomed to speaking in a low voice, walking along quietly, and staying silent and motionless on a chair, looking blankly with wide-open eyes. Yet, when she did raise an arm or take a step, there was a feline suppleness in her, a mass of energy and passion dormant within her torpid frame. One day, her cousin had fallen over in a faint. She picked him up and carried him off brusquely, this sudden outburst of strength putting large patches of red on her face. The cloistered life that she led and the debilitating regime imposed on her could not weaken her sturdy, slender body, but her face did assume a pale, slightly yellowish tint, and she became almost ugly through being kept from daylight. Sometimes, she would go to the window and look at the houses opposite across which the sun cast its golden rays.

When Mme Raquin sold her business and retired to the little house by the water, Thérèse felt secret shivers of joy run through her. Her aunt had so often told her: 'Don't make a fuss, keep quiet,' that she carefully kept all her natural impulses concealed deep inside. She had an immense capacity for coolness and an appearance of calm that hid violent fits of passion. She felt herself to be constantly in her cousin's room, beside this dying child; she had the gentle manner, stillness, placidity and stammering voice of an old woman. When she saw the garden, the pale river and the huge green slopes rising up on the horizon, she had a mad impulse to run around, shouting. She felt her heart beat furiously in her breast; but not a muscle moved on her face and she merely smiled when her aunt asked her whether she liked this new home.

So life improved for her. She had the same suppleness of movement, the same calm and indifferent expression: she was still the child brought up in the bed of an invalid. But inside, she lived an ardent and passionate existence. When she was alone, in the long grass by the river, she lay flat on her stomach like an animal, her eyes dark and wide, her body flexed, ready to pounce. And she would stay there for hours on end, thinking of nothing, with the sun burning into her, delighted at being able to dig her fingers into the earth. She had wild dreams; she would look defiantly at the river as it rumbled past and imagine that the water was going to leap out and attack her; so she stiffened and prepared to defend herself, wondering angrily how to overcome the waves.

In the evening, Thérèse, now calm and silent, would sew beside her aunt; her face seemed to be dozing in the light that oozed softly from under the shade of the lamp. Camille, slumped in an armchair, thought about his sums. Only the occasional word, spoken in a low voice, would disturb the tranquillity of this sleepy scene.

Mme Raquin contemplated her children with serene goodwill. She had decided to marry them to each other. She still considered her son to be on the point of death and was terrified by the thought that she would one day die, leaving him alone and ill. So she was counting on Thérèse, telling herself that the girl would keep good watch over Camille. There were no limits to the confidence she felt in her niece, with her quiet manners and silent devotion. She had seen her at work, and she wanted to give her to Camille as a guardian angel. The marriage was decided upon, a foregone conclusion.

The children had long known that they were to marry one day. They had grown up in the idea, so it had become quite natural and familiar to them. In the family, the alliance was spoken of as something necessary, inevitable. Mme Raquin had said: 'We'll wait until Thérèse is twenty-one.' And they waited, patiently, without shame or eagerness.

Camille's blood had been impoverished by illness and he felt none of the urgent desires of adolescence. With his cousin, he remained a little boy, kissing her as he would kiss his mother, as a matter of habit, abandoning none of his egotistical composure. He saw her as an obliging companion who prevented him from getting too bored and who, from time to time, made him a herbal tea. When he played with her or held her in his arms, he felt as though he were holding a boy; not a shudder passed through him. And it never occurred to him on such occasions to kiss Thérèse's hot lips as she struggled free with a nervous laugh.

The girl, too, seemed to remain cold and indifferent. Sometimes she would fix her large eyes on Camille and watch him for several minutes with a supremely untroubled stare. Only her lips made slight, barely perceptible movements. There was nothing to be read on this closed face, kept ever sweet and attentive by her implacable will. When there was talk of her marriage, Thérèse took on a serious look and merely nodded approval of everything that Mme Raquin said. Camille fell asleep.

In the evening, in summer, the two young people would make off to the river. Camille was irritated by his mother's constant attentions; he had moments of rebellion, he wanted to run about, make himself ill, escape from all the petting that nauseated him. So he would drag Thérèse along with him, provoke her to wrestling bouts and rolling around in the grass. One day, he pushed his cousin and she fell over. She leaped up in a single bound, like a wild animal, her face blazing and her eyes red, and rushed at him with both fists raised. Camille slumped to the ground. He was afraid of her.

Months and years went by. The day fixed for the wedding arrived. Mme Raquin took Thérèse aside, spoke to her about her father and mother, and told her the story of her birth. The young woman listened to her aunt, then kissed her without saying a word.

That night, instead of going to her own bedroom on the left of the staircase, Thérèse went to her cousin's, on the right. This was the only alteration that took place in her life that day. The next morning, when the young couple came down, Camille still had his sickly languor and his saintly, self-centred calm, while Thérèse retained her mild indifference and her restrained expression, terrifying in her impassivity.

III

A week after his wedding, Camille stated plainly to his mother that he intended to leave Vernon and go to live in Paris. Mme Raquin protested: she had arranged her life for herself and did not want to change a single thing in it. Her son threw a tantrum and threatened to fall ill if she did not give in to his whim.

'I've never got in the way of your plans,' he told her. 'I've married my cousin, I've taken all the medicines you gave me. Now, the least you can do is to allow me one wish and see it from my point of view . . . We'll leave at the end of the month.'

Mme Raquin did not sleep that night. Camille's decision was turning her life upside down and she tried desperately to see how she could right it. Little by little, she calmed down. She told herself that the young couple might have children and that, if that happened, her small capital would not be enough. She had to make more money, go back into business, find a lucrative employment for Thérèse. By the next morning, she had grown accustomed to the idea of leaving and drawn up her plans for a new life.

Over breakfast, she was quite merry.

'Here's what we'll do,' she told her children. 'I'll go to Paris tomorrow. I'll look for a little haberdasher's business and

Thérèse and I will go back to selling needles and thread. It will keep us occupied. As for you, Camille, you can do what you like: you can stroll around in the sunshine, or find yourself a job.'

'I'll find a job,' the young man replied.

The truth was that only a silly ambition had driven Camille to leave Vernon. He wanted to be an employee in a large department; he blushed with pleasure when he imagined himself in the middle of a huge office, with glazed cotton sleeves and a pen behind his ear.

Thérèse was not consulted. She had always shown such passive obedience that her aunt and her husband no longer bothered to ask her opinion. She went where they went, she did what they did, without complaint, without reproach, without even seeming to realize that anything had altered.

Mme Raquin came to Paris and went directly to the Passage du Pont-Neuf. An old spinster in Vernon had directed her to a relative who had a haberdashery business in the arcade which she wanted to dispose of. Being an experienced haberdasher, Mme Raquin found the shop rather small and a bit dark; but as she was crossing Paris, she had been horrified by the noise in the streets and the richness of the window displays, while this narrow passage with its modest shop fronts reminded her of her old shop, which had been so quiet and so peaceful. She could imagine herself still in the provinces; she breathed again, thinking that her dear children would be happy in this backwater. The cheapness of the business decided her; it was on offer for two thousand francs. The rent of the shop and the first floor was only twelve hundred francs. Mme Raquin, who had nearly four thousand francs in savings, calculated that she could pay the purchase price and the first year's rent without breaking into her capital. Camille's wages and the profits from the haberdashery would be enough, she thought, to cover everyday expenses. In that way she would not draw any further on her income and would allow the capital to grow for the benefit of her grandchildren.

She returned to Vernon radiant, saying that she had found a pearl, a charming corner in the centre of Paris. Little by little, after a few days, as she chatted about it in the evening, the damp, dark shop in the arcade became a palace; in memory, she saw it as spacious, wide and quiet, full of a thousand inestimable qualities.

'Oh, my dear Thérèse!' she said. 'You see how happy we shall be in that spot! There are three fine rooms upstairs ... The arcade is full of people ... We'll create some delightful displays ... Be sure of it, we won't get bored.'

There was no end to it. All her business instincts were re-awakened and she prepared Thérèse with advice on selling, buying and all the little tricks of the retail trade. At length, the family left its house on the banks of the Seine and the same evening settled into the Passage du Pont-Neuf.

When Thérèse entered the shop where she was to spend her life from then on, she felt as though she were going down into the clammy earth of a pit. She shuddered with fear and a feeling of nausea rose in her throat. She looked at the damp, dirty passageway, toured the shop, went up to the first floor and examined each room; these bare rooms, without furniture, were terrifyingly lonely and decrepit. The young woman could not make a gesture or speak a word. She was rigid. When her aunt and her husband had gone downstairs, she sat down on a trunk, her hands stiff and her throat full of sobs, though she could not weep.

Confronted with the reality, Mme Raquin was embarrassed, ashamed of her dreams. She tried to defend her purchase. She found an answer to every new drawback as it appeared, explaining the darkness by the fact that the weather was dull, and summed up by saying that all that was needed was a good sweep.

'Huh!' Camille replied. 'It's all quite satisfactory. In any case, we'll only come up here in the evenings. I won't be home before five or six o'clock. The two of you will have each other for company, so you won't get bored.'

The young man would never have agreed to live in such a hovel if he had not been counting on the cosy comfort of his office. He told himself that he would be warm all day in his department and that, in the evenings, he could go to bed early.

For a whole week, the shop and living quarters remained in

disorder. From the first day onwards, Thérèse sat behind the counter and did not move from her place. Mme Raquin was astonished by this attitude of resignation. She had imagined that the young woman would try to beautify her home, put flowers on the window-sills and ask for new wallpaper, curtains and carpets. When she suggested some improvement or a repair, her niece just replied calmly:

'What's the use? We're very well as we are, we don't need any luxuries.'

It was Mme Raquin who had to arrange the bedrooms and put some order into the shop. Eventually, Thérèse got tired of seeing her constantly moving around the place; she hired a cleaner and forced her aunt to come and sit beside her.

It was a month before Camille found a job. He spent as little time as possible in the shop, wandering the streets all day long. He became so bored that he even spoke of going back to Vernon. Finally, he got a place in the offices of the Orléans Railway Company,[1] where he earned a hundred francs a month. He had realized his dream.

In the morning, he left at eight. He went down the Rue Guénégaud and arrived on the banks of the river. Then, walking along slowly with his hands in his pockets, he followed the Seine from the Institut to the Jardin des Plantes.[2] This long walk, which he took twice a day, never bored him. He watched the river flow by and paused to see a string of barges going along it. His mind was blank. He would often station himself opposite Notre-Dame and stare at the scaffolding around the church, which was then being restored; these huge timbers amused him, though he did not know why. Then, as he went on, he glanced into the Port aux Vins[3] and counted the number of cabs coming from the station. In the evening, worn out and with his head full of some silly story he had heard at the office, he went through the Jardin des Plantes and had a look at the bears, if he was not in too much of a hurry. He would stay there for half an hour, leaning over the pit and watching the bears as they ambled heavily around. It amused him to see how these big creatures walked. He stared at them, with his jaw hanging, wide-eyed, like an idiot enjoying the sight of them as they moved about.

Finally, he would make up his mind to go home, dragging his feet and taking in the passers-by, the carriages and the shops.

When he got home, he would eat and then start to read. He had bought the works of Buffon[4] and every evening he would set himself the task of reading twenty or thirty pages, even though it bored him. He would also read the *History of the Consulate and the Empire* by Thiers and Lamartine's *History of the Girondins*,[5] which he got in parts at ten centimes each, or else some work of popular science. He thought he was improving himself. Sometimes, he would force his wife to listen as he read a few pages or told a particular story out of them. He was very surprised that Thérèse could remain thoughtful and silent for a whole evening, without being tempted to pick up a book. When it came down to it, he decided that his wife was none too clever.

Thérèse impatiently rejected his books. She preferred to remain idle, staring, her thoughts vaguely wandering. Meanwhile, she remained even-tempered and easygoing; all her will was bent on the effort to make herself into a passive instrument, supremely compliant and self-denying.

Business was slow. The profits remained steadily the same every month. The clientele was made up of women who worked in the district. Every five minutes, a young woman would come in and buy a few sous' worth of goods. Thérèse served the customers always with the same words and a mechanical smile on her lips. Mme Raquin was more flexible and talkative; and, to tell the truth, she was the one who attracted and kept the customers.

For three years, the days went on, one like the next. Camille was not absent from his office for a single day; his mother and his wife hardly left the shop. Thérèse, living in this dank darkness, in this dreary, depressing silence, would see life stretching in front of her, quite empty, bringing her each evening to the same cold bed and each morning to the same featureless day.

IV

Once a week, on Thursday evenings, the Raquin family received guests. They would light a big lamp in the dining room and put a kettle on to make tea. It was a whole palaver. This evening stood out from all the rest; it had become one of the family customs – a madly jolly (though respectable) orgy. They would go to bed at eleven.

In Paris Mme Raquin met up with one of her old friends, police commissioner Michaud, who had been in the force in Vernon for twenty years and lived in the same house as her. So they had got to know one another very well; then, when the widow sold up to go and live in her house by the river, they gradually lost sight of one another. Michaud came up from the provinces a few months later, to enjoy the fifteen hundred francs of his pension peacefully in Paris, in the Rue de Seine. One rainy day, he met his old friend in the Passage du Pont-Neuf and that very same evening, he went round for a meal at the Raquins.

This was the start of their Thursdays. The retired police commissioner got in the habit of coming regularly once a week. After a while, he brought his son, Olivier, a tall lad of thirty, dry and thin, who had married a rather small, slow, sickly woman. Olivier had a job with a salary of three thousand francs at the Préfecture de Police, which made Camille exceptionally jealous; he was head clerk in the department of security and order. From the very first, Thérèse hated this stiff, cold young man who felt he was honouring the shop in the arcade by bringing along the dryness of his lanky body and the weakness of his poor little wife.

Camille introduced another guest, a veteran employee of the Orléans Railway. Grivet had served there for twenty years; he was head clerk and earned two thousand one hundred francs. He was the one who handed out the work in Camille's office and the younger man showed him a degree of respect. In his dreams, he imagined that Grivet would die some day and that he might replace him, after ten years. Grivet was delighted with the welcome Mme Raquin gave him and would come back every

week without fail. Six months later, his Thursday visit had
become a duty and he would go to the Passage du Pont-Neuf as
he went every morning to the office, mechanically, with the
instinct of an animal.

From that time on, the gatherings became delightful. At seven
o'clock, Mme Raquin would light the fire, put the lamp in the
middle of the table, place a set of dominoes beside it and wipe
the tea service which stood on the dresser. At eight o'clock
precisely, Old Michaud and Grivet met in front of the shop, one
coming from the Rue de Seine, the other from the Rue Mazarine.
They used to come in and the whole family would go up to the
first floor. They sat down around the table, waiting for Olivier
Michaud and his wife, who always arrived late. When everyone
was there, Mme Raquin poured out the tea, Camille emptied
the box of dominoes on the oiled tablecloth and everyone settled
into the game. Not a sound was heard except the click of
dominoes. After each game, the players argued for two or three
minutes, then silence fell once more, broken by sharp clicks.

Thérèse played with an unconcern that irritated Camille. She
used to pick up François, the big tabby cat that Mme Raquin
had brought with her from Vernon, and stroke him with one
hand while putting down her dominoes with the other. Thursday
evenings were torture for her and she often complained of not
feeling well, of having a bad headache, in order to avoid playing,
so that she could sit by idly and half asleep. With one elbow on
the table and her cheek resting on the palm of her hand, she
would watch her aunt's and her husband's guests, seeing them
through a kind of smoky yellow mist that came out of the lamp.
All these faces drove her crazy. She looked from one to the
other with feelings of profound disgust and dull irritation. Old
Michaud had a pallid complexion with red blotches: the dead
face of an old man in his second childhood. Grivet had the
narrow mask, round eyes and thin lips of a halfwit. Olivier,
whose cheekbones protruded, gravely bore a stiff, insignificant
head on his ridiculous body. As for Suzanne, Olivier's wife, she
was quite pale, with dull eyes, white lips and a soft face. And
Thérèse could not see a single human, not a living creature,
among these grotesque and sinister beings with whom she was

shut up. At times she would suffer hallucinations, thinking that she was buried in a vault together with mechanical bodies whose heads moved and whose arms and legs waved when their strings were pulled. The heavy atmosphere of the dining room stifled her, and the eerie silence and yellowish glow of the lamp filled her with a vague sense of terror, an inexpressible feeling of anxiety.

Downstairs, on the front door, they had put a bell which gave a high-pitched tinkle as customers came in. Thérèse kept her ears open and when the bell rang she would hurry down, relieved and happy to get out of the dining room. She took her time serving the customer. When she was alone again, she would sit behind the counter and stay there for as long as possible, apprehensive of going back upstairs and feeling real joy at not having Grivet and Olivier in front of her. The damp air of the shop calmed the fever that burned her hands, and she slipped back into the solemn reverie that was her habitual state of being.

But she could not stay like this for long. Camille would be annoyed by her absence. He could not understand how anyone might prefer the shop to the dining room on a Thursday evening, so he would lean over the banisters and look around for his wife.

'Hey, there!' he would shout. 'What are you doing? Why don't you come back up? Grivet is having the devil's own luck. He's just won again.'

The young woman would get up painfully and return to her place opposite Old Michaud, whose drooping lips would form into a repulsive smile. And from then until eleven o'clock, she used to stay slumped in her chair, looking at François as he lay in her arms, so as not to see these paper dolls grimacing around her.

V

One Thursday, when he got home from the office, Camille brought with him a tall, square-shouldered young fellow, whom he pushed into the shop with a familiar pat on the back.

'Mother,' he asked Mme Raquin, showing the lad to her, 'do you recognize this gentleman?'

The old shopkeeper looked at the tall fellow and rummaged around in her memory, but found nothing. Thérèse observed the scene placidly.

'What!' Camille continued. 'You don't recognize Laurent, little Laurent, the son of Old Laurent, who has those fine fields of wheat over near Jeufosse?[1] Don't you remember? I used to go to school with him. He'd come to fetch me in the morning, as he left the house of his uncle, our neighbour, and you would give him bread and jam.'

Mme Raquin suddenly remembered little Laurent, who seemed to her to have grown up considerably; it was at least twenty years since she had seen him last. She tried to make up for her astonishment with a flood of memories and some quite maternal endearments. Laurent had sat down and was smiling serenely. He spoke out clearly and examined his surroundings with a calm and relaxed expression.

'Just imagine,' Camille said, 'this joker has been working at the Orléans Railway Station for eighteen months, and it was not until this evening that we met and recognized one another. That's how big and important the office is!'

The young man said this wide-eyed, pursing his lips, so proud was he to be a humble cog in such a huge mechanism. He went on, shaking his head:

'Oh, but he's well off, this one. He's done his studies and he's earning fifteen hundred francs already. His father sent him to boarding school where he did law and learned how to paint. Isn't that right, Laurent? You must stay for dinner . . .'

'I'd be delighted,' Laurent said, without further ado.

He took off his hat and settled down in the shop. Mme Raquin hurried away to attend to her saucepans. Thérèse, who had not spoken a word, was looking at the newcomer. She had never before seen a real man. Laurent amazed her: he was tall, strong and fresh-faced. She looked with a kind of awe at his low forehead with its rough black hair, at his plump cheeks, his red lips and his regular features with their sanguine beauty.[2] Her gaze paused for a moment on his neck, a broad, short neck, thick and powerful. Then she became absorbed in the contemplation of the large hands resting on his knees; their fingers were squared off and the closed fist, which must be huge, could have stunned a bull. Laurent came of true peasant stock, with a somewhat heavy manner, rounded back, slow, studied movements and a calm, stubborn look about him. You could sense the swelling, well-developed muscles beneath his clothes, and the whole body, with its thick, firm flesh. Thérèse examined him curiously from his hands to his face, feeling a little shudder pass through her when she reached his bull's neck.

Camille got out his volumes of Buffon and his ten-centime instalments, to show his friend that he, too, was working. Then, as though replying to a question that he had been asking himself for a few minutes, he said: 'But, Laurent, you must know my wife? Don't you remember the little cousin who used to play with us, in Vernon?'

'I recognized Madame straight away,' Laurent replied, staring Thérèse in the eyes.

The young woman felt somehow uneasy beneath this direct gaze, which seemed to penetrate right inside her. She gave a forced smile and exchanged a few words with Laurent and her husband, then hurried off to join her aunt. She was not comfortable.

They sat down to dinner. From the soup onwards, Camille thought he should look after his friend.

'How is your father?' he asked.

'I really don't know,' Laurent replied. 'We fell out. We haven't written to one another for five years.'

'Well, I never!' the clerk exclaimed, amazed by this monstrous behaviour.

'Yes, the dear man has his own ideas about things . . . As he is always in dispute with his neighbours, he sent me off to boarding school, imagining that he would later have me as a lawyer who could win all his suits for him. Oh, Old Laurent only has useful ambitions! He wants to take advantage of every notion, however idiotic!'

'But didn't you want to be a lawyer?' Camille asked, still more amazed.

'Good Lord, no,' his friend answered, with a laugh. 'For two years, I pretended to be attending lectures so that I could collect the grant of twelve hundred francs that my father was giving me. I lived with one of my friends from school who's a painter and I started to paint as well. It was fun; it's a jolly business, not too tiring. We used to smoke and lark around all day long.'

The Raquin family stared in astonishment.

'Unfortunately,' Laurent went on, 'it couldn't last. The old man learned that I had been lying to him and stopped my hundred francs a month just like that, telling me to come back and till the earth like him. So I tried to paint religious pictures, but it's not a good market. When it became clear to me that I would starve to death, I said to hell with art and looked for a job . . . My father's sure to die one of these days, and I'm waiting until he does so that I can live without working.'

Laurent spoke quite calmly. In a few words, he had just made a quite typical statement that entirely summed up his character. Underneath, he was lazy, with strong appetites and a well-defined urge to seek easy, lasting pleasures. His great, powerful body asked for nothing better than to lie idle, wallowing in constant indolence and gratification. He would have liked to eat well, sleep long and fully satisfy his desires, without moving from the spot or running the risk of exhausting himself in any way.

He had been appalled at the prospect of becoming a lawyer and shuddered at the idea of tilling the soil. He had thrown himself into art, hoping to find it a profession for the idle: the brush seemed a light tool to handle and he also believed that success would come easily. He dreamed of a life of fleshly pleasures, cheaply purchased, a life full of women, of resting on sofas, eating and getting drunk. The dream lasted as long as Old Laurent kept on supplying the readies; but when the young man, who was thirty by then, saw poverty looming, he started to think. He had no stomach for privation; he would not have gone through a single day without food for the greater glory of art. As he said, he let painting go to hell as soon as he realized that it would never satisfy his large appetites. His first attempts had been worse than mediocre: his peasant's eye observed

Nature as awkward and dirty; his canvases, muddy, badly composed and grimacing, were beneath criticism. In any event, his artistic ambition did not extend far and he was not too depressed when he had to put down his brushes. His only real regret was at leaving his schoolfriend's studio, a huge studio in which he had lounged about so self-indulgently for four or five years. He did still miss the women who came there to pose, whose favours were within reach of his purse. This world of animal pleasures had left him with urgent lusts. None the less, he did enjoy his job as a clerk; where his basic needs were concerned, he lived very well, liking the routine work which took little out of him and lulled his mind. Only two things got on his nerves: the lack of women and the food in eighteen-sou restaurants which did not satisfy the cravings of his greedy stomach.

Camille listened to him and looked at him with naïve astonishment. This feeble boy, whose soft, prostrate body had never felt a shudder of desire, childishly imagined the studio life that his friend was describing. He conjured up the spectacle of those women exhibiting their naked flesh. He questioned Laurent about it.

'So,' he asked, 'were there really women who took off their blouses in front of you like that?'

'Certainly there were,' Laurent replied, with a smile, looking at Thérèse, who had gone quite pale.

'It must give you an odd feeling,' Camille went on, with a childish titter. 'I'd be embarrassed. The first time, you must have wondered where to look.'

Laurent had opened up one of his large hands and was looking closely at the palm. His fingers trembled slightly and a flush of red rose to his cheeks.

'The first time,' he repeated, as though talking to himself, 'I think I found it quite natural ... It's great fun, that art game; just a pity it doesn't pay ... As my model I had a redhead who was quite adorable: firm, gleaming flesh, superb bosom and hips as wide –'

Laurent looked up and saw Thérèse in front of him, silent and motionless. The young woman was staring at him intently.

Her eyes, dull black, looked like two bottomless pits, and there were glimpses of pinkness shining in her mouth through half-open lips. She seemed to be hunched and gathered into herself; she was listening.

Laurent looked alternately from Thérèse to Camille. The former painter suppressed a smile. He concluded his sentence with a gesture, a wide, voluptuous gesture that the young woman followed with her eyes. They were at the dessert and Mme Raquin had gone downstairs to attend to a customer.

When the table had been cleared, Laurent, who had been thoughtful for a moment or two, suddenly turned to Camille.

'I'll tell you what,' he said. 'I must paint your portrait.'

Mme Raquin and her son were delighted by this idea. Thérèse remained silent.

'It's summer,' Laurent went on. 'So, as we get out of the office at four, I'll come here and you can pose for me for two hours, in the evening. It will take a week.'

'That's it!' said Camille, blushing with pleasure. 'You can have dinner with us. I'll have my hair curled and put on a black topcoat.'

The clock struck eight. Grivet and Michaud arrived. Olivier and Suzanne came behind them.

Camille introduced his friend to the company. Grivet pursed his lips. He disliked Laurent, because in his view he had been promoted too fast. In any case, it was no trivial matter bringing in a new guest. The Raquins' circle could not make way for a newcomer without a little show of disapproval.

Laurent behaved himself. He understood the situation and wanted to be liked, to be accepted at once. He told stories, cheered them all up with his loud laugh and even won over Grivet himself.

That evening, Thérèse made no attempt to go down to the shop. She stayed on her chair until eleven, playing and chatting, avoiding Laurent's eye; anyway, he took no notice of her. The young man's sanguine nature, his resonant voice, his hearty laughter and the sharp, strong smells that he emitted disturbed the young woman and plunged her into a kind of nervous anxiety.

VI

From that day onwards, Laurent came back to the Raquins' almost every evening. He lived in a little furnished room which he rented for eighteen francs a month, in the Rue Saint-Victor,[1] opposite the Port aux Vins. This attic room, under the roof, with a narrow skylight at the top half opening on the sky, was barely six metres across. Laurent would stay out as late as possible before he went home to this garret. Before he met Camille, since he had no money to spend hanging around in cafés, he would linger for as long as he could in the cheap restaurant where he took dinner in the evening, smoking a pipe and sipping a *gloria*,[2] which cost him three sous. Then he would amble slowly back to the Rue Saint-Victor, strolling along the riverside and stopping to sit on a bench, when it was warm.

The shop in the Passage du Pont-Neuf became a delightful retreat for him, warm, peaceful and full of friendly words and kindnesses. He saved the three sous on his *gloria* and savoured Mme Raquin's excellent tea. He stayed there until ten o'clock, nodding off, digesting his dinner and making himself at home. He would not leave until he had helped Camille to shut up the shop.

One evening, he brought his easel and box of paints. He was to start on Camille's portrait the next day. A canvas was bought and minute preparations made. Finally the artist got to work, in the couple's own bedroom. The light was better there, he said.

It took him three evenings to draw the head. He carefully drew the charcoal pencil across the canvas, in short strokes, meanly; his technique was stiff, dry, like a parody of the primitive masters. He copied Camille's face as a pupil copies a nude model, with a hesitant hand and a naïve precision that gave the face a sulky look. On the fourth day, he put tiny little spots of colour on the palette and began to paint with the tips of the brushes. He spotted the canvas with dirty little marks, making short, tight hatching strokes, as he might when using a pencil.

At the end of every session, Mme Raquin and Camille

expressed their delight. Laurent said that they had to wait, that the likeness would come.

Once the portrait had been started, Thérèse spent all her time in the bedroom, now the studio. She left her aunt behind the counter and used the slightest excuse to go upstairs and become absorbed in watching Laurent paint.

Always solemn and subdued, paler and more silent, she would sit down and watch the brushes at work. However, the spectacle did not seem to entertain her very much; she came there as though drawn by some force, and stayed as though pinned to the spot. Sometimes, Laurent would turn round, give her a smile and ask if she liked the portrait. She barely answered him, trembling, before lapsing back into her contemplative absorption.

One evening, on his way home to the Rue Saint-Victor, Laurent had a long debate with himself. He was wondering whether or not to become Thérèse's lover.

'Now there's a little woman,' he thought, 'who will be my mistress whenever I like ... She's always there, at my back, examining me, sizing and weighing me up ... She shivers, she has a funny little face, silent and passionate. She definitely needs a lover, you can see that in her eyes ... You have to admit that Camille is a poor specimen.'

He laughed to himself, remembering his friend's scrawny pallor. Then he went on:

'She's bored in that shop. I go there because I have nowhere else to go. Otherwise, you wouldn't often catch me in the Passage du Pont-Neuf. It's so damp and depressing. A woman must find it deadly there ... I'm sure that she likes me; so, why shouldn't it be me rather than anyone else?'

He paused, imagined some fanciful things and, with a preoccupied air, watched the Seine flow by.

'Hell, yes, why not?' he exclaimed. 'I'll kiss her at the first chance I get. I bet she'll fall straight into my arms.'

He started to walk on, but then he was seized with doubts.

'Though she is ugly, when it comes down to it,' he thought. 'Her nose is long, her mouth large. I'm not at all in love with her. I might get myself mixed up in something unpleasant. I'll have to think.'

Laurent, who was quite cautious, juggled these thoughts around in his head for a full week. He calculated all the possible outcomes of a liaison with Thérèse, and decided to take the risk only when he had demonstrated to his own satisfaction that he would gain from it.

It was true that, in his view, Thérèse was ugly and he did not love her, but she would cost him nothing. The cheap women that he paid for were certainly no prettier or more loveable. So even economics told him to take his friend's wife. Meanwhile, it had been a long time since he had satisfied his needs; money was short, he had been depriving his flesh and did not want to lose an opportunity to indulge it a little. Finally, when you thought about it, this affair was one that could not have undesirable consequences: it would be in Thérèse's interests to keep it hidden and he could drop her whenever he felt like it. And even if Camille did discover everything and lost his temper, he could knock him down easily if he tried to do anything about it. From whatever way you looked at it, the prospect seemed simple and attractive to Laurent.

From that moment on, he lived in an agreeable state of confidence and passivity, biding his time. He had decided to act decisively at the first opportunity. He saw before him a future of warm evenings. All the Raquins would be attending to his enjoyment: Thérèse would appease the fire in his blood, Mme Raquin would cosset him like a mother and Camille would chat with him, in the evening, in the shop, to prevent him getting too bored.

The portrait was finished and still the opportunity did not arise. Thérèse was always there, oppressed and anxious, but Camille, too, never left the room and Laurent despaired of being able to get rid of him for an hour. At last, however, he had to announce that the portrait would be finished the next day. Mme Raquin proclaimed that they would have dinner together and celebrate the painter's work.

The next day, when Laurent had placed the final brushstroke on the canvas, the whole family gathered to admire the likeness. The portrait was vile, a dirty grey colour, with large, bluish-purple blotches. Laurent was unable to use the brightest colours

without making them dull and muddy. Unintentionally, he had
exaggerated his model's pale features, and Camille's face looked
like the greenish mask of a drowned man. The twisted line
of the drawing contorted the features and made the sinister
resemblance even more striking. But Camille was delighted: he
said that the painting made him look distinguished.

When he had admired his face, he announced that he was
going to fetch two bottles of champagne. Mme Raquin went
back down to the shop, and the artist remained alone with
Thérèse.

The young woman was still crouching in front of the picture,
staring vaguely ahead of her. She seemed to be quivering and
waiting. Laurent hesitated; he looked at the picture, and played
with his brushes. Time passed. Camille might come back and
the opportunity might not arise again. Suddenly, the painter
swung round and found himself face to face with Thérèse. They
looked at one another for a few seconds.

Then, with a violent gesture, Laurent leaned down and pulled
the young woman against his chest. He bent her head back,
crushing her lips with his. She recoiled, wildly, furiously, then,
suddenly, gave in, slipping down on to the floor. They did not
exchange a word. The act was silent and brutal.

VII

From the start, the lovers considered their relationship to be
necessary, inevitable and entirely natural. At their first meeting,
they called each other 'tu'[1] and kissed without awkwardness or
blushing, as though they had been intimate for several years.
They settled easily into their new situation, quite calmly and
shamelessly.

They arranged meetings. Since Thérèse could not go out, it
was decided that Laurent would go to her. In a precise, self-
assured voice, the young woman explained what she had worked
out. They would meet in the couple's bedroom. The lover would
arrive through the alleyway that led into the arcade and Thérèse

would open the staircase door to him. In the meantime, Camille would be in his office and Mme Raquin down below in the shop. It was a bold plan and bound to succeed.

Laurent agreed. In his prudence, there was a kind of brutal temerity, the temerity of a man with large fists. His mistress's calm and solemn manner induced him to come and taste the passion so boldly offered. He found an excuse, obtained two hours' leave from his boss and hurried round to the Passage du Pont-Neuf.

As soon as he got into the arcade, he felt the pangs of desire. The woman who sold costume jewellery was sitting right opposite the entrance; he had to wait for her to be busy, for a young shop girl to come and buy a ring or some copper earrings from her. Then, quickly, he slipped into the alleyway and climbed the dark, narrow staircase, steadying himself against walls that were oozing damp. His feet knocked on the stone stairs; at the sound of each step, he felt a burning pain across his chest. A door opened. On the threshold, in a patch of white light, he saw Thérèse in her camisole and petticoat, shining, with her hair tied tightly behind her head. She shut the door and put her arms around him. She exuded a warm smell, a smell of white linen and freshly washed flesh.

Laurent was amazed at finding his mistress beautiful. He had never seen this woman. Thérèse was lithe and strong; she grasped him, throwing her head back, while burning lights and passionate smiles flickered across her face. This lover's face seemed transfigured; she had a look at once mad and tender; she was radiant, with moist lips and gleaming eyes. The young woman, sinuous and twisting, possessed a strange beauty, an utter abandon. It was as though her face had been lit from inside and flames were leaping from her flesh. And around her, her burning blood and taut nerves released hot waves of passion, a penetrating, acrid fever in the air.

With the first kiss, she revealed the instincts of a courtesan. Her thirsting body gave itself wildly up to lust. It was as though she were awakening from a dream and being born to passion. She went from the feeble arms of Camille to the vigorous arms of Laurent, and the approach of a potent man gave her a shake that woke her flesh from its slumber. All the instincts of a highly-strung woman burst forth with exceptional violence. Her mother's blood, that African blood burning in her veins, began to flow and pound furiously in her thin, still almost virginal body. She opened up and offered herself with a sovereign lack of shame. From head to toe, she was shaken by long shudders of desire.

Laurent had never known such a woman. He was astonished, uneasy. Normally, his mistresses did not welcome him with such ardour; he was used to cold, indifferent kisses and to languid, sated loving. Thérèse's sobs and fits almost scared him, even as they excited his voluptuous curiosity. When he left her, he would be staggering like a drunken man. The following day, when he recovered his sly mood of calm caution, he wondered if he should go back to this lover, whose kisses inflamed him. At first, he firmly decided to stay at home. Then he wavered. He tried to forget, not to see Thérèse, naked, with her soft, urgent caresses; but she was always there, relentless, holding out her arms. The physical pain that he felt from this spectacle became intolerable.

He gave in, made a new arrangement to meet her and went back to the Passage du Pont-Neuf.

From that day onwards, Thérèse became part of his life. He did not yet accept her, but he gave in to her. He experienced hours of terror and moments of caution; and, in brief, the liaison disturbed him considerably; but his fears and uneasiness ceded to his desires. Their meetings multiplied, one after another.

Thérèse had no such doubts. She gave herself to him without reserve, going directly where her passions drove her. This woman, who had bowed to circumstances, was now standing up to reveal her whole being, to lay her life bare.

Sometimes she would put her arms round Laurent's neck, rest her head against his chest and say, in a voice still breathless:

'If only you knew how I've suffered! I was brought up in the damp warmth of a sickroom. I used to sleep beside Camille; in the night, I would move away from him, disgusted by the musty smell of his body. He was spiteful and stubborn. He wouldn't take any medicine unless I shared it with him, so to please my aunt I had to drink all sorts of potions . . . I don't know why I didn't die ... They made me ugly, my poor dear, they stole everything I had, and you can't love me as I love you.'

She cried, she kissed Laurent and she continued, speaking with an undertone of hatred in her voice:

'I don't wish them any harm. They brought me up, they took me in and protected me from poverty. But I would rather have been abandoned than endure their welcome. I had a ravenous hunger for fresh air; even when I was small, I dreamed of wandering the roads, barefoot in the dust, begging and living like a gypsy. They told me my mother was the daughter of a tribal chief in Africa. I have often thought about her. I realize that I belong to her in my blood and my instincts, I used to wish I had never left her, but was crossing the deserts, slung on her back ... Oh, what a childhood I had! I still feel revulsion and outrage when I remember the long days I spent in that room with Camille gasping away ... I had to crouch in front of the fire, watching like an idiot as his herb tea boiled and feeling the cramp in my limbs. But I couldn't move, because my aunt would scold me if I made a noise ... Later on, I was terribly happy, in the little house by the river, but I was already stupefied, I could hardly walk and I fell over if I ran. Then they buried me alive in this vile shop.'

Thérèse was breathing heavily and hugging her lover tightly; she was getting her revenge. Her thin, supple nostrils gave little nervous twitches.

'You wouldn't believe how bad they made me,' she continued. 'They turned me into a hypocrite and a liar. They stifled me with their bourgeois comfort and I don't understand why there is any red blood left in my veins. I would lower my eyes and put on a sad, imbecilic face like them, leading the same dead life. When you first met me, huh, didn't I look like a fool? I was earnest, I was crushed, I was like an idiot. I no longer hoped for anything, I used to think about throwing myself into the Seine one day ... But before I got to that point, you don't know how many nights I spent in fury! There, in Vernon, in my cold room, I would bite my pillow to stifle my cries, I would hit myself and call myself a coward. My blood was boiling, I could have torn myself apart. Twice, I thought of running away, just walking away, anywhere, in the sunlight. But I couldn't do it: they had turned me into a docile creature with their weak kindness and their repulsive tenderness. So I lied, I kept on lying. I stayed there, sweet and silent, dreaming about how I could hit and bite.'

The young woman stopped, wiping her damp lips on Laurent's neck. Then, after a pause:

'I can't remember why I agreed to marry Camille. I didn't refuse, out of a sort of contemptuous indifference. I felt sorry for the boy. When I played with him, I could feel my fingers sink into his arms as though into clay. I took him, because my aunt offered him to me and I thought I would never have to bother about him ... And I found a husband who was no different from the ailing little boy I used to sleep with when I was six. He was just as frail, as whining, and he still had that smell of a sick child that used to disgust me so much in the old days. I'm telling you all this so that you won't be jealous ... A sort of nausea would rise in my throat, I thought of all the medicines I'd taken and I shrank from him; I spent dreadful nights ... But you, you ...'

Thérèse sat upright and bent over backwards, her fingers caught in Laurent's large hands, looking at his broad shoulders and his huge neck ...

'I love you. I've loved you from the moment when Camille pushed you into the shop ... Perhaps you don't respect me, because I gave myself to you, entirely, all at once ... It's true, I don't know how it happened. I'm proud, I got carried away. I wanted to hit you, that first day when you kissed me and threw me on the ground in this room. I don't know how I loved you; if anything, I hated you. The sight of you upset me, it hurt to look at you. When you were there my nerves were at breaking-point, my mind went blank and a red film floated before my eyes. Oh, how much I suffered! And I looked for that suffering, I used to wait for you to come, I would walk round your chair so that I could pick up your breath and rub my clothes against yours. It was as though your blood was sending waves of heat towards me as I went by, and this sort of burning mist that wrapped around you drew me and kept me beside you, much as I tried, inside me, to break away . . . Do you remember when you were painting here? An irresistible force drew me to your side and I breathed in your atmosphere, feeling a cruel delight. I knew that I seemed to be begging for kisses and I was ashamed of my slavery, feeling that I would fall if you so much as touched me. But I gave in to my cowardice and shook with cold as I waited for you to deign to take me in your arms.'

At this, Thérèse paused, shivering, as though proud and avenged. She was intoxicated, holding Laurent against her breast; and the bare, icy room witnessed scenes of burning ardour and sinister brutality. Each new meeting between them brought still more passionate ecstasies.

The young woman seemed to enjoy her daring and impudence. She had no misgivings, no fear. She was throwing herself into adultery with a kind of urgent candour, careless of danger, feeling a sort of pride in taking risks. When her lover was due, her only precaution would be to tell her aunt that she was going upstairs for a rest. And while he was there, she walked around, talked and acted unheedingly, without ever thinking about the noise. At the start, it would sometimes worry Laurent.

'For heaven's sake!' he would whisper to Thérèse. 'Don't make such a racket. Mme Raquin will come up.'

'Pooh!' she would reply, with a laugh. 'You're always scared. She's stuck behind the counter, what would she be coming up here for? She'd be too afraid that someone would rob her. Anyway, let her come if she wants. You can hide . . . I don't give a damn about her. I love you.'

Laurent did not find this speech the least bit reassuring. Passion had not yet subdued his sly peasant caution. But soon habit induced him, without too much anxiety, to accept the boldness of these meetings in broad daylight, in Camille's room, just feet away from the old haberdasher. His mistress kept telling him that danger spared those who confronted it directly, and she was right. The lovers could never have found a safer place than this room where no one thought to look for them. There, they would satisfy their desires, amazingly undisturbed.

One day, however, Mme Raquin did come up, concerned that her niece might be ill. The young woman had been upstairs for almost three hours. She was foolhardy enough not even to bolt the door which led off the dining room to the bedroom.

When Laurent heard the old woman's heavy footsteps coming up the wooden staircase, he panicked and hurriedly looked for his waistcoat and hat. Thérèse started to laugh at the funny face he was making. She seized his arm and thrust him down, into a corner at the foot of the bed, telling him in a quiet, calm voice:

'Stay there and don't move.'

She threw the man's clothing that was lying around over him and on top of it all spread a white petticoat that she had taken off herself. All this she did with measured, careful gestures, not losing any of her calm. Then she lay down in the bed, her hair untidy, half naked, still flushed and shaking.

Mme Raquin gently opened the door and came over to the bed, walking as softly as she could. The younger woman pretended to be asleep. Laurent was sweating under the white petticoat.

'Thérèse, are you ill, child?' the haberdasher asked, in a voice full of concern.

Thérèse opened her eyes, yawned, turned round and replied in a pained voice that she had a terrible migraine. She begged her aunt to let her sleep. The old woman left as she had come, without a sound.

The two lovers, laughing silently, kissed with violent passion.

'You see!' Thérèse said triumphantly. 'We've nothing to fear here. All these people are blind. They are not in love.'

Another day, the young woman had an odd idea. Sometimes she would rave, behaving as though she were mad.

The tabby cat, François, was sitting on his bottom right in the middle of the room. Solemn and motionless, he was looking at the two lovers with wide-open eyes. He seemed to be examining them carefully, without blinking, lost in a sort of diabolical trance.[2]

'Look at François,' Thérèse said to Laurent. 'You'd think he understood and that he was going to tell Camille everything this evening. Why, wouldn't it be odd if he were to start speaking in the shop one of these days? He could tell some fine stories about us.'

The young woman was exceptionally amused by the idea that François might speak. Laurent looked at the cat's large green eyes and felt a shudder run through him.

'Here's what he'd do,' Thérèse went on. 'He'd stand up and, pointing at me with one paw and at you with the other, he'd exclaim: "Monsieur and Madame here were kissing one another very hard in the bedroom; they didn't bother about me, but since their criminal affair disgusts me, I beg you to have both of them thrown into gaol, and then they won't disturb my afternoon sleep again."'

Thérèse joked like a child, miming the cat, extending her hands like claws and moving her shoulders with a feline undulation. François, sitting still as a rock, kept on looking at her. Only his eyes seemed to be alive and, in the corners of his mouth, there were two deep folds that made this stuffed animal's face seem to break out laughing.

Laurent felt a chill in his bones. He found Thérèse's joke ridiculous. He got up and put the cat out of the door. In fact, he was afraid. Thérèse was not yet entirely mistress of him. Deep inside, he felt a little of the unease that he had experienced from the young woman's first embrace.

VIII

In the evenings, in the shop, Laurent was perfectly happy. Normally, he came back from the office with Camille. Mme Raquin had conceived a maternal affection for him; she knew that he was not well off, that he ate poorly and slept in an attic, so she told him once and for all that there would always be a place for him at their table. She liked the boy with that effusive love that old women have for people from their own part of the world who carry with them memories of the past.

The young man took full advantage of this hospitality. On leaving the office, before coming back, he would take a bit of a walk with Camille along the river. Both of them appreciated this friendship; they suffered less from boredom and chatted as they went. Then they would agree to go and eat Mme Raquin's supper. Laurent opened the door of the shop as though he owned it. He sat himself down, astride his chair, smoking and spitting, just as though he were at home.

He was not at all bothered by the presence of Thérèse. He treated the young woman with a friendly lack of formality, teasing her and paying her routine compliments, without a hint of a smile. Camille laughed and, since his wife would reply to his friend only in monosyllables, he was quite convinced that they hated each other. One day, he even reproached Thérèse with what he called her coldness towards Laurent.

Laurent had been right: he had become the wife's lover, the husband's friend and the mother's spoiled child. Never had his appetites been so well satisfied. He luxuriated in the infinite pleasures provided for him by the Raquin family. In any case, his position in this family seemed quite natural to him. He was on intimate terms with Camille, but felt no anger or remorse towards him. He was not even cautious about what he did or said, so certain was he of his prudence and composure; the egotism with which he enjoyed this happiness protected him against any feeling of sin. In the shop, his mistress became a woman like any other, whom he might not kiss and who did not exist for him. The reason he did not kiss her in front of everyone was that he was afraid of not being allowed to come back. This was the only thing that stopped him. Otherwise, he would not have cared at all about the feelings of Camille and his mother. He was blissfully unaware of any consequences that the discovery of his affair might bring. He thought that he was acting naturally, as anyone would have done in his place, being a poor and hungry man. Hence his smug complacency, his prudent daring and his mocking attitude of unconcern.

Thérèse, who was more nervous and anxious, was obliged to play a part. She did so to perfection, thanks to the training in hypocrisy that she owed to her upbringing. She had lied for more than fifteen years, repressing her passions and applying her implacable will to appear dull and listless. She had no difficulty in freezing her features behind a dead mask. When Laurent arrived, she appeared to him serious, grumpy, her nose longer and her lips thinner. She was ugly, surly and unapproachable. In reality, she was not putting it on; she was simply playing her old self, without attracting attention by exaggerating her brusqueness. As far as she was concerned, she felt a bitter pleasure in fooling Camille and Mme Raquin. She was not like Laurent, wallowing in a state of dull contentment at the satisfaction of his desires and oblivious of duty. She knew that what she was doing was wrong, and she had violent urges to leap up from the table and kiss Laurent full on the mouth, to show her husband and her aunt that she was not an animal, and that she had a lover.

At times, warm feelings of joy rose within her and, accomplished actress though she was, she could not refrain from singing, when her lover was not there and she was not afraid of giving herself away. These sudden outbursts of merriment delighted Mme Raquin, who used to accuse her niece of being too solemn. The young woman bought pots of flowers and arranged them on the window sills of her room. Then she had new wallpaper put up; she wanted a carpet, curtains, new rosewood furniture. All this luxury was for Laurent's benefit.

Nature and circumstances seemed to have made this man for this woman, and to have driven them towards one another. Together, the woman, nervous and dissembling, the man, lustful, living like an animal, they made a strongly united couple. They complemented one another, they protected one another. In the evening, at table, in the pale light of the lamp, you could feel the strength of the bond between them, seeing Laurent's heavy, smiling face and the silent, impenetrable mask of Thérèse.

These were sweet and tranquil evenings. In the silence, in the warm, transparent half-light, friendly words passed between those pressed around the table; after dessert they spoke about the dozens of trivial events of the day, their memories of the past and their hopes for the future. Camille loved Laurent as much as such a self-satisfied egotist could love, and Laurent seemed to have an equal affection for him; they would exchange expressions of devotion, considerate gestures and looks of concern. Mme Raquin observed them with placid features, imbued the very air that they breathed with tranquillity, spreading her peace around her children. It looked like a reunion of old acquaintances who knew each other's inmost thoughts and had total confidence in their friendship.

Thérèse, as still and peaceful as the rest, would study these bourgeois joys and this complacent indolence. And, in her inner depths, she laughed, savagely. Her whole being mocked, while her face retained its cold rigidity. She felt an exquisite pleasure in telling herself that, only a few hours earlier, she had been in the room next door, half naked, her hair loose, lying on Laurent's chest; she remembered everything about her afternoon of insane desire, went through each detail in her mind's eye and compared that passionate scene with the lifeless one before her eyes. Oh, how she was deceiving these good folk! And how happy she was to deceive them with such triumphal impudence! It was there, a few feet away, behind that thin partition, that she would greet her man; it was there that she would writhe in the grim throes of adultery. And, for that moment, her lover would become a stranger to her, a friend and colleague of her husband, a kind of imbecile, an intruder who did not have to concern her. This frightful play-acting, this life of deception and this contrast between the burning kisses of daytime and the feigned indifference of evening, made the young woman's heart pound with new ardour.

When Mme Raquin and Camille went downstairs, for some reason or other, Thérèse would leap up and silently, with savage force, press her lips against those of her lover and stay like that, panting, suffocating, until she heard the wooden stairs creak. Then, with an agile movement, she went back to her place and resumed her grudging scowl. In a calm voice, Laurent carried on the chat he had been having with Camille. It was like a lightning flash of passion, swift, blinding, across a leaden sky.

On Thursdays, the evening would be a little more lively. Laurent was mortally bored on that day of the week and made sure that he did not miss a single meeting; he thought it prudent to be known and respected by Camille's friends. He had to listen to the ramblings of Grivet and Old Michaud. Michaud would always tell the same stories of murder and theft, while Grivet spoke at the same time about his workmates, his bosses and his department. The young man would take refuge with Olivier and Suzanne, whose brand of idiocy he found less boring. In any case, he was not slow to suggest a game of dominoes.

It was on Thursday evening that Thérèse would settle the day and time of their meetings. In the confusion at the end, when Mme Raquin and Camille were taking their guests to the front door, the young woman would go up to Laurent and whisper to him, squeezing his hand. Sometimes, when everyone's back was turned, she would even kiss him, from a kind of bravado.

This life of alternating storm and calm lasted for eight months. The lovers lived in a state of complete beatitude. Thérèse was no longer bored and no longer desired anything, while Laurent, sated, cosseted and even plumper, feared nothing except the end of this delightful existence.

IX

One afternoon, when Laurent was about to leave work and hurry off to see Thérèse, who was expecting him, his boss called him in and informed him that in future he was forbidden to go out of the office. He had been having too much time off and the management had decided to sack him if he was away one more time.

Tied to his desk, he was in desperation until the evening. He had to earn his living, he could not afford to lose his job. When evening came, Thérèse's wrathful look was a torture for him. He had no idea how to explain to his mistress why he had failed in his promise. While Camille was shutting up shop, he quickly went over to the young woman.

'We can't see one another any more,' he whispered. 'My boss won't let me out again.'

Camille came back and Laurent had to go without any further explanation, leaving Thérèse stunned by this abrupt remark. In exasperation, refusing to admit that her pleasure could be denied, she spent a sleepless night devising ridiculous plans for them to meet. The following Thursday, she talked to Laurent for a minute longer. Their anxiety was increased by the fact that they did not even know where to meet so that they could talk it over. The young woman gave her lover a new rendezvous which, for the second time, he failed to keep. From then on, she had only one idea in her mind, which was to see him at all costs.

For a fortnight, Laurent had not been able to go near Thérèse, and he realized how essential the woman had become to him. Indulging his lusts had created new appetites in him, which urgently demanded satisfaction. He no longer felt any awkwardness at his mistress's love-making, but sought it with the determination of a starving animal. A raging of the blood had infected his flesh and now that his mistress was being taken away from him, his passion burst out with blind fury; he loved her to distraction. Everything in the blossoming of this animal being seemed unconscious: he was obeying his instincts, letting himself be driven by the will of his body. If anyone had told him, a year earlier, that he would be enslaved by a woman, to the point of destroying his peace of mind, he would have burst out laughing. Desire had been working silently inside him, without his realizing it, and had eventually cast him, bound hand and foot, into the savage embraces of Thérèse. Now he was afraid of stepping beyond the bounds of prudence and did not dare come to the Passage du Pont-Neuf in the evenings, fearful that he might do something crazy. He was no longer his own master; his mistress, with her feline sinuosity and nervous flexibility, had gradually insinuated herself into every fibre of his body. He needed that woman to live as one needs to eat and drink.

He would surely have done something foolish had he not received a letter from Thérèse telling him to stay at home the next day. His mistress promised to come and see him at around eight o'clock in the evening.

On leaving the office, he got rid of Camille by saying that he was tired and wanted to go back to bed straight away. After dinner, Thérèse also played a part; she said something about a customer who had left without paying, pretended to be a resolute creditor and announced that she was going to claim her money. The customer lived at Batignolles. Mme Raquin and Camille thought it was a long way to go and that the outcome was uncertain, but they were not excessively surprised and let Thérèse leave quietly.

She hurried to the Port aux Vins, slipping on the greasy pavements and bumping into people on the street in her haste. Her face was damp with sweat and her hands were burning; she was like a drunken woman. She quickly ran up the stairs in the lodging house. On the sixth floor, breathless, through blurred eyes, she saw Laurent leaning over the banisters, waiting for her.

She came into the garret. The space was so small that her wide skirts could hardly fit inside it. She tore off her hat with one hand and leaned against the bed, swooning . . .

The skylight was wide open and poured the cool of the evening on to the burning heat of the bed. The lovers stayed for a long time in this hovel, as though at the bottom of a hole. Suddenly, Thérèse heard the clock on La Pitié[1] strike ten. She wished she had been deaf. She raised herself painfully off the bed and looked round the garret, which she had not yet examined. She looked for her hat, tied the ribbons and sat down again, saying in a measured voice:

'I have to go.'

Laurent had come over and was kneeling in front of her. He took her hands.

'Goodbye,' she said, without moving.

'Don't just say goodbye,' he insisted. 'That's too vague. When will you come back?'

She looked straight in his eyes.

'Do you want the truth?' she said. 'Well, the truth is that I don't think I shall come back. I don't have any excuse, I can't invent one.'

'So we must say farewell, for good?'

'No! I don't want to!'

She spoke the words with a mixture of fury and terror. Then, without knowing what she was saying and without getting up, she added in a quieter voice:

'I'm leaving.'

Laurent thought. His mind turned to Camille.

'I've got nothing against him,' he said finally, without saying the man's name. 'But he really is too much of a nuisance.

Couldn't you get rid of him for us, send him on a journey somewhere, a long way off?'

'Oh, yes! Send him on a journey!' she replied, shaking her head. 'Do you think a man like that would agree to go on a journey? There's only one journey from which no one returns ... But he will bury the lot of us. All those types with one foot in the grave never seem to die.'

There was a pause. Laurent remained on his knees, pressed against his mistress, his head leaning on her breast.

'I had a dream,' he said. 'I wanted to spend a whole night with you, to go to sleep in your arms and wake up the next morning to your kisses. I want to be your husband ... Do you understand?'

'Yes, yes,' Thérèse answered, trembling.

She suddenly leaned over Laurent's face, covering it with kisses. The laces on her hat caught on the young man's rough beard; she had forgotten that she was dressed and that she would crease her clothes. She was sobbing, panting as she murmured between her tears.

'Don't say such things,' she said. 'Don't say such things, because I won't have the strength to leave you, I'll stay here ... You should give me courage. Tell me that we'll see one another again. It's true, isn't it: you do need me? One day we'll find a way of living together, won't we?'

'So come back, come back tomorrow,' Laurent insisted, his trembling hands stroking her waist.

'But I can't come back ... I told you, I don't have any excuse.' She was wringing her hands. She continued:

'It's not the scandal that bothers me! If you like, when I get home, I'll tell Camille that you are my lover and I'll come back here to sleep ... I'm worried about you. I don't want to upset your life, I want to make you happy.'

The young man's instinctive caution came to the fore.

'You're right,' he said. 'We mustn't behave like children. Now, if your husband were to die ...'

'If my husband were to die,' Thérèse repeated slowly.

'We would get married, we wouldn't fear a thing, we would revel in our love ... What a good, sweet life it would be!'

She was sitting up now, her cheeks pale, looking with dark eyes at her lover. Her lips were twitching.

'People do die sometimes,' she murmured, at length. 'Only, it's dangerous for those who survive.'

Laurent said nothing.

'You see,' she went on, 'all the usual methods are no good.'

'I didn't mean that,' he said calmly. 'I'm not a fool, I want to love you in peace. I was just thinking that accidents do happen every day, that a foot can slip or a tile fall off the roof . . . Do you understand? In that last case, only the wind is to blame.'

His voice was strange. He gave a smile and added, in a caressing tone:

'Now then, don't worry, we'll love one another, we shall live together happily . . . Since you can't come here, I'll arrange it somehow . . . If we should stay without seeing one another for several months, don't forget me, but know that I am working for our happiness.'

He put his arms around Thérèse as she was opening the door to go.

'You are mine, aren't you?' he went on. 'Swear to me that you will give yourself to me entirely, at any time, whenever I want –'

'Yes!' she cried. 'I belong to you. Do what you wish with me.'

They stayed there for a moment, fierce, wild and silent. Then Thérèse roughly tore herself away from him and, without turning round, left the attic and went down the stairs. Laurent listened to the sound of her receding footsteps.

When the sound had died away, he went back into his little room and lay down. The bedclothes were warm. He felt suffocated in this narrow cage, which Thérèse had left full of the heat of her passion. He seemed to be still breathing something of her, she had been there, leaving behind a pervasive scent of herself, a smell of violets; but now all he had to press in his arms was his mistress's intangible ghost, present all around him; he was in a fever of reviving, unsatisfied desire. He did not close the window, but lay on his back, his arms bare and his hands unclenched, drinking in the cool air, while pondering it all as he gazed at the square of dark blue outlined above him by the skylight.

Until daybreak, he turned the same idea over in his mind. Before Thérèse came, he had not considered the murder of Camille. It was under pressure of events, annoyed at the idea of not seeing his mistress again, that he had spoken about the man's death. And, at that, a new corner of his unconscious being had come to light. In the passion of adultery, he had begun to dream about killing.

Now, calmer, alone in the peace of night, he was reviewing the notion of murder. The idea of death, uttered in desperation between two kisses, came back keenly, relentlessly. Driven by insomnia, aroused by the pungent scents that Thérèse had left behind, he devised traps, working out what could go wrong and enumerating all the benefits to be derived from becoming a murderer.

He had everything to gain from the crime. He told himself that his father, the peasant in Jeufosse, was never going to die; he might have to spend another ten years working in the department, eating in cheap restaurants and living, without a wife, in an attic. The idea infuriated him. On the other hand, with Camille dead, he would marry Thérèse, become the heir to Mme Raquin, resign from his job and stroll around in the sunshine. It pleased him to imagine this lazy existence; he could already see himself as a man of leisure, eating and sleeping, waiting patiently for his father to die. And when reality invaded his dream, he bumped into Camille and clenched his fists, as though to strike him down.

Laurent wanted Thérèse. He wanted her for himself alone, always within reach. If he did not get rid of the husband, the wife would elude him. She had told him that she could not come back. He would happily have kidnapped her and carried her off somewhere, but then they would both die of hunger. There was less risk in killing the husband. There would be no scandal, he would just push a man out of the way in order to take his place. With his brutal peasant reasoning, he considered this solution both an excellent and a natural one. It was in fact his innate prudence that suggested adopting this quick expedient.

He lay sprawling on his bed, flat on his belly, pressing his damp face into the pillow where Thérèse's chignon had spread.

He grasped the material between his dry lips and drank in the faint scents still clinging to it; and he stayed there, breathless, panting, watching strips of fire cross his closed eyelids. He was wondering how he could kill Camille. Then, when he was out of breath, he would suddenly turn round until he was lying on his back, eyes wide open, with the cold air from the window full on his face, as he stared up at the stars and at the bluish square of sky, seeking for advice on murder, a plan for how to kill.

Nothing came to him. As he had told his mistress, he was not a child or an idiot. He did not want to use a dagger or poison. He needed a sly, cunning sort of crime, one that involved no danger, a kind of sinister snuffing out, without screams or terror – a simple disappearance. Even though he was shaken and driven forward by passion, his whole being imperiously demanded caution. He was too much of a coward, too much of a sensualist, to risk his own tranquillity. He was killing in order to live in peace and happiness.

Little by little, sleep overcame him. The cold air had driven the warm, sweet-smelling ghost of Thérèse out of the attic. Exhausted, calmed, Laurent allowed a kind of vague, gentle numbness to sweep over him. As he was falling asleep, he decided to wait for a suitable opportunity, and his mind, growing drowsier and drowsier, cradled him with the thought: 'I shall kill him, I shall kill him.' In five minutes, he was at rest, breathing with untroubled regularity.

Thérèse had got home at eleven. She arrived at the Passage du Pont-Neuf, her head burning and her mind racing, without any knowledge of the journey she had taken. Her ears were so full of the words she had heard that she felt as though she had just come down the stairs from Laurent's room. She found Mme Raquin and Camille anxious and full of concern. She answered all their questions curtly, telling them that she had had a useless journey and stayed for an hour waiting for an omnibus.

When she got into bed, the clothes felt cold and damp. Her limbs, still burning, shivered in repulsion. Camille soon went to sleep and for a long time Thérèse looked at the pale face idiotically resting on the pillow, with its mouth open. She moved away from him and felt an urge to stick her clenched fist into that mouth.

X

Almost three weeks went by. Laurent came back to the shop every evening. He seemed weary, as though sick. There was a faint, bluish circle around his eyes, while his lips were pale and cracked. But otherwise, he still had his usual heavy passivity about him; he looked Camille straight in the face and behaved in the same open, friendly way. Mme Raquin spoiled the family friend even more, seeing him relapse into a sort of dull fever.

Thérèse had resumed her dumb, sullen look. She was more unmoving, more impenetrable and more passive than ever. It seemed that Laurent did not exist for her; she hardly glanced at him, spoke to him only occasionally and treated him with utter indifference. Mme Raquin, whose good nature was pained by this attitude, would sometimes tell the young man: 'Take no notice of my niece's coldness. Her face looks unfriendly, I know, but her heart is warm with every kind of affection and devotion.'

The two lovers no longer made any assignations. Since the day at the Rue Saint-Victor, they had not once met alone. In the evening, when they were face to face, apparently calm and indifferent to one another, waves of passion, terror and desire seethed beneath the unruffled surfaces of their faces. And inside Thérèse there were moments of fury, baseness and cruel sneering, while in Laurent there was dark brutality and anguished indecision. They themselves did not dare to look into the depths of their beings, to plumb this feverish unrest that filled their brains with a kind of thick, acrid vapour.

When they could, behind a door, without saying a word, they would exchange a brief, rough grasp of hands. They would have liked to carry off shreds of the other's flesh clinging to their fingers. There was only this hand squeeze to quench their desire; they put their whole bodies into it. They asked for nothing else from one another. They were waiting.

One Thursday evening, before they started their game, Mme Raquin's guests, as usual, had a bit of a chat. One of the main subjects of conversation was talking to Old Michaud about his former job and asking him about the strange and sinister happenings in which he had supposedly been involved. Grivet and Camille would listen to the police commissioner's tales with the scared, open-mouthed expressions of little children hearing *Bluebeard* or *Tom Thumb*. They were terrified and entertained at the same time.

That particular day, Michaud, who had just told them about a frightful murder, the details of which had sent shivers up their spines, added with a shake of the head: 'And we don't know everything . . . How many crimes remain undetected! How many murderers escape justice!'

'What!' exclaimed Grivet, in astonishment. 'Do you think that there are villains, like that, in the streets, who have killed people and not been arrested?'

Olivier gave a pitying look and smiled.

'My dear sir,' he replied, curtly, 'if they have not been arrested, that is because no one knows that they have killed someone.'

This argument did not seem to convince Grivet. Camille came to his assistance.

'I'm of one and the same opinion as Monsieur Grivet,' he said, with ridiculous pomposity. 'I need to believe that the police is doing its job and that I shall never rub shoulders with a murderer in the street.'

Olivier took these words as a personal affront.

'Of course the police does its job!' he exclaimed, in an irritated voice. 'But we can't achieve the impossible. There are scoundrels who got their education in crime at the Devil's own school; they would elude God Himself . . . Isn't that right, Father?'

'Yes, yes,' Old Michaud agreed. 'Now, when I was in Vernon – you may remember this, Madame Raquin – a carter was murdered on the highway. The body was found cut in pieces at the bottom of a ditch. We never did manage to get our hands on the guilty party. He may still be alive today, he could be our next-door neighbour . . . and Monsieur Grivet might even meet him on his way home.'

Grivet went as white as a sheet. He did not dare turn round:
he thought that the carter's murderer was right behind him.
Despite that, he was delighted at feeling this fear.

'No, no,' he stammered, without knowing quite what he was
saying. 'Well, no, I really can't bring myself to believe that . . . I
have a story of my own. Once upon a time there was a servant
girl who was thrown into prison for stealing a silver knife and
fork from her masters. Two months later, when they were
cutting down a tree, they found the silver in a magpie's nest.
The bird was the thief. The servant was released . . . so you see,
the guilty party is always punished.'

Grivet was triumphant. Olivier tittered.

'So, you're saying they put the magpie in prison?'

'That's not what Monsieur Grivet meant,' Camille said, not
wanting to see his boss made to look a fool. 'Mother, give us
the dominoes.'

While Mme Raquin went to get the box, the young man
continued, talking to Michaud:

'So you admit that the police is powerless? There are
murderers walking around in the full light of day?'

'I'm sorry to say there are,' the commissioner replied.

'It's immoral,' Grivet concluded.

Thérèse and Laurent had said nothing during this conversation. They did not even smile at Grivet's stupidity. Both leaning on their elbows on the table, they listened, with a distant
look on their rather pale faces. For a moment, their eyes met,
dark and burning. Little beads of sweat shone at the roots of
Thérèse's hair and a chill draught made Laurent's skin shiver
imperceptibly.

XI

Sometimes, on Sundays, when it was fine, Camille obliged
Thérèse to go out with him and take a short walk down the
Champs-Elysées. The young woman would have preferred to
stay in the damp shadows of the shop; it tired her and bored her

being on her husband's arm as he strolled along the pavement, stopping in front of the shop windows, with the astonishment, the remarks and the silences of an imbecile. But Camille insisted. He liked to show off his wife, and when he met one of his colleagues, especially one of his superiors, he would be so proud to exchange greetings in the company of Madame. In any case, he would walk for the sake of walking, almost without saying a word, stiff and misshapen in his Sunday best, dragging his feet, dim-witted and vain. It pained Thérèse to have a man like that on her arm.

On days when they went out for a walk, Mme Raquin would accompany the children to the end of the arcade. She kissed them as though they were leaving on a journey, giving endless instructions and expressing earnest wishes.

'Above all,' she would tell them, 'beware of accidents. There is so much traffic in Paris! Promise me you won't go among crowds.'

Eventually, she would let them go, looking after them until they disappeared. Then she went back into the shop. Her legs were getting heavy and she could not walk any great distance.

At other times, though less often, the couple would escape from Paris; they would go to Saint-Ouen or Asnières,[1] and eat a fried meal in one of the restaurants by the Seine. These were real occasions, talked about for a month in advance. Thérèse agreed more readily – almost with joy – to such outings, which would keep her out in the open air until ten or eleven at night. Saint-Ouen, with its green islands, reminded her of Vernon; there, all the wild affection that she had felt for the river when she was a girl revived in her. She would sit down on the bank, dipping her hands in the water and feeling truly alive in the heat of the sun, moderated by the cool breeze in the shade of the trees. While she was tearing and dirtying her dress on the pebbles and the muddy ground, Camille would carefully spread out his handkerchief and crouch down beside her, taking a dozen different precautionary measures. Recently, the young couple had almost always taken Laurent with them; he would brighten up the walk with his jokes and his peasant vigour.

One Sunday, Camille, Thérèse and Laurent set out for Saint-Ouen at about eleven o'clock, after lunch. They had planned the trip for a long time and it was to be their last that season. Autumn was coming and cold gusts were starting to freeze the evening air.

That morning, however, the sky was still blue and serene. It was hot in the sun and warm under the shade. They decided that they should take advantage of the last fine day.

The three trippers took a cab, pursued by the old haberdasher's anxious outpourings and lamentations. They crossed Paris and left the cab at the fortifications,[2] carrying on to Saint-Ouen on foot. It was midday. The road, brightly lit by the sun and covered in dust, had the dazzling brightness of snow. The air was thick, acrid and scorching. Thérèse walked along on Camille's arm, with little steps, protected by his sunshade, while he mopped his brow with a huge handkerchief. Behind them came Laurent, with the sun beating down on the back of his neck, though he showed no sign of feeling it. He was whistling, knocking aside the pebbles with his foot and, from time to time, glancing at the swaying of his mistress's hips with a fierce glint in his eye.

As soon as they got to Saint-Ouen, they set about finding a clump of trees with a carpet of green grass in the shade. They crossed over to an island and pushed their way into the undergrowth. The fallen leaves lay on the ground in a reddish layer, which snapped under their feet with a dry crackling sound. The tree trunks were standing upright, numberless, like clusters of Gothic columns, and the branches dipped right down to their foreheads, so that their only horizon was the bronze vault of dying leaves and the black-and-white shafts of the aspens and oaks.[3] The walkers were in a wilderness, a melancholy pit in the silence and cool of a narrow clearing. All around, they could hear the Seine rumbling by.

Camille had chosen a dry spot and sat down, lifting up the skirts of his coat. Thérèse had just dropped on to the leaves with a lot of noise from her rustling skirts; she was half smothered by the folds of her dress billowing out around her and uncovering one of her legs up to the knee. Laurent, lying face down with his chin on the ground, was looking at this leg and listening to his friend railing against the government, saying that all the islands in the Seine should be changed into English gardens, with benches, sanded paths and pruned trees, as in the Tuileries.[4]

They spent nearly three hours in the clearing, waiting for the sun to cool before going for a walk in the country, then dinner. Camille talked about his office and told them silly stories; then he got tired, flopped down and went off to sleep. He had placed his hat over his eyes. Thérèse, with her eyes closed, had been pretending to snooze for a long time.

At this, Laurent slipped quietly over to the young woman; he kissed her shoe, then her ankle. The leather and the white stocking burned his mouth as he kissed them. The bitter scent of the earth mingled with the light perfume of Thérèse and seeped into him, heating his blood and arousing his lust. For the past month, he had been living in a state of resentful celibacy. Now, the walk in the sun on the road to Saint-Ouen had aroused him. He was there, in this isolated pit, surrounded by the great voluptuous stillness and shade, and he could not clasp his arms around this woman who belonged to him. The husband might wake up and see him, which would mean that all his caution had been wasted. That man was a constant obstacle. The lover, lying flat on the ground, hidden by her skirts, trembling and eager, placed his silent kisses on the shoe and the white stocking. Thérèse lay absolutely still. Laurent thought that she was asleep.

He got up, his back aching and leaned against a tree. Then he saw that the young woman was staring upwards with her eyes shining and wide open. Her face, between her raised arms, was dull and pale, cold and stiff. Thérèse was thinking. Her staring eyes were like a deep abyss which held only darkness. She did not move or look towards Laurent, who was standing behind her.

Her lover stared at her, almost fearful at seeing her so still and so unresponsive to his caresses. This head, white and lifeless, sunk in the folds of her skirts, aroused in him a sort of terror, shot through with chafing lusts. He would have liked to bend down and close those great open eyes with a kiss. But, almost in the same skirts, Camille, too, was sleeping. This poor creature, with his thin, twisted body, was snoring lightly and under the hat half covering his face you could see his mouth open, deformed by sleep, gaping in a foolish grimace. Little reddish hairs were scattered around his skinny chin, staining the pallid flesh and, now that his head was thrown back, you could see his thin, wrinkled neck, in the middle of which the Adam's apple stood out, brick red, rising with each snore. Sprawled out like this, Camille was an undignified and irksome sight.

Looking at him, Laurent swiftly lifted up his foot. He was about to crush the face with a single blow.

Thérèse stifled a cry. She paled and closed her eyes, turning her head away, as though to avoid the splash of blood.

And Laurent, for a few seconds, stayed there, his foot raised, poised above the sleeping Camille's face. Then he slowly withdrew his leg and walked a few steps away. It occurred to him that this would be a stupid murder: the crushed head would bring the whole police force down on him. The only reason he wanted to do away with Camille was to live with Thérèse. After committing the crime, he wanted a life of pleasure, like the person who killed the carter in the story that Old Michaud had told them.

He went over to the river bank and watched the water flowing past, with a mindless look. Then, suddenly, he went back into the undergrowth. He had finally devised a plan, worked out a murder that would be convenient and without risk to himself.

So he woke the sleeping man by tickling his nose with a straw. Camille sneezed and got up, thinking it a very good trick. He liked Laurent because of such jokes, which made him laugh. Then he shook his wife, who had her eyes closed. When Thérèse had got up and shaken her skirts, which were crumpled and covered in dry leaves, the three of them left the clearing, breaking the small branches in their path.

They left the island and walked along the roads, down paths full of groups of people in their Sunday best. Between the hedges, girls were running along in brightly coloured dresses; a team of oarsmen went by, singing; lines of bourgeois couples, old folk and employees with their wives, were strolling, beside the ditches. Every path seemed like a populous, noisy street. Only the sun remained aloof and calm. It was declining towards the horizon, casting vast expanses of pale light over the reddening trees and white roads. A sharp chill was starting to descend from the shimmering sky.

Camille was no longer giving Thérèse his arm. He was talking to Laurent, laughing at his friend's jokes and tricks as he jumped over the ditches and lifted up heavy stones. The young woman, on the other side of the road, was walking on, her head lowered, bending down from time to time to pick a blade of grass. When she had fallen behind, she stopped and looked at her lover and her husband in the distance.

'Hey! Aren't you hungry?' Camille shouted, eventually.

'Yes,' she replied.

'Well, come on then!'

Thérèse was not hungry, but she was weary and uneasy. She was not sure what Laurent had in mind and her legs were trembling beneath her with anxiety.

The three of them came back to the river's edge and looked around for a restaurant. They sat down on a sort of wooden terrace at a cheap eating-house that stank of grease and wine. The place was full of shouting, songs and the clink of dishes. In every alcove, in every private room, there were groups talking in loud voices and the thin walls vibrated, magnifying the din. The staircase shook as the waiters went up and down.

Up on the terrace, the smell of grease was dispelled by the river breeze. Thérèse, leaning against the balustrade, looked out over the landing stage. A double row of cafés and fairground stalls stretched off to right and left. Under the arbours, between a few yellow vine leaves, there were glimpses of white table-cloths, the black patches of men's jackets and women's bright skirts. People were coming and going, bareheaded, running and laughing; and the dreary tunes of barrel organs mingled with the loud voices of the crowd. A smell of frying oil and dust hung on the still air.

Below Thérèse, some whores from the Latin Quarter were dancing round on a worn piece of lawn, singing a childish ditty. Their hats had fallen on to their shoulders and their hair was loose; they were holding hands and playing like little girls. Their voices had recaptured a hint of childish freshness and their pale faces, stamped with brutal kisses, were blushing tenderly with a virginal pinkness. Their wide, unchaste eyes were clouded with sentimental tears. Some students, smoking clay pipes, were watching them as they danced and shouting crude jokes at them.

Meanwhile, beyond, on the Seine, on the hillsides, the quiet of evening was falling, a vague, blue atmosphere wrapping the trees in a transparent mist.

'Hey, there, waiter!' said Laurent, leaning over the banisters. 'What about our dinner?'

Then, as if changing his mind, he went on:

'I say, Camille, how about going for a boat trip before we eat? That would give them time to roast our chicken. We'll get bored if we have to wait for an hour.'

'As you like,' said Camille, not caring one way or the other. 'But Thérèse is hungry.'

'No, no, I can wait,' said the young woman quickly, seeing that Laurent was staring at her.

All three of them went down. As they passed the counter, they booked a table, ordered their meal and said that they would be back in an hour. Since the owner hired out boats, they asked him to come and untie one for them. Laurent chose a narrow skiff, so light that it scared Camille.

'Dammit,' he said, 'we'd better not move around in that. We'd get a right soaking.'

The fact is that he was terribly afraid of water. In Vernon, his sickly state had meant that as a boy he had not been able to splash around in the Seine. When his schoolmates were running down to leap in the river, he would be tucked up between warm blankets. Laurent had become a fearless swimmer and indefatigable rower, while Camille had never lost the dread of deep water felt by women and children. He tested the bottom of the skiff with his foot as though to make sure it was firm.

'Come on, in you go,' said Laurent, laughing. 'You're always such a scaredy cat.'

Camille stepped over the edge and went unsteadily to take a seat in the stern. Feeling the boards under his feet, he was reassured and made a joke, to show he was not afraid.

Thérèse had stayed on the bank, serious and not moving,

beside her lover, who was holding the painter. He bent down and quickly whispered to her:

'Look out . . . I'm going to push him in . . . Do as I say . . . I'll look after everything.'

The young woman went dreadfully pale and stayed as though pinned to the ground. She stiffened, her eyes staring wide.

'Get in the boat, then,' Laurent muttered to her again.

She did not move. A frightful struggle was going on inside her. She had to use all her strength to control herself, because she was afraid she would burst into tears and fall in the water.

'Ah! Look!' Camille shouted. 'Laurent, look at Thérèse, now . . . She's the one who's scared! Will she, won't she, get in . . .'

He was sprawled on the rear bench, with his two elbows on the sides of the skiff, lolling around and showing off. Thérèse gave him an odd look; the jeers of this poor creature were like the crack of a whip stinging her and driving her on. She suddenly jumped into the boat, staying at the bow. Laurent took the oars. The skiff left the bank and proceeded gently towards the islands.

Dusk was coming. Great shadows fell from the trees and the water was black at the edge. In the middle of the river, there were wide streaks of pale silver. Soon, the boat was in the middle of the Seine. Here, all the sounds from the banks were muted: the shouts and singing were vague and melancholy as they drifted across, with sad, languid notes. The smells of fried food and dust had gone. There was a chill in the air. It was cold.

Laurent stopped rowing and let the boat drift with the current.

Rising opposite them was the great reddish mass of the islands. The two banks, dark brown in colour, flecked with grey, were like two broad bands meeting at the horizon. The sky and the water seemed to have been cut out of the same whitish material. Nothing is more painfully calm than dusk in autumn. The daylight pales in the quivering air and the ageing leaves fall from the trees. The countryside, scorched by the burning sun of summer, feels death approaching with the first cold winds; and, in the sky, there are plaintive murmurs of despair. Night falls, bringing shrouds in its shadows.

The three trippers fell silent. Sitting in the boat as it drifted along with the current, they were watching the last glimmers of light leave the tops of the trees. They were getting closer to the islands. The great reddish masses were darkening and the whole landscape was simplified by the dusk: the Seine, the sky, the islands and the hills were now only brown and grey smudges, merging into a milky fog.

Camille, who had ended up lying flat with his head over the water, dipped his hands in the river.

'Crikey, it's cold!' he exclaimed. 'It wouldn't be much fun to take a dive into that stuff!'

Laurent said nothing. For a while, he had been looking anxiously at both banks. He was sliding his large hands down towards his knees, clenching his teeth. Thérèse, stiff and motionless, her head tilted back a little, waited.

The boat was about to enter a little channel, dark and narrow, which ran between two islands. From behind one of these, you could hear the muffled singing of a boating party that must have been coming back up the Seine. Beyond that, upstream, the river was clear.

Then Laurent got up and grasped Camille around the waist. The clerk started to laugh.

'No, don't! You're tickling me,' he said. 'Stop messing around . . . Seriously, you'll make me fall.'

Laurent grasped him harder and shook him. Camille turned and saw the terrifying, contorted face of his friend. He could not understand what was going on, but was gripped by a vague sense of terror. He tried to cry out and felt a rough hand around his throat. With the instinct of a struggling animal, he got up on his knees and gripped the side of the boat. For a few seconds, he struggled like that.

'Thérèse! Thérèse!' he called, in a whistling, half-suffocated voice.

The young woman watched, gripping a bench in the skiff with both hands as it creaked and swayed on the river. She could not shut her eyes. A terrifying contraction kept them wide open, staring at the dreadful scene of struggle. She was silent and rigid.

'Thérèse! Thérèse!' the unfortunate victim cried, croaking.

At this final plea, Thérèse burst into tears. Her nerves broke and the crisis that she had been anticipating threw her shaking into the bottom of the boat. There she stayed, bent double, swooning, lifeless.

Laurent was still shaking Camille, with one hand gripped around his throat. Eventually, he managed to prise him away from the side of the boat with his other hand. He held him up like a child in his powerful arms. As he bent his head forward, leaving his neck uncovered, his victim, mad with fear and fury, twisted round, bared his teeth and dug them into the neck. And when the murderer, choking back a cry of pain, briskly threw Camille into the river, his teeth took away a piece of flesh.

He fell into the water with a scream. He came back to the surface two or three more times, giving increasingly muffled cries.

Laurent did not waste a second. He turned up the collar of his jacket to hide the wound. Then he grasped the swooning Thérèse, turned the skiff over with a kick and let himself fall into the Seine with his mistress in his arms. He supported her in the water, calling for help in a pathetic voice.

The oarsmen, whose singing they had heard behind the island, rowed swiftly towards them. They realized that a disaster had taken place: they set about rescuing Thérèse, lying her down on a bench, and Laurent, who began to lament the death of his friend. He jumped back in the water, looked for Camille in places where he could not be, came back weeping, wringing his hands and tearing out his hair. The oarsmen tried to calm him and console him.

'It's my fault,' he cried. 'I shouldn't have let the poor lad dance around and shake the boat as he did ... Suddenly, we were all three of us on the same side, and we capsized. As he was falling, he called out to me to save his wife ...'

As always happens, there were two or three young people among the oarsmen who claimed to have witnessed the accident.

'We saw it clearly,' they said. 'Heavens, you know, a boat is not as solid as a dance floor ... Oh, this poor little woman, it'll be frightful for her when she comes round!'

They picked up their oars, took the skiff in tow and brought Thérèse and Laurent to the restaurant, where the dinner was waiting. In a few minutes, all of Saint-Ouen knew about the accident. The oarsmen described it as though they were eye-witnesses. A sympathetic crowd gathered around the cabaret.

The restaurant owner and his wife were good people, who made some spare clothes available to the shipwrecked pair. When Thérèse revived, she had a nervous crisis and burst into terrible sobs. She had to be put to bed. Nature was assisting in the sinister piece of play-acting that had just taken place.

When the young woman was calmer, Laurent entrusted her to the care of the restaurant owners. He wanted to go back to Paris alone, to tell Mme Raquin the dreadful news, softening the blow as much as possible. The truth was that he was mistrust-ful of Thérèse's nervous excitement. He wanted to give her time to think things over and learn her part.

It was the oarsmen who ate Camille's dinner.

XII

In the dark corner of the public omnibus taking him back to Paris, Laurent put the final touches to his plan. He was almost certain of getting away with it. He was filled with a heavy, anxious feeling of joy, joy at having accomplished the crime. When they got to the Barrière de Clichy, he took a cab and told the driver to take him to Old Michaud's house in the Rue de Seine. It was nine o'clock in the evening.

He found the retired police commissioner at dinner, together with Olivier and Suzanne. He had come here in order to cover himself, in the event of anyone suspecting him, and to avoid having to announce the frightful news to Mme Raquin alone. He found the idea of doing that oddly repugnant; he was expecting such despair that he was afraid he could not produce enough tears for his part; and then, the mother's grief weighed on him, though when it came down to it, he was not much concerned.

When Michaud saw him come in wearing coarse clothes a few sizes too small, he looked questioningly at him. Laurent told him what had happened, in a breaking voice, as though breathless with grief and tiredness.

'I came to you,' he said, in the end, 'because I didn't know what to do about those two poor women who have suffered such a cruel blow. I didn't dare to go to the mother by myself. I beg you, come with me.'

As he spoke, Olivier was staring hard at him, with a directness that he found very disconcerting. The murderer had plunged, head first, among these policemen, in a bold move that ought to save him. But he could not help shuddering as he felt their eyes fixed on him; where there was only amazement and pity, he saw suspicion. Suzanne, the most frail and palest of them, was on the point of swooning. Olivier, terrified by the idea of death, though his heart was in fact quite indifferent, made a pained grimace of surprise as he examined Laurent's face, though without the slightest suspicion of the sinister truth. As for Old Michaud, he gave exclamations of horror, commiseration and amazement; he twisted around on his chair, clasped his hands and raised his eyes heavenwards.

'Oh, my God!' he said, in a strangled voice. 'Oh, my God, what a dreadful thing! You go out and you die, like that, all at once. It's frightful ... And that poor Madame Raquin, the mother, what are we to tell her? You were quite right to come and fetch us ... We'll go with you.'

He got up, walked about the room, shuffling as he looked for his cane and his hat; then, as he hurried around, got Laurent to repeat the full story of the disaster, punctuating each remark with an exclamation.

All four of them went downstairs. At the entrance to the Passage du Pont-Neuf, Michaud stopped Laurent.

'Don't come in,' he said. 'Your presence would be a kind of brutal announcement – just what we want to avoid ... The poor mother would suspect something wrong and force the truth out of us sooner than we would like. Wait here for us.'

The murderer was relieved by this arrangement: he had been trembling at the idea of going inside the shop. Calm descended on him and he began to step on and off the pavement, walking easily backwards and forwards. At times, he forgot what was going on and looked in the shop windows, hummed to himself and turned round to stare after women as they went past. He stayed for a full half-hour like this in the street, his nerve returning more and more.

He had not eaten since the morning. He had a sudden feeling of hunger, went into a pastry shop and stuffed himself with cakes.

In the shop in the arcade, a heart-rending scene was taking place. Even though Old Michaud did his best, with friendly words, making every attempt to soften the blow, there came a moment when Mme Raquin realized that something dreadful had happened to her son, whereupon she demanded to know the truth, in a fury of despair, a violent fit of tears and cries that overcame her old friend's resistance. When she did learn the truth, her grief was tragic. She heaved with sobs, great shudders threw her body backwards and she suffered a mad seizure of horror and anguish. She remained gasping for breath, from time to time giving out a piercing cry in the aching depths of her sorrow. She would have thrown herself on the ground, if Suzanne had not seized her by the waist and wept on her knees, looking up towards her with her pale face. Olivier and his father remained standing, irritated and silent, turning away from this spectacle which affected them in a way unpleasantly threatening to their self-esteem.

The poor mother saw her son tumbled along in the murky waters of the Seine, his body stiff and horribly swollen; and, at the same time, she saw him as a little baby in his cot, when she used to defend him from death as it tried to claim him. She had brought him into the world more than ten times and she loved him for all the love she had shown him in the previous thirty years. And now he had died far away from her, all of a sudden, in cold, dirty water, like a dog. She remembered the warm blankets that she used to wrap around him. How much care, what a warm childhood, how many endearments and expressions of affection – all this, only to see him one day miserably drowned! At this thought, Mme Raquin felt her throat tightening and hoped that she was about to die, stifled by so much grief.

Old Michaud hurried out. He left Suzanne with the haber-dasher and went back with Olivier to look for Laurent, so that they could go directly to Saint-Ouen.

On the way, they barely exchanged a couple of words. Each had retreated into a corner of the cab which was shaking them along over the cobbles. They stayed silent and unmoving in the depth of the shadows that filled the carriage. From time to time, the swift ray of a gas lamp threw a flash of light across their faces. The dreadful event that had brought them together envel-oped them in a sort of melancholy dejection.

When they finally reached the restaurant on the river bank, they found Thérèse lying down, her hands and head burning with fever. The café owner told them quietly that the young lady was running a high temperature. The truth was that Thérèse, feeling weak and cowardly, was afraid that she would have a fit and confess to the murder, so she had decided to fall ill. She remained fiercely mute, keeping her lips and eyelids tight closed and refusing to see anyone, because she was afraid to speak. With the bedclothes up to her chin and her face half buried in the pillow, she curled up like a baby and listened anxiously to everything that was being said around her. And, in the reddish light that filtered through her closed eyelids, she could still see Camille and Laurent struggling at the edge of the boat and her husband, pale, frightful, taller than life, rising straight up out of the muddy water. This inescapable vision fuelled the fever in her blood.

Old Michaud tried to talk to her, to console her. She shrugged him off, turned round and started to sob again.

'Leave her, Monsieur,' said the restaurant owner. 'She shivers at the slightest noise. What she surely needs, you see, is rest.'

Downstairs, in the dining room, a policeman was taking statements about the accident. Michaud and his son came down, followed by Laurent. Once Olivier let it be known that he was an important official at the Préfecture, everything was over in ten minutes. The oarsmen were still there, giving minute details of the drowning, describing how the three trippers had fallen in and claiming to be eyewitnesses. If Olivier and his father had had the slightest suspicion, it would have disappeared as soon as they heard these statements. But they had not for a moment doubted Laurent's honesty. On the contrary, they described him to the policeman as the victim's best friend, and they were at pains to insist that the official report should include the fact that the young man had jumped into the water to save Camille Raquin. The following day, the newspapers described the event with a wealth of details: the despairing mother, the inconsolable widow, the noble, courageous friend . . . it was all there, in the report which did the rounds of the Parisian papers, then finally got buried in the provincial press.

When the taking of the statements was finished, Laurent felt a wave of warm joy filling his flesh with new life. From the time when the victim had buried his teeth into his neck, it was as though he had been stiffened, acting mechanically, according to a plan laid down long in advance. He was possessed by the sole instinct of self-preservation which dictated his words and advised him how to act. Now, with the certainty that he would get away with it, the blood started to flow through his veins with sweet tranquillity. The police had gone past his crime and seen nothing; they were fooled, they had just acquitted him. He was saved. At this thought, he felt a sweat of pleasure along the length of his body, and a warmth that restored free movement to his limbs and to his mind. He continued in his role as the grieving friend with incomparable skill and self-assurance. Underneath, he felt an animal satisfaction; he thought of Thérèse, lying in the room upstairs.

'We can't leave that poor young woman here,' he said to Michaud. 'She may be in danger of serious illness, we really must take her back to Paris . . . Come on, we'll persuade her to come with us.'

Upstairs, he himself spoke to Thérèse, begging her to get up and let them take her to the Passage du Pont-Neuf. When she heard the sound of his voice, she shuddered, opened her eyes wide and looked at him. She was haggard and trembling. Painfully and without answering, she sat up. The men left the room, leaving her alone with the restaurant owner's wife. When she was dressed, she came unsteadily down the stairs and got into the cab, supported by Olivier.

No one spoke during the journey. Laurent, with supreme daring and insolence, slid one hand along the young woman's skirts and grasped her fingers. He was sitting opposite her, in the shifting shadows. He could not see her face, which she kept sunk on her breast. When he had taken her hand, he pressed it strongly and kept it in his until they reached Rue Mazarine. He felt her hand tremble, but she did not take it away; on the contrary, she squeezed his quickly a few times. And, one held in the other, the hands burned, the damp palms stuck together and the clenched fingers bruised one another whenever the cab shook. It seemed to Laurent and Thérèse that the blood of the other was flowing into their chests through their joined hands; their fists became the burning hearth on which their life seethed. Wrapped in the darkness and the desolate silence around them, this furious squeezing of hands was like a crushing weight bearing down on Camille's head to keep it under the water.

When the cab stopped, Michaud and his son were the first to get down. Laurent leaned over towards his mistress and softly murmured: 'Be strong, Thérèse. We have a long time to wait. Remember . . .'

The young woman had still not spoken. She opened her lips for the first time since her husband's death.

'Oh, I'll remember!' she said, trembling, in a voice as soft as a sigh.

Olivier gave her his hand, to help her down. This time, Laurent went as far as the shop. Mme Raquin was lying down, in the throes of delirium. Thérèse dragged herself to her own bed and Suzanne hardly had time to undress her. Feeling reassured and seeing that everything was working out as he hoped, Laurent left. He went slowly back to his dingy attic in the Rue Saint-Victor.

It was after midnight. A cool breeze was blowing down the silent, empty streets. The young man could hear nothing but the regular sound of his footsteps on the stone pavements. The cool air filled him with a sense of well-being, while the silence and the dark gave him brief sensations of pleasure. He strolled along . . .

At last, he was done with his crime. He had killed Camille.

All that was finished business and would not be spoken about again. He would live quietly and wait until he could take possession of Thérèse. He had sometimes found the idea of the murder oppressive; but now that the murder was accomplished, his chest felt lighter, he breathed freely and he was cured of the sufferings imposed by hesitation and fear.

In reality, he was slightly dazed, his body and thoughts weighed down with tiredness. He got home and slept deeply. As he slept, little nervous twitches flicked across his face.

XIII

The next day, Laurent woke up feeling bright and cheerful. He had slept well. The cold air coming through the window sent the sluggish blood coursing in his veins. His could hardly remember what had happened the previous evening. Had it not been for the burning sensation on his neck, he might have thought that he had gone to bed at ten o'clock after a calm evening. Camille's bite was like a hot iron on his skin; when he considered the pain that this injury was causing him, he deeply resented it. It was as though a dozen pins were gradually piercing his flesh.

He turned down his shirt collar and looked at the wound in a tawdry, fifteen-sou mirror hanging on the wall. The wound was a red hole, as wide as a small coin. The skin had been torn off and the flesh was visible, pinkish, with black patches. Trails of blood had run down as far as the shoulder in slender threads, congealing as they went. The bite stood out on the white neck in dull, powerful brown; it was on the right, below the ear. Leaning back and craning his neck, Laurent looked, as the greenish mirror gave his face a frightful grimace.

He splashed water over it, pleased with the results of his examination, telling himself that the wound would heal over in a few days. Then he dressed and went to his office, calmly, as usual. He described the accident in a voice full of feeling. When his colleagues read the account in the press, he became a real hero. For a week, this was the only subject of conversation for the staff of the Orléans Railway: they were quite proud that one of their fellow workers had been drowned. Grivet held forth at length on the folly of venturing into the midst of the river when you can so easily watch the Seine go by as you cross one of its bridges.

Laurent had one vague source of unease. It had not been possible to confirm Camille's death officially. Thérèse's husband was certainly dead, but his murderer would like his body to have been recovered so that a formal certificate could be made out. They had looked in vain for the drowned man's corpse on the day after the accident; it was considered that it must have gone down into one of the holes under the banks of the islands. Scavengers were already actively searching the river in order to collect the bounty.

Laurent made it his business to go by the Morgue[1] every morning on his way to the office. He had sworn to look after everything himself. Despite a revulsion that made him feel sick and despite the shudders that would sometimes pass through him, he went regularly for more than a week to examine the faces of all the drowned people laid out on the slabs.

When he went in, he was sickened by a stale smell, a smell of washed flesh, and cold draughts blew across his skin. His clothes hung against his shoulders, as though weighed down by the humidity of the walls. He would go directly to the window that separates the spectators from the bodies, and press his pale face against the glass, looking. In front of him were the ranks of grey slabs on which, here and there, naked bodies stood out as patches of green and yellow, white and red. Some bodies kept their virginal flesh in the rigidity of death, while others seemed like heaps of bloody, rotten meat. At the end, against the wall, hung pitiful rags: skirts and trousers, grimacing against the bare plaster. At first, Laurent saw only the general greyness of stones and walls, spotted with red and black from the clothes and the corpses. There was a tinkling of running water.

Bit by bit he could distinguish the bodies. He proceeded from one to the next. Only drowned men interested him; when there were several bodies swollen and blue from the water, he looked eagerly at them, trying to recognize Camille. Often the flesh was peeling off their faces in shreds, the bones had broken through the drenched skin and the face seemed to have been boiled and boned. Laurent found it hard to be certain; he examined the bodies and tried to identify his victim's skinny frame. But all drowned bodies are fat; he saw huge bellies, puffy thighs, arms round and strong. He couldn't tell for sure, so he remained shivering and staring at these greenish rag dolls whose frightful grimaces seemed to mock him.

One morning, he got a real fright. For some minutes, he had been looking at a drowned man, short in stature and horribly disfigured. The flesh of this body was so soft and decayed that the water running over it was taking it away bit by bit. The stream pouring on the face was making a hole to the left of the nose. Then, suddenly, the nose collapsed and the lips fell off, revealing white teeth. The drowned man's head broke into a laugh.

Every time he thought he recognized Camille, Laurent felt a burning sensation in his heart. He desperately wanted to find his victim's body, yet he was overcome with cowardice when he thought that he saw it in front of him. His visits to the Morgue filled him with nightmares and shudders that left him panting. He shook off his fears, called himself a child and tried to be strong, but in spite of that his flesh rebelled, and feelings of disgust and horror seized him as soon as he came into the humidity and the stale smell of the hall.

When there were no drowned men on the last row of slabs, he breathed more easily and felt less disgust. Then he became a simple, curious onlooker, taking a strange pleasure in staring violent death in the face, in its dolefully peculiar and grotesque shapes. He enjoyed the spectacle, especially when there were women showing their naked busts. These brutal, outstretched naked bodies, spotted with blood, pierced in places, attracted him and held his gaze. Once, he saw a young woman of twenty, a working-class girl, strong, heavily built, who seemed to be sleeping on the stone. Her fresh, plump body was paling with very delicate variations of tint; she was half smiling, her head slightly to one side, offering her bosom in a provocative manner. You would have taken her for a courtesan lying on a bed if there had not been a black stripe on her neck, like a necklace of shadow:[2] the girl had just hanged herself because of a disappointment in love. Laurent looked at her for a long time, studying her flesh, absorbed in a kind of fearful lust.

Every morning, while he was there, he heard people coming and going behind him as they entered and left.

The Morgue is a show that anyone can afford, which poor and rich passers-by get for free. The door is open, anyone can come in. There are connoisseurs who go out of their way not to miss one of these spectacles of death. When the slabs are empty, people go out disappointed, robbed, muttering under their breath. When the slabs are well filled, and when there is a fine display of human flesh, the visitors crowd in, getting a cheap thrill, horrified, joking, applauding or whistling, as in the theatre, and go away contented, announcing that the Morgue has been a success that day.

Laurent soon came to know the regulars who attended the place, a mixed, diverse group of people who came to sympathize with one another or snigger together. Some workmen would come in on their way to their jobs, with a loaf of bread and some tools under their arms; they found death amusing. Among them were jokers who would play to the gallery by making a facetious remark about the expression on each body's face. They nicknamed the victims of fires 'coalmen', while those who had been hanged, murdered or drowned, and bodies that had been wounded or crushed, excited their ridicule; and their voices, which trembled a little, stammered out comic remarks in the shivering silence of the hall. Then came the lower-middle classes, thin, dry old men, and casual passers-by who came in here because they had nothing better to do, looking at the bodies with the blank eyes and distasteful expressions of men of sensitive feelings and placid natures. Women came in great numbers: pink, young working girls, with white blouses and clean skirts, who went briskly from one end of the window to the other, attentive and wide-eyed, as though looking at the display in a fashion store; there were working-class women, too, haggard, with doleful expressions, and well-dressed ladies, nonchalant, trailing their silk dresses.

One day, Laurent saw one of these ladies standing a few paces back from the window, pressing a cambric handkerchief to her nostrils. She was wearing a delightful grey silk skirt with a large, black lace mantelet. She had a veil over her face and her gloved hands seemed quite small and delicate. There was a gentle scent of violets around her. She was looking at a corpse. On a slab, a short distance away, was the body of a hefty lad, a builder who had died instantly when he fell off some scaffolding. He had a barrel chest, short, thick muscles and greasy, white flesh; death had made a marble statue of him. The lady was examining him, turning him round, as it were, with her eyes, weighing him up, engrossed by the sight of this man. She raised a corner of her veil, took another look, and left.

From time to time, gangs of kids would come in, children aged between twelve and fifteen, running along the window and stopping only by women's bodies. They would put their hands on the glass and stare impudently at the naked breasts. They would nudge one another and make crude remarks, learning about vice in the school of death. It is in the Morgue that young street urchins have their first mistress.

After a week of this, Laurent was sickened by it. At night, he would dream about the bodies he had seen that morning. This daily dose of suffering and disgust that he imposed on himself eventually disturbed him so much that he decided to make only two more visits. The next day, on coming into the Morgue, he felt a vicious blow in his chest: opposite him, on a slab, Camille was staring at him, lying on his back with his head raised and his eyes half open.

The murderer slowly went over to the window as though drawn by a magnet, unable to take his eyes off his victim. He was not in pain, but he did feel a great inner chill and a slight tingling on his skin. He would have expected to shake more. He stayed motionless for five whole minutes, lost in unconscious contemplation, involuntarily marking in the depths of his memory all the frightful lines and foul colours of the scene before his eyes.

Camille was hideous. He had spent a fortnight in the water. His face still seemed firm and stiff, the features were preserved, but the skin had taken on a muddy, yellowish tint. The head, thin and bony, slightly puffy, was twisted into a grimace; it was leaning a bit to one side, the hair stuck to the temples, the eyelids raised, revealing the pallid globe of the eyes; the lips were twisted, drawn to one side of the mouth, giving a horrible sneer; the blackish tip of the tongue was visible between the whiteness of the teeth. This head, tanned and stretched, was even more terrifying in its pain and horror since it retained an appearance of humanity. The body seemed like a heap of decayed flesh; it had been horribly battered. You could tell that the arms were no longer joined to it; the shoulder blades were breaking through the skin. The ribs stood out on the greenish chest as black lines. The left side, open and broken, had a gaping hole surrounded by dark-red strips. The whole torso was decayed; the legs were more solid, stretched out, spotted with repulsive blotches. The feet were falling off.

Laurent looked at Camille. He had never seen such a horrifying drowned body. More than that: the corpse had a skimped look, a shrunken, mean appearance; it was huddled up in its own decay; it amounted to just a small heap. You might have guessed that this was a clerk on twelve hundred francs, sickly and stupid, whose mother had fed him on herbal teas. This meagre body, which had grown up between warm blankets, was shivering on its cold marble.

When Laurent did manage to tear himself away from the poignant curiosity that kept him there, motionless and gaping, he went out and began to walk quickly along the river bank. And as he went, he repeated: 'That's what I've made of him. He's repulsive.' He felt as though a pungent odour were following him around, the odour that this putrefying corpse must be giving off.

He went to see Old Michaud and told him that he had just recognized Camille on a slab in the Morgue. The formalities were completed, the drowned man was buried and a death certificate made out. Laurent, with nothing to worry about now, threw himself with delight into forgetting his crime and the annoying, distressing scenes that had followed the murder.

XIV

The shop in the Passage du Pont-Neuf stayed closed for three days. When it reopened, it seemed darker and damper. The window display, yellow with dust, appeared to be wearing the family's mourning; everything was scattered haphazardly in the dirty windows. Behind the linen bonnets hanging from rusted hooks, the pallor of Thérèse's face was duller and more earthy. Its immobility took on a sinister calm.

All the old wives in the arcade were full of sympathy. The woman who sold costume jewellery pointed out the young woman's emaciated profile to each of her customers as an interesting and regrettable object of curiosity.

For three days, Mme Raquin and Thérèse stayed in their beds without speaking or even seeing one another. The old haberdasher was propped upright on her pillows, staring vacantly in front of her with the gaze of an idiot. Her son's death had given her a massive blow to the head and she fell as though bludgeoned. For hours on end she remained, calm and motionless, swallowed up by the bottomless gulf of her despair; then, at times, a crisis seized her and she wept and cried out in delirium. Thérèse, in the next room, seemed to be asleep; she had turned her head to the wall and drawn the blanket over her face; and she lay there, stiff and silent, not one sob moving her body or the sheet that covered it. It was as though she were hiding the thoughts that kept her pinned, rigid, in the darkness of the alcove. Suzanne, who looked after the two women, went softly from one to the other, shuffling her feet, but she could not get Thérèse to turn round, only to react with sudden movements of irritation, nor could she console Mme Raquin, whose tears started to flow as soon as a voice roused her in her despondency.

On the third day, Thérèse threw back the blanket and sat up in bed, swiftly, with a sort of feverish resolve. She brushed her hair aside and held her hands against her temples, staying like that for a moment, with her hands up and her eyes staring, as though still reflecting. Then she jumped down on to the carpet.

Her limbs were shivering and red with fever; there were broad, livid patches on her skin, which was wrinkled in places, as though it had no flesh under it. She had aged.

Suzanne, just coming into the room, was quite surprised to find her up. In a placid, drawling voice, she advised her to get back into bed and rest some more. Thérèse took no notice; she was looking for her clothes and putting them on with hurried, trembling hands. When she was dressed, she went to examine herself in a mirror, rubbed her eyes and ran her hands across her face, as though to obliterate something. Then, without a word, she walked quickly across the dining room and into Mme Raquin's room.

The older woman was temporarily in a state of stunned calm. When Thérèse came in, she turned her head and looked at the young widow as she came across and stood in front of her, silent and depressed. The two stared at one another for a few seconds, the niece with growing anxiety and the aunt making a painful effort of memory. At last it came back to her and she held out her trembling arms, hugging Thérèse around the neck and saying:

'My poor child! My poor Camille!'

She was weeping and the tears dried on the burning skin of the young woman, who was hiding her face in the folds of the sheet. Thérèse stayed there, bending over, letting the mother weep out her tears. Ever since the murder, she had been dreading this first conversation, and she had stayed in bed so that she could delay the moment and have time to consider the terrible part she had to play.

When she saw that Mme Raquin was calmer, she started to fuss around her, advising her to get up and come down into the shop. The old haberdasher had almost reverted to childhood. The sudden appearance of her niece had brought about a positive crisis in her which had restored her memory and awareness of the people and things around her. She thanked Suzanne for caring for her, speaking in a weak voice, but no longer delirious, full of a sadness that sometimes stifled her. She watched Thérèse walking about, giving in to sudden fits of weeping. On such occasions she would call her over, kiss her, still sobbing, and tell her in a choking voice that she had nothing but her left in the world.

That evening, she agreed to get up and try to eat. When she did so, Thérèse saw what a dreadful blow her aunt had suffered. The poor old woman's legs had grown heavy, she needed a stick to drag herself into the dining room and it seemed to her that the walls were shaking around her.

However, the next day she already wanted them to reopen the shop. She was afraid of going mad if she stayed alone in her room. She walked heavily down the wooden stairs, stopping with both feet at each one, and went to sit down behind the counter. From that day on, she remained fixed there in a passive state of grief.

Beside her, Thérèse waited and thought. The shop was once more quiet and dark.

XV

Laurent would sometimes come back in the evening, every two or three days. He stayed in the shop, talking to Mme Raquin for half an hour. Then he would leave, without having looked Thérèse directly in the face. The old haberdasher considered him as the man who had saved her niece, a noble soul who had done everything he could to bring her son back to her. She welcomed him with affectionate goodwill.

One Thursday evening, Laurent was there when Old Michaud and Grivet came in. Eight o'clock was striking. The office worker and the former police chief had each decided separately that they could resume their old routine without appearing to intrude, and they arrived at the same minute, as though driven by a single mechanism. Behind them, Olivier and Suzanne also made their appearance.

They went up to the dining room. Mme Raquin, who was not expecting anyone, hurried to light the lamp and make some tea. When everyone was seated around the table, each in front of his or her cup, and when the box of dominoes had been emptied out, the poor mother was suddenly transported back into the past and burst into tears. One place was empty: her son's.

This grief threw a pall over the proceedings and made them feel awkward. Every face had a look of egotistical self-satisfaction. These people were embarrassed, none of them having in their minds the slightest living memory of Camille.

'Come, come, dear lady,' Michaud exclaimed, with a hint of impatience. 'You mustn't give way to it like that. You'll make yourself ill.'

'We're all mortal,' Grivet remarked.

'Your tears will not bring back your son,' said Olivier, sententiously.

'Please,' said Suzanne, 'don't upset all of us.'

And since Mme Raquin was sobbing all the more, unable to hold back her tears, Michaud continued:

'Now, then, come on, be brave. You must realize that we've come here to take your mind off it. So, darn it all, let's not be miserable; let's try to forget . . . We'll play for two sous a game. There! What do you say?'

With a supreme effort, the haberdasher swallowed her tears. Perhaps she was aware of the fatuous egotism of her guests. She wiped her eyes, still very upset. The dominoes shook in her poor hands and she could not see through the tears that remained just behind her eyelids.

They played.

Laurent and Thérèse had watched this brief scene with a serious and impassive air. The young man was delighted to see their Thursday evenings revived. He eagerly wanted them to take place, knowing that he would need these meetings to reach his goal. And, then, without wondering why, he felt more at ease among these few people that he knew and so dared to look directly at Thérèse.

The young woman, dressed in black, pale and thoughtful, possessed a beauty that he had not previously seen in her. He was happy to meet her eyes and to see them stop and gaze at his with unblinking courage. Thérèse still belonged to him, body and soul.

XVI

Fifteen months went by. The anguish of the first moments was mitigated, and every day brought greater peace and relaxation. Life resumed its course with weary languor, taking on that state of monotonous lethargy that follows a great crisis. And, at the start, Laurent and Thérèse allowed themselves to be carried along by this new life as it transformed them, working away secretly inside them in a way that will have to be analysed very minutely if one is to establish all its phases.

Soon Laurent was coming back every evening to the shop, as in the past. But he no longer dined there or settled down for a whole evening. He would arrive at half past nine and leave after closing the shop. It appeared as though he was fulfilling a duty by coming in to help the two women. If he neglected this task for one day, he would apologize the next as humbly as a servant. On Thursday, he helped Mme Raquin to light the fire and welcome her guests. He was quietly attentive in a way that charmed the old woman.

Thérèse would calmly watch him fussing around her. Her face had lost its pallor and she seemed more well, more cheerful and more gentle. Only very occasionally did her mouth twist in a nervous contraction, making two deep lines that gave her a strange expression of pain and terror.

The two lovers did not try to see one another alone. Neither of them ever asked the other for a meeting and they never exchanged a furtive kiss. It was as though the murder had, for the time being, calmed the lustful fever of their flesh and, in killing Camille, they had managed to assuage the raging and insatiable desire that they had been unable to satisfy in one another's arms. They experienced in their crime a sensation of gratification so intense that it sickened them and made their embraces repulsive.

None the less, they could have had a thousand opportunities to lead the very life of free love that they had dreamed about and which had driven them to murder. Mme Raquin, confused and debilitated, was not an obstacle. The house was theirs; they could leave it and go wherever they wished. But love no longer appealed to them, their appetite had faded, and they stayed there, calmly chatting, looking at one another without blushing, without trembling, having apparently forgotten the wild embraces that had bruised their flesh and made their bones crack. They even avoided being alone together; when they were, they could find nothing to say and each of them was afraid of appearing too cold towards the other. When they shook hands, they felt a kind of unease at the touch of their skin.

Anyway, they both thought they could explain what made them so indifferent and fearful towards one another. They put their coldness down to caution. In their view, this calm and abstinence were the fruit of great wisdom. They claimed that the passivity of their flesh and the sleep in their hearts were voluntary. Moreover, they considered the repugnance and anxiety that they felt as a vague, lingering fear of punishment. Sometimes they would force themselves to hope, trying to recover the ardent dreams of former times, only to be quite amazed when they found that their imaginations were empty. So they clung to the idea of their forthcoming marriage. Once they had reached their goal, with nothing more to fear, belonging to one another, they would rediscover their passion and enjoy the delights that they had imagined. This hope soothed them and prevented them from plumbing the depths of the void that had opened up inside them. They persuaded themselves that they loved one another as they had done in the past and awaited the moment that would make them perfectly happy by uniting them for ever.

Never had Thérèse known such peace of mind. She was certainly a better person: all the implacable willpower in her being was relaxed.

At night, alone in her bed, she felt happy. She could no longer sense the thin face and puny body of Camille beside her, inflaming her flesh and plaguing her with unsatisfied desires. For herself, she became a little girl again, a virgin under her white curtains, peaceful amid the silence and the darkness. She liked her huge, rather cold room, with its high ceiling, its dark corners and its scents of the cloister. She had even come to like the great black wall outside her window; one whole summer, every evening, she would stay looking for hours on end at the grey stones of this wall and the narrow slivers of starry sky outlined by the chimneys and the roofs. She would think of Laurent only when a nightmare woke her up with a start; and then, sitting bolt upright, shaking and with staring eyes, she would wrap her nightdress around her and tell herself that she would not suffer from these sudden terrors if she had a man lying beside her. She thought of her lover as being like a dog that would guard and protect her. Her cool, calm skin felt no shudder of desire.

By day, in the shop, she took an interest in things around her; she came out of herself, no longer living in a state of dumb rebellion, wrapped up in thoughts of hatred and vengeance. She was bored by day-dreaming; she needed to act and to see. From morning to night, she watched the people who went through the arcade, entertained by the noise and the comings and goings. She became inquisitive and chatty, in short, a woman, for up to then she had only ever acted and thought like a man.

From her observations, she noticed a young man, a student, who lived in rented accommodation near by and came past the shop several times a day. He had a pale beauty, with the long hair of a poet and an officer's moustache. Thérèse thought him distinguished. She was in love with him for a week, like a boarding-school girl. She read novels and compared this young man to Laurent, finding the latter quite coarse and heavy. Reading novels opened horizons that were new to her; until now, she had loved only with her blood and her nerves; now she started to love with her head. Then, one day, the student vanished; no doubt, he had moved house. Thérèse forgot him in a matter of hours.

She subscribed to a lending library and became passionately fond of all the heroes of the stories that she read. This sudden love of reading had a considerable influence on her temperament.[1] She acquired a nervous sensibility which made her laugh or cry for no reason. The equilibrium that had started to be achieved inside her was shattered. She fell into a sort of vague reverie. At times, she was shaken by thoughts of Camille and she remembered Laurent with new desire, but full of fear and misgiving. So she relapsed into her mood of anxiety; sometimes she tried to find some way of marrying her lover that very moment, at others she thought of running away or never seeing him again. When novels talked to her about chastity and honour, they set up a kind of barrier between her instincts and her will. She was still the unmanageable creature that wanted to wrestle with the Seine and had thrown herself head first into adultery; but she became aware of goodness and gentleness, she under-stood the soft features and lifeless attitude of Olivier's wife, and she knew that she could not kill her husband and be happy. As a result, she could no longer see clearly inside herself and she lived in a state of cruel uncertainty.

Laurent, for his part, went through various phases of calm and excitement. At first, he enjoyed a feeling of profound tran-quillity, as though he had been relieved of a huge weight. At times, he would wonder in astonishment: it was as though he had had a bad dream and he asked himself whether it was really true that he had thrown Camille into the water and seen his corpse on a slab in the Morgue. He was uncommonly surprised by the memory of his crime. Never would he have considered himself capable of a murder. All his caution and his cowardice shuddered when it occurred to him that his crime might have been discovered and he might have been guillotined. He felt the cold edge of the blade on his neck. While he was doing it, he had gone straight ahead, with the obstinacy and blindness of an animal. Now he turned round and, seeing the abyss that he had crossed, was seized by a dizzying sense of terror.

'I must certainly have been drunk,' he thought. 'That woman intoxicated me with her caresses. Good Lord, what an idiot, what a madman I was! I was risking the scaffold by doing that ... Well, in the end it turned out all right; but if I had the time again, I'd never do it.'

Laurent lapsed into inactivity, becoming more feeble, more cowardly and more cautious than ever. He got fat and lazy. No one who looked at this great body, slumped in on itself, seeming to have no bones or nerves, would have thought to accuse him of violence and cruelty.

He went back to his old ways. For several months, he was a

model employee, carrying out his duties in a perfectly mechanical way. In the evenings, he dined in an eating-house in the Rue Saint-Victor, cutting his bread into small slices, chewing slowly, dragging out his meal as long as possible. Then he pushed his chair back, leaned against the wall and smoked his pipe. He looked like some fat married man. In the daytime, he thought about nothing; at night, he slept a deep and dreamless sleep. With his face pink and plump, his belly full and his head empty, he was happy.

His flesh seemed dead and his mind hardly ever turned to Thérèse. At times he did think about her as one thinks about a woman whom one is to marry later on, in some indeterminate future. He waited patiently for the time of his marriage, forgetting the woman, but dreaming of the new position he would then acquire. He would leave the office, he would do some amateur painting and he would stroll around. Every evening, such thoughts brought him back to the shop in the arcade, despite the vague sense of unease that he felt as he went in.

One Sunday, feeling bored and not knowing what to do, he went round to see his old schoolfriend, the young painter with whom he had shared a room for a long time. The artist was working on a painting that he intended to send to the Salon:[2] it showed a naked Bacchante[3] stretched out on a piece of drapery. At the back of the studio, the model, a woman, was lying, her head bent back, her upper body twisted and her hip raised. Now and then, she would laugh, sticking out her chest, extending her arms and stretching, to relieve the stiffness. Laurent, sitting opposite her, watched her, smoking and talking to his friend. The sight made his heart pound and set his nerves on edge. He stayed until evening and took the woman home with him. He kept her as his mistress for nearly a year. The poor girl began to love him, considering him a handsome fellow. In the morning, she would leave, go and model all day, then come back regularly every evening at the same time. With the money that she earned, she would feed, dress and maintain herself, so she did not cost Laurent a penny, and he was not bothered where she came from or what she might have done. This woman brought a further element of balance into his life; he took her for granted, as a useful and necessary object that kept his body quiet and healthy. He never knew whether he loved her and it never occurred to him that he was being unfaithful to Thérèse. He just felt more fat and contented. That was all.

Meanwhile, Thérèse's period of mourning was over. The young woman would put on bright dresses and one evening Laurent happened to find her younger-looking and prettier. But he still felt a certain uneasiness with her; for some time she had seemed excitable and full of strange whims, laughing or becoming sad for no reason. When he saw her wavering, it worried him, because he partly guessed her inner turmoil. He started to hesitate, horribly afraid that he would upset his tranquil existence: he was living peacefully, sensibly catering for his needs, and he was scared to risk this balance by tying himself to a woman whose passion had already driven him mad. In any case, he did not reason these things out, he instinctively felt the upheaval that it would create in him if he were to have Thérèse.

The first shock that struck him, shaking him out of his complacency, was the idea that he would at last have to think about marriage. It was now almost fifteen months since Camille died. For a short while, Laurent considered not marrying at all, dumping Thérèse and keeping the model, whose undemanding and inexpensive love was quite enough for him. Then, it occurred to him that he could not have killed a man for nothing; when he recalled his crime and the dreadful effort that he had made to gain sole possession of this woman who now disturbed him so much, he felt that the murder would become useless and horrible if he did not marry her. It seemed ludicrous to him to throw a man in the water so that you could steal his widow, to wait fifteen months, and after that to make up one's mind to live with some girl who hawked her body round all the artists' studios ... He smiled at the notion. In any event, was he not bound to Thérèse by ties of blood and horror? He felt her somehow crying out and twisting inside him, he belonged to her. He was afraid of his accomplice; perhaps, if he did not marry her, she would go and confess everything to the Law, for revenge and out of jealousy. These ideas were pounding in his head. Once again, he was stricken with fever.

Meanwhile, the model left him abruptly. One Sunday, she failed to return; no doubt she had found warmer and more comfortable digs. Laurent was only mildly put out, but he had grown accustomed to having a woman lying beside him at night and he suddenly felt there was a gap in his life. A week later, his nerves could bear it no longer. He went back to the shop in the arcade for whole evenings on end, once more looking at Thérèse with eyes that glinted occasionally. The young woman, who was excited by long hours with her books, returned his gaze with languid and surrendering eyes.

In this way, both of them found their way back to anguish and desire, after a long year of waiting in a state of disgust and indifference. One evening as he was closing the shop, Laurent stopped Thérèse in the passageway.

'Would you like me to come to your room this evening?' he asked, in a passionate voice.

The young woman threw up her hands in horror.

'No, no, let's wait,' she said. 'We must be careful.'

'I've been waiting long enough, I think,' said Laurent. 'I'm fed up, I want you.'

Thérèse looked at him wildly. The blood rushed to her hands and to her face. She seemed to hesitate, then said abruptly:

'Let's get married. I'll be yours.'

XVII

Laurent left the Passage, anxious in his mind and uneasy in his body. Thérèse's warm breath and her compliance had brought back all the keen urges of earlier times. He went down to the river and walked along with his hat in his hand, so that he could get the full benefit of the fresh air on his face.

When he reached Rue Saint-Victor, he paused at the entrance to his lodgings, afraid to go up, afraid of being alone. An inexplicable, childish terror made him dread that he might find a man hiding in his garret. He had never suffered from such faint-heartedness. He did not even try to argue against the strange fit of trembling that came over him. He went into a wine shop and stayed there for an hour, mechanically drinking large glasses of wine. He thought of Thérèse and felt cross with the young woman because she had not wanted to have him that same night in her room and it occurred to him that he would not have been afraid had he been with her.

They closed the wine shop and showed him the door. He came back to ask for some matches. The concierge in his house was on the first floor. Laurent had a long alleyway to go down and a few steps to go up before he could take his candle. This alleyway and small flight of stairs, horribly black, appalled him. Normally, he went through the darkness here quite happily. This evening, he did not dare ring; he thought that there might be some murderers, hiding in a particular recess formed by the entrance to the cellar, who would suddenly leap out at his throat as he went by. Finally, he rang, lit a match and made up his mind to venture into the alleyway. The match went out. He stayed motionless, panting, not daring to run, striking the matches on the damp wall so nervously that his hand shook. He thought he could hear voices and the sound of footsteps in front of him. The matches broke in his fingers. He managed to light one. The sulphur began to boil and catch on the wood, but so slowly that it increased Laurent's terror: in the pale, bluish light from the sulphur, in the lights flickering around, he imagined he could see monstrous shapes. Then the match fizzed, and the light became white and clear. Relieved, Laurent went forward cautiously, taking care not to let the light go out. When he should have walked past the cellar, he pressed against the opposite wall; the cellar was a mass of darkness that scared him. Then he went quickly up the few steps to the concierge's lodge and thought he was saved when he had his candle. He went more slowly up the other floors, holding his candle high and lighting every corner that he had to walk past. Those huge, strange shapes that come and go when you are in a staircase with a light filled him with a vague sense of unease as they swiftly rose up and disappeared in front of him.

When he got upstairs, he opened his door and quickly shut himself inside. The first thing he did was to look under his bed and to search the room thoroughly, to make sure that no one was hidden in it. He closed the skylight, thinking that someone could easily come down through there. When he had taken these precautions, he felt calmer and got undressed, amazed at his own faint-heartedness. Eventually, he smiled, calling himself a baby. He had never been timid and could not explain this sudden rush of fear.

He went to bed. Once he was in the warmth of the sheets, he thought again of Thérèse, whom his anxieties had made him forget. Keeping his eyes obstinately closed and trying to go to sleep, he found that his thoughts were working involuntarily, forcing themselves on him and connecting with one another to show him the advantages that he would get by marrying as soon as possible. Sometimes, he would turn round and tell himself: 'Don't think any more, let's sleep; I have to be up at eight o'clock tomorrow to go to the office.' And he made an effort to slide off into sleep. But, one by one, the ideas would return and his mind would resume its silent inner debate. Soon he found himself in a sort of anxious reverie, which listed at the back of his brain the reasons why he should marry, and the alternate arguments that lust and caution gave for and against possessing Thérèse.

So, realizing that he could not sleep, that insomnia was keeping his body in a state of irritation, he turned over on to his back, opened his eyes wide and let his mind fill with the memory of the young woman. The balance was upset and the hot fever of earlier times shook him once more. He thought of getting up and going back to the Passage du Pont-Neuf. He would have the outer gate opened for him, he would knock on the little door of the staircase and Thérèse would welcome him in. At this idea, the blood rushed to his neck.

His daydream was astonishingly clear. He saw himself in the street, walking quickly beside the houses and saying to himself: 'I'm taking this boulevard, crossing this crossroads, to get there sooner.' Then the gate to the arcade grated on its hinges and he went down the narrow passage, dark and empty, congratulating himself on the fact that he could go to Thérèse without being

seen by the woman who sold costume jewellery; then he imagined being in the alleyway and going up the little staircase as he
had so often done. Once there, he felt again the searing delight
that he used to feel; he recalled the delicious fears and voluptuous charms of adultery. His memories became a reality that
impregnated his every sense: he could smell the musty odour of
the corridor, touch the slimy walls and see the grimy shadows
that lingered there. And he went up every step, panting, straining
his ears and already satisfying his desires in this fearful approach
to the woman he desired. Finally, he was scratching on the door
and the door opened: Thérèse was there, waiting for him, in her
petticoat, all white . . .

He could really watch his thoughts as they unfolded in front
of him. With his eyes focused on the gloom, he could actually
see. When, after running through the streets, entering the arcade
and going up the little staircase, he imagined he could make
out Thérèse, eager and pale, he jumped quickly out of bed,
muttering: 'I must go, she's waiting for me.' His sudden movement dispelled the vision. He felt the cold of the floor and was
afraid. For a moment, he stayed without moving, barefoot,
listening. He thought he could hear a noise outside. If he went
to see Thérèse, he would once again have to go past the cellar
door downstairs, and this idea sent a great cold shudder up his
back. Once again, he felt terrified, with a stupid, overwhelming
dread. He looked defiantly round his room and saw some whitish streaks of light; and so, gently, cautiously, but at the same
time with anxious haste, he got back into bed and curled up,
hiding himself under the blanket, as though getting out of the
way of a weapon, a knife that was threatening him.

The blood had rushed suddenly to his neck and his neck was
burning. He put a hand to it, feeling the scar from Camille's bite
beneath his fingers. He had almost forgotten the bite, and now
he was terrified to find it on his skin. He imagined it eating into
his flesh. He quickly pulled his hand away so that he would not
have to feel it, but he did feel it still, pressing in, devouring his
neck. So he tried to scratch it gently, with the end of a nail, but
the dreadful burning increased. To prevent himself from tearing

off his skin, he pressed his hands between his knees, which were drawn up under him. And there he remained, stiff, on edge, his neck burning and his teeth chattering with fear.

Now his mind became fixed on Camille, with terrifying intensity. Until then, the drowned man had not troubled Laurent's sleep. But now the thought of Thérèse brought with it the spectre of her husband. The murderer did not dare reopen his eyes: he was afraid of seeing the victim in a corner of the room. At one point, he thought that his bed was shaking in some odd way; he imagined Camille hiding under it and shaking it like that, so that Laurent would fall out and he could bite him. Crazed with fear, his hair standing on end, he grasped his mattress, imagining that the shaking was getting stronger and stronger.

Then he perceived that the bed was not moving. This brought about a reaction in him. He sat up, lit his candle and called himself an idiot. To calm his fever, he drank a large glass of water.

'I was wrong to drink at that wine shop,' he thought. 'I don't know what's wrong with me tonight. It's silly. I'll be knocked out later on in the office. I should have gone to sleep straight away when I got into bed, and not thought about a load of things. That's what's keeping me awake ... Now let's go to sleep.'

He blew out the light again and put his head into the pillow, slightly cooler and fully determined not to think any more or be afraid. Tiredness began to relax his nerves.

He did not sleep his usual, heavily weighted sleep. He slipped gradually into a sort of drowsiness. He was like someone merely numbed, plunged in a sweet, voluptuous state of insensibility. He could feel his drowsing body and, in his insensate flesh, his mind remained awake. He had chased away the ideas in his head and struggled against wakefulness, and now that he was numbed, when he had no strength and no willpower, the ideas slowly came back, one by one, to take possession of his weakened self. His daydreams began again. He went back over the journey between himself and Thérèse: he went downstairs, ran past the cellar and found himself outside. He walked down all the streets he had already taken earlier, when he was day-dreaming with open eyes. He went into the Passage du Pont-Neuf, climbed the little staircase and knocked on the door. But instead of Thérèse, instead of the young woman in a petticoat with her breasts naked, it was Camille who opened to him, Camille as he had seen him in the Morgue, greenish and horribly disfigured. The corpse held out its arms to him with a ghastly laugh, showing the tip of a blackened tongue between the whiteness of its teeth.

Laurent gave a cry and woke up with a start. He was bathed in a cold sweat. He pulled the blanket over his eyes, cursing and angry with himself. He wanted to go back to sleep.

He fell asleep as before, slowly, and the same heaviness seized him, so that when his will had once again been relaxed in the languor of half-sleep, he started to walk once more, returning to the place where his obsession led him: he hurried to see Thérèse. And once more it was the drowned man who opened the door.

In terror, the wretch sat up in bed. The thing he most wanted in the world was to drive away this unrelenting dream. He longed for a leaden sleep that would crush his thoughts. Provided he was awake, he had enough energy to drive away the ghost of his victim, but as soon as he was no longer in control of his mind, even while his mind was leading him to pleasure, it led him on to horror.

He tried to sleep once again. There followed a succession of sensual drowsings and sudden, agonized awakenings. In his furious obstinacy, he kept on going towards Thérèse and kept on coming up against Camille's corpse. More than ten times, he went along the same path, starting out with his flesh ablaze with desire, followed the same route, experienced the same feelings, performed the same actions, with minute precision; and more than ten times, it was the drowned man that he saw waiting for his embrace when he reached out to grasp and hug his mistress. His desire was not lessened by this same sinister ending that woke him up every time; a few minutes later, as soon as he went back to sleep, his desire forgot the ghastly corpse that awaited him, and hurried once more to find the lithe, warm body of a woman. For an hour, Laurent lived through this series of nightmares, this bad dream constantly repeated, continually unforeseen, which, at every shocked awakening, left him shattered by an ever sharper sense of terror.

One shock, the last, was so violent and painful that he decided to get up and stop struggling. Dawn was coming. A dismal grey light filtered through the attic window, which marked out a whitish square against the sky, the colour of ashes.

Laurent got dressed slowly, with a dull feeling of annoyance. He was irritated at not having slept and at having given way to a fear that he now considered childish. As he was putting on his trousers, he stretched, rubbed his limbs and felt his face, beaten and puffy from a feverish night. And he kept saying:

'I wouldn't have thought of all that. I would have slept and then I'd be fresh and ready for anything by now . . . Oh, if only Thérèse had wanted to, yesterday evening, if only Thérèse had slept with me!'

This idea – that Thérèse would have prevented him from being afraid – calmed him a little. Underneath lay the fear of having to spend other nights like the one that he had just endured.

He threw some water on his face and gave his hair a comb. This simple wash cleared his head and drove away his last fears. He was reasoning clearly and now felt only a great sense of tiredness in all his limbs.

'I'm not a coward, though,' he thought, as he finished dressing. 'I really don't give a damn about Camille. It's quite ridiculous to think that the poor devil is under my bed. Now perhaps I'm going to be thinking that every night. I really do have to get married as soon as I can. When Thérèse is holding me in her arms, I won't think about Camille. She will kiss my neck and I won't feel that frightful burning sensation. Now, then, let's look at that bite.'

He went over to his mirror, stretched his neck and looked. The scar was light pink. As Laurent was making out his victim's tooth marks, he felt quite moved by it and the blood rushed to his head. It was then that he noticed something odd. The scar was turned purple by the rising flow; it became bright and blood-filled, standing out red against the plump white neck. At the same time, Laurent felt sharp pricks, as though someone were sticking pins into the wound. He quickly turned up his shirt collar.

'Pooh!' he said. 'Thérèse will cure that ... A few kisses will be all it takes. How stupid I am to think about such things!'

He put on his hat and went downstairs. He needed to get some fresh air, to walk around. As he went past the cellar door, he smiled; but at the same time he tested the strength of the hook that kept the door shut. Outside, he walked slowly in the fresh morning air on the empty pavements. It was about five o'clock.

Laurent spent a dreadful day. He had to fight against an overwhelming urge to sleep that overtook him in the afternoon in his office. His head was aching and heavy. He could not stop it falling forward, so that he had to jerk it upright when he heard one of his bosses coming along the corridor. The struggle with these sudden movements left his body completely exhausted and caused him a lot of anxiety.

That evening, tired as he was, he wanted to go and see Thérèse. He found her as feverish, as dejected and as weary as he was.

'Poor Thérèse had a bad night,' said Mme Raquin, when he had sat down. 'It appears that she had nightmares and frightful insomnia. I heard her cry out several times and this morning she was quite ill.'

While her aunt was speaking, Thérèse was staring at Laurent. Each of them doubtless guessed the terror they had shared, because the same nervous shudder passed across both their faces. They stayed looking at each other until ten o'clock, exchanging commonplaces, but understanding one another and both conspiring through their looks to hasten the moment when they could unite against the drowned man.

XVIII

Thérèse, too, had been visited by the ghost of Camille in that night of fever.

She had been suddenly aroused by Laurent's ardent plea for them to meet, after more than a year of indifference. Her flesh began to ache when, lying in bed alone, she considered that the wedding was soon to take place. And then, struggling in the throes of insomnia, she saw the drowned man rise up in front of her. Like Laurent, she had twisted around in a frenzy of desire and horror and, like him, told herself that she would no longer be afraid, no longer experience such suffering, when she held her lover between her arms.

At the same moment, this man and this woman had felt a kind of failing of the nerves, which brought them back, gasping and terrified, to their terrible love. An affinity of blood and lust had been established between them. They shuddered the same shudders, and their hearts, in a sort of agonizing fellowship, ached with the same terror. From then on, they had only one body and one soul to feel pleasure and pain. This community, this mutual interpenetration, is a psychological and physiological fact that often occurs between those who are thrown violently together by great nervous shocks.

For more than a year, Thérèse and Laurent carried the chain lightly that was clamped to their limbs, binding them together. In the mental collapse that followed the acute crisis of the murder, in the feelings of disgust and the need for calm and forgetting that came after that, the two prisoners could imagine that they were free and that no iron link bound them together. The chain lay slack on the ground, while they rested, stricken with a kind of happy stupor, and tried to find love elsewhere, to lead sensibly balanced lives. But on the day when circumstances drove them once more to exchange words of desire, the chain suddenly tightened and they experienced such a shock that they felt attached to one another for ever.

The very next day, Thérèse started her campaign, working away in secret to bring about her marriage to Laurent. The task

was a difficult one, fraught with danger. The lovers were afraid
that they might do something rash and awake suspicion by
revealing too suddenly what they had had to gain from Camille's
death. Realizing that they could not talk about marriage, they
devised a very sensible plan that consisted in getting Mme
Raquin and the Thursday evening guests to offer them what
they dare not ask for themselves. Their one idea from now on
was to get the idea of Thérèse's remarriage into the heads of
these good people and above all to make them think that the
idea originated with themselves and was theirs alone.

The play-acting involved was long and delicate. Both Thérèse
and Laurent had taken on the role that suited them and they
went forward with extreme caution, weighing every little word
and gesture. Underneath, they were consumed by an impatience
that wore and stretched their nerves. They lived in a state of
continual irritation; only their terror of the consequences kept
them smiling and calm.

They were in a hurry to get it over with, because they could
no longer remain alone and separate. Every night, the drowned
man came to them, while insomnia kept them lying on a bed of
burning coals, and turned them over and over with iron pincers.
Every evening, the state of nervous agony in which they lived
drove up the fever in their blood, raising frightful spectres before
them. When evening came, Thérèse no longer dared go up to
her room. She experienced strong waves of terror at the idea of
locking herself up until morning in that great room which was
filled with strange glimmerings and peopled by ghosts as soon
as the light went out. Eventually, she would leave her candle
alight, not even wanting to go to sleep, so that it kept her eyes
wide open. And when tiredness made her eyelids close, she saw
Camille in the darkness and would reopen them with a start. In
the morning, she would drag herself around in the daylight,
shattered, after only a few hours' sleep. As for Laurent, he had
become quite timorous since the evening when he had been
afraid while walking in front of the cellar door. Before that, he
had lived with the self-confidence of an animal, but now he
shook and went pale at the slightest noise, like a little boy. A
shudder of fear had suddenly run through him and it had not

left him since. At night, he suffered even more than Thérèse did: fear profoundly ravaged this great, soft, cowardly body, and he watched the close of day with a cruel sense of unease. Quite often he found that he did not want to go home and would spend whole nights walking through the deserted streets. Once, he remained until morning under a bridge in the pouring rain, and there, crouching down, freezing cold, not daring to get up and return to the embankment, he watched the dirty water flowing past in the pale shadows for almost six hours, during which his terrors would sometimes flatten him against the damp ground. He imagined he could see long lines of drowned people carried along with the current under the arch of the bridge. When exhaustion finally drove him home, he double-locked the door, and tossed and turned until dawn, a prey to frightful attacks of fever. The same nightmare would persistently return: he thought he was falling out of the hot, passionate arms of Thérèse into the cold and slimy arms of Camille. He dreamed that his mistress was stifling him in her warm embrace and then that the drowned man was pressing him to his rotting chest in an icy hug. These sudden, alternating sensations of desire and disgust, the successive touch of flesh burning with love and of cold flesh softened by the mud, made him pant and shudder, gasping in horror.

And, every day, the two lovers' panic grew, every day their nightmares crushed and appalled them more. Each now believed that nothing but the other's kisses would ever kill their insomnia. Out of prudence, they did not dare to meet, but waited for the day when they got married as a day of salvation that would be followed by a happy night.

In this way they longed for their union with all the desire they felt within them to have a night's tranquil sleep. During the period of indifference, they had wavered, each forgetting the arguments of selfishness and desire which had, as it were, faded, after having driven the two of them to murder. Now the fever was burning them again and, behind their desire and their selfishness, they rediscovered the reasons that had originally made them decide to kill Camille, in order to taste the joys that, to their minds, a legitimate marriage would surely procure them.

And yet, it was with a feeling of vague despair that they took the final decision to get married openly. Deep inside, they were scared. Their desire trembled. They leaned over one another, so to speak, as over an abyss that held a horrible fascination for them; each of them bent above the other's being, clinging on silently, while sharp, delicious waves of vertigo relaxed their grip and gave them the urge to let go. But confronted with the present moment, with their anxious waiting and their fearful desires, they felt an overwhelming need to close their eyes and dream of a future of affectionate happiness and quiet pleasures. The more they trembled at the sight of one another, the more they guessed the horror of the chasm into which they were about to plunge, the more they tried also to make promises of happiness to themselves and set out the unavoidable arguments that were leading them, inevitably, to marry.

Thérèse wanted to get married solely because she was afraid and her organism demanded Laurent's violent embrace.[1] She was suffering from a nervous crisis that made her almost mad. In truth, she was not thinking reasonably, but flinging herself into passion, her mind distracted by the romances that she had been reading and her flesh aroused by the cruel nights of insomnia that had been keeping her awake for several weeks now.

Laurent, whose temperament was more stolid, tried to rationalize his decision, even as he was giving way to his terrors and his desires. To prove that his marriage really was necessary and that he would finally be quite happy, and to dispel the vague fears that were getting a grip on him, he reworked all his earlier arguments. His father, the peasant in Jeufosse, obstinately refused to die, so he told himself that the inheritance could be a long time in coming. He was even afraid that this inheritance might escape him altogether and end up in the pockets of one of his cousins, a large lad who farmed the land, much to the satisfaction of Old Laurent. In which case, he would remain poor and live without a wife, in a garret, sleeping badly and eating worse still. In any case, he was counting on not having to work all his life. He was starting to get singularly bored with his office, where even the light duties assigned to him became a heavy burden on his laziness. Whenever he thought about it, he came to the conclusion that the supreme happiness was to do nothing. Then he recalled that he had drowned Camille in order to marry Thérèse and then do nothing afterwards. Certainly, the desire to have his mistress to himself alone had played a large part in the idea of his crime, but he had perhaps been led to murder still more by the hope of putting himself in Camille's place, of being looked after as he was and enjoying unending bliss. If he had been driven by passion alone, he would not have shown such cowardice and caution. The truth was that, through this killing, he had sought to guarantee a tranquil and idle life for himself and the satisfaction of all his appetites. All these ideas, whether he was conscious of them or not, came back into his mind. To encourage himself, he kept thinking that it was now time to profit from Camille's death as he had planned. He set out in his mind the advantages and pleasures of his future life: he would leave his office, and live in a state of delightful idleness; he would eat, drink and sleep to his heart's content; he would have constantly at hand a passionate woman who would restore the balance of his blood and his nerves; he would soon inherit Mme Raquin's forty or so thousand francs, because the poor old soul was dying a little day by day; and finally, he would create for himself the life of a contented animal and forget all the rest. Constantly, once Thérèse and he had decided to get married, Laurent told himself these things. He expected still further benefits and he was happy as anything when he thought he had found a new argument, based on his own selfish interests, that would oblige him to marry the drowned man's widow. But much as he forced himself to hope and much as he dreamed of a future oozing with idleness and the pleasures of the flesh, he still felt a sudden icy shudder chill his flesh and still, from time to time, was seized with a feeling of anxiety that seemed to stifle the joy in his throat.

XIX

Meanwhile, Thérèse and Laurent's secret campaign was bring-ing results. Thérèse had adopted an attitude of despair and melancholy, which started, after a few days, to disturb Mme Raquin. The old haberdasher wanted to know what was making her niece so sad. At this, the young woman played to perfection her part as the inconsolable widow; she spoke vaguely of bore-dom, listlessness and nervous pain, without mentioning any-thing specific. When her aunt pressed her on it, she replied that she was well, that she did not know what was making her so depressed, but that she kept crying without knowing why. Then there was her constant sighing, her pale, pathetic smiles, and those silences, oppressive in their emptiness and despondency. Eventually, faced with this young woman who had retreated into herself and seemed to be dying slowly of some unknown sickness, Mme Raquin became seriously alarmed. She had no one left in the world except her niece and she prayed God every night to preserve this child so that there would be someone to close her eyes. There was a bit of egotism in this last love of her old age. She felt she would be deprived of the few meagre consolations that still helped her to live when it occurred to her that she might lose Thérèse and die alone at the back of the damp shop in the arcade. From then on, she kept her eyes constantly on her niece and was appalled to observe the young woman's sorrows, wondering what she could do to cure her of these silent feelings of despair.

The situation being so grave, she thought she should consult her old friend Michaud. One Thursday evening, she kept him behind in the shop and confided her fears in him.

'Good heavens, don't you see?' the old man said, with the brutal frankness that came from his former occupation. 'It's been clear to me for a long time that Thérèse was in a sulk and I know very well why her face is all yellow and downcast like that.'

'You know why?' said Mme Raquin. 'Tell me quickly. If only we could make her better.'

'Pooh! The treatment's easy,' Michaud went on, with a laugh. 'Your niece is unhappy because she's been alone every night in her room for almost two years now. She needs a husband. You can see it in her eyes.'

The old police chief's straight talking hurt Mme Raquin deeply. She thought that the wound which had been constantly bleeding in her since the frightful accident at Saint-Ouen burned as sharply and as cruelly in the heart of the young widow. With her son dead, she thought that there could not possibly be another man for her niece. And now Michaud, with his coarse laugh, was saying that Thérèse was sick because she needed a husband.

'Marry her off as quick as you can,' he said as he left. 'Unless you want to see her dry up altogether. That's my opinion, dear lady, and believe me, I'm right.'

Mme Raquin could not at first get used to the idea that her son had been forgotten already. Old Michaud had not even spoken Camille's name and he had started to joke when talking about Thérèse's supposed illness. The poor mother realized that she alone kept the memory of her dear child alive in the depths of her being. She wept and felt as though Camille had just died a second time. Then, when she had had a good cry, when she was tired out from grief, she thought despite herself about what Michaud had said and got used to the idea of purchasing a little happiness at the cost of a marriage that, according to the fine scruples of her memory, would kill her son a second time. She lost her nerve when she found herself confronted with Thérèse, weighed down with misery, in the icy silence of the shop. She was not one of those stiff, dry creatures who take a bitter joy at living in eternal despair. She was demonstrative, capable of flexibility and devotion, with her chubby, affable, good woman's temperament which impelled her to express her affection. Since her niece had stopped speaking and remained there, pale and weak, life had become intolerable for her and the shop seemed like a tomb. She wanted warm feelings about her, life, caresses, something soft and merry that would help her to await death with equanimity. These unconscious desires made her accept the idea of remarrying Thérèse and she even forgot about

her son a little. She experienced something like a rebirth in the
dead existence that she led, with a new will to act and new
things to occupy her mind. She was looking for a husband for
her niece and could think of nothing else. This choice of a
husband was an important matter and the poor old woman was
considering herself rather than Thérèse: she wanted to marry
her off in a way that would ensure her own happiness and was
desperately afraid that the young woman's new husband would
upset the last moments of her old age. She was terrified by the
idea that she was going to bring a stranger into her everyday
life. The thought itself gave her pause and prevented her from
speaking openly about marriage to her niece.

While Thérèse, with the perfect hypocrisy that she owed
to her upbringing, was playing at boredom and depression,
Laurent took the part of the sensitive and obliging man. He
catered to the little needs of the two women, especially Mme
Raquin, on whom he showered delicate little marks of his consideration. Little by little, he became indispensable around the
shop and he was the only one to bring a touch of merriment to
this dark hole. When he was not there, in the evenings, the old
lady would look around her uneasily, as though something was
missing, almost afraid to find herself alone with Thérèse and
her misery. In fact, Laurent would stay away for the occasional
evening only in order to reinforce his power. He came to the
shop every day after leaving work and stayed until the arcade
closed. He ran errands and he would fetch any little thing
that Mme Raquin needed, as she could not walk very easily.
Then he would sit down and chat. He had found an actor's
voice, soft and penetrating, which he used to soothe the good old
woman's ears and heart. Most of all, he seemed very concerned
about Thérèse's health, as a friend and as a sympathetic man
whose own soul suffers because of the sufferings of others.
Several times, he took Mme Raquin aside and terrified her,
by pretending to be himself very worried at the changes and
the effects of depression that he claimed to see on the young
woman's face.

'We're going to lose her soon,' he would mutter with tears in
his voice. 'We can't hide from ourselves the fact that she is very

ill. Oh, dear! What will happen to our little bit of happiness, our nice, quiet evenings!'

Mme Raquin listened to him in dismay. Laurent even went as far as to risk talking about Camille.

'You see,' he would also tell the old woman, 'my poor friend's death was a dreadful blow for her. She has been dying for the past two years, ever since the fateful day when she lost Camille. Nothing will console her, nothing will heal her. We must be resigned to it.'

These brazen lies made her weep bitterly. She was upset and blinded by the memory of her son. Every time that Camille's name was spoken, she burst into tears, she let herself go, and she wanted to embrace the person who mentioned her poor child. Laurent had noticed the way that the name made her upset and softened her heart. He could get her to cry at will, subjecting her to an emotion that took away her clear perception of things, and he misused this power in order to keep her constantly grieving and pliable in his hands. Every evening, even though it gave him a sickening feeling in the pit of his stomach, he would bring the conversation round to Camille, to his exceptional qualities, warm heart and sharp wit, extolling his victim with perfect cynicism. Occasionally, when he caught Thérèse giving him a strange look, he shuddered and eventually himself came to believe all the good things he was saying about the drowned man. At that, he would fall silent, suddenly gripped with a frightful feeling of jealousy because he feared that the widow might be in love with the man whom he had thrown in the water and whom he was now praising with the conviction of a person in the grip of some hallucination. Throughout the conversation, Mme Raquin was in tears and saw nothing around her. Even as she wept, she felt that Laurent had a loving and generous heart; he alone remembered her son, he alone still spoke of him in a voice trembling with emotion. She wiped her tears and looked at the young man with infinite tenderness, loving him like her own child.

One Thursday evening, Michaud and Grivet were already in the dining room when Laurent came in and went over to Thérèse, asking her about her health in a voice of gentle concern.

For a moment, he sat down beside her, playing his role of affectionate and worried friend, for the benefit of the onlookers. As the young people were next to one another, exchanging a few words, Michaud, who was looking at them, leaned over, pointed at Laurent and said very quietly to the old haberdasher:

'There you are! That's the husband your niece wants. Quickly arrange for them to marry. We'll help you if necessary.'

He smiled in a suggestive way: in his view Thérèse must be in need of a good, lusty husband. The idea struck Mme Raquin like a shaft of light and she suddenly noticed all the benefits that would accrue to her personally from a marriage between Thérèse and Laurent. Such a marriage would only strengthen the ties that already bound her and her niece to her son's friend, that kind-hearted being who came to cheer them up in the evenings. In that way, she would not be bringing a stranger into the family or risking her own happiness; on the contrary, while providing support for Thérèse, she would introduce a new joy into her own old age, finding a second son in this young man who had been showing her such filial love for the past three years. And then, she felt that Thérèse would be less unfaithful to Camille's memory if she were to marry Laurent. Religions of the heart make these strangely nice distinctions. Mme Raquin, who would have wept at the sight of a stranger kissing the young widow, felt no inner revulsion at the idea of delivering Thérèse to the embraces of her son's former colleague. She thought, as they say, that this would keep it in the family.

Throughout the evening, while her guests were playing dominoes, Mme Raquin gave the couple looks of such tenderness that the young man and the young woman guessed that their play-acting had succeeded and that the end was in sight. Before leaving, Michaud had a short, whispered conversation with the old haberdasher and then ostentatiously took Laurent by the arm and announced that he would accompany him for part of the way. As Laurent left, he exchanged a brief glance with Thérèse; it was a look full of urgent admonitions.

Michaud had taken it on himself to find out the lie of the land. He found the young man very devoted to the ladies, but very surprised by the plan for marriage between himself and

Thérèse. Laurent added, in a broken voice, that he loved the
widow of his poor friend like a sister and that he would feel he
was committing a veritable sacrilege if he were to marry her.
The retired police commissioner insisted. He gave a hundred
good reasons for him to agree, even speaking of devotion, and
went so far as to tell the young man that his duty obliged him
to give Mme Raquin back a son and Thérèse a husband. Little
by little, Laurent allowed himself to be won over. He pretended
to give in to his feelings, to accept the idea of marriage as one
that had fallen out of the sky, and was required by devotion and
duty, as Old Michaud was telling him. When the latter had
extracted a formal 'yes', he left his companion, rubbing his
hands and thinking he had just won a great victory. He congratulated himself on being the first to have the idea of this marriage
which would bring all the former enjoyment back to their Thursday evenings.

While Michaud was talking with Laurent as they slowly
walked along beside the river, Mme Raquin was having a quite
similar conversation with Thérèse. Just as her niece was going
to bed, pale and uneasy on her feet as usual, the old woman
kept her back for a moment. She questioned her in a gentle
voice, begging her to be frank and to tell her the reason for the
dark mood that was oppressing her. Then, getting only vague
answers, she talked about the void left by widowhood and
gradually worked her way round towards the possibility of a
remarriage and finally asked Thérèse straight out if she did not
secretly long to get married again. Thérèse protested, saying
that this was not on her mind and that she would remain faithful
to Camille. Mme Raquin began to cry. She argued against her
own belief, suggesting that despair need not be eternal; and
finally, in answer to an exclamation by the young woman that
she would not replace Camille, Mme Raquin named Laurent.
After that, she expounded at length, with a flood of words, upon
the suitability and advantages of such a match. She bared her
soul and repeated aloud what she had been thinking during the
evening. With unselfconscious egotism, she painted a picture of
her last happy days surrounded by her two dear children.

Thérèse listened with bowed head, resigned and docile, ready to satisfy her aunt's least desire.

'I love Laurent like a brother,' she said, in a pained voice, when her aunt had finished. 'Since that is what you want, I shall try to love him as a husband. I want to make you happy ... I had hoped that you would let me mourn in peace, but I shall dry my tears, since your happiness is involved.'

She embraced the old lady, who was surprised and anxious at having been the first to forget her son. As she got into bed, Mme Raquin wept bitterly, accusing herself of being weaker than Thérèse and wanting a match out of egotism that the young widow herself would accept for reasons of simple self-denial.

The following morning, Michaud and his old friend had a brief conversation in the arcade in front of the shop. They told each other the results of their manoeuvres and agreed to go right ahead, obliging the young people to get engaged that very evening.

In the evening, at five o'clock, Michaud was already in the shop when Laurent arrived. As soon as the young man was seated, the retired police commissioner whispered in his ear:

'She accepts.'

This bald statement was overheard by Thérèse, who went pale, staring shamelessly at Laurent. The two lovers looked at one another for a few seconds, as though discussing the matter. Both of them realized that they had to accept the position without further ado and get it all over with. Laurent got up and went over to take the hand of Mme Raquin, who was making every effort to hold back her tears.

'Dear Mother,' he said with a smile. 'I talked with Monsieur Michaud yesterday evening about your future well-being. Your children want to make you happy.'

When the old lady heard herself addressed as 'dear Mother', her tears flowed. She grasped Thérèse's hand and pressed it into Laurent's, unable to utter a word.

The two lovers shuddered at each other's touch. They stayed there, with fingers gripped and burning, in a nervous embrace. The young man went on in a hesitant voice:

'Thérèse, would you like us to create a happy, peaceful life for your aunt?'

'Yes,' the young woman replied, weakly. 'We have a duty to fulfil.'

At that, Laurent turned towards Mme Raquin and added, very pale:

'When Camille fell into the water, he called out to me: "Save my wife, I entrust her to you." I feel that I am carrying out his final wish by marrying Thérèse.'

When she heard this, Thérèse let go of Laurent's hand. It was as though she had received a blow in the chest. She was over-whelmed by her lover's effrontery. She stared at him with haggard eyes while Mme Raquin, choking with sobs, stammered out:

'Yes, yes, my dear, marry her, make her happy; my son will thank you from the depths of his grave.'

Laurent felt that he was weakening, and leaned against the back of a chair. Michaud, also moved to tears, pushed him towards Thérèse, saying:

'Kiss one another. This will be your engagement.'

The young man had a strange feeling as he put his lips on the widow's cheeks, and she shrank back as though burned by the two kisses that her lover had given here. This was the first time that the man had kissed her before witnesses. The blood rushed to her face and she felt hot and uncomfortable – though she had no feelings of shame and had never blushed at the intimacies of their love-making.

After this crisis was over, the two murderers relaxed. Their marriage was fixed and they were at last reaching the goal that they had been pursuing for so long. Everything was agreed upon that very evening. On the following Thursday, the engagement was announced to Grivet, Olivier and his wife. Michaud was delighted to relay the news, rubbing his hands and saying again and again:

'It was my idea, I married them . . . You see what a fine couple they'll make!'

Suzanne came over in silence to kiss Thérèse. This poor crea-ture, pale and lifeless, had conceived a feeling of friendship for the dark, rigid young widow. She loved her as a child might, with a sort of respectful terror. Olivier complimented the aunt and the niece, while Grivet risked a few vulgar jokes, which did not go down well. In short, they were all thoroughly delighted and declared that everything was for the best. To be honest, they already saw themselves at the wedding.

Thérèse and Laurent maintained an attitude that was restrained and cautious. They demonstrated feelings for one another that were nothing more than considerate and affectionate. They gave the impression of carrying out an act of supreme self-sacrifice. Nothing in their appearance betrayed the terrors and desires that agitated them. Mme Raquin gave them faint smiles, and gentle, grateful looks of benevolence.

There were a few formalities to complete. Laurent had to write to his father to ask for the old man's consent. The peasant of Jeufosse, who had almost forgotten that he had a son in Paris, replied in four lines that he could marry or get himself hanged if he wished. He let it be known that, since he had resolved never to give him a penny, he left him to look after himself and authorized him to commit any act of folly that he wished. Laurent was peculiarly unsettled by this kind of authorization.

After Mme Raquin had read the letter from this unnatural father, she had a surge of generosity that drove her to do something silly. She settled on her niece the forty-odd thousand francs that she owned, renouncing everything for the sake of the young couple and entrusting herself to their goodwill, because she wanted all her happiness to flow from them. Laurent was contributing nothing to their finances, and even suggested that he would not stick at his job for ever, but might go back to painting. In any event, the little family's future was assured: the income from the forty-odd thousand francs, together with the profits from the haberdashery business, should be enough to let three people live comfortably. They would have just enough to be happy.

The preparations for the wedding were speeded up. The formalities were reduced to a minimum. You might have thought that everyone was in a hurry to drive Laurent into Thérèse's bed. At last the longed-for day arrived.

XX

On the morning, Laurent and Thérèse both woke up in their separate rooms with the same profoundly joyful thought: they told themselves that their last night of terror was over. They would no longer sleep alone and could protect one another against the drowned man.

Thérèse looked around her and gave a strange smile as she mentally assessed the size of her large bed. She got up and dressed slowly, while waiting for Suzanne, who was to come and help to get her ready for her wedding.

Laurent sat upright in bed. He stayed like that for a few minutes, saying farewell to the attic that he considered so demeaning. At last, he would be leaving this dog's kennel and have a wife of his own. It was December. He shuddered and stepped down on the tiled floor, telling himself that he would be warm that night.

A week earlier, Mme Raquin, knowing that he was broke, had slipped a purse into his hand containing the sum of five hundred francs, which was all her savings. The young man had accepted it without demur and fitted himself out in new clothes. The old haberdasher's money had also allowed him to give Thérèse the customary gifts.

The black trousers, the tailcoat and white waistcoat, the fine linen shirt and tie, were laid out on two chairs. Laurent washed and scented his body from a bottle of eau de Cologne, then started to get dressed with minute care. He wanted to look good. While he was attaching his collar, a high, stiff, detachable collar, he felt a sharp pain in his neck. The collar stud slipped from his fingers. He got impatient with it and felt as though the starched material of the collar were cutting into his flesh. He wanted to look and lifted his chin; and it was then that he saw that Camille's bite was quite red: the collar had grazed the scar. Laurent gritted his teeth and went pale. The sight of this blemish standing out on his neck was upsetting and annoying for him at this particular moment. He screwed up the collar and picked out another, putting it on very carefully. Then he finished dressing.

When he went downstairs, his new clothes kept him quite stiff, so that he did not dare turn his head, with his neck imprisoned in starched cloth. At every move he made, a fold in this cloth would pinch the wound that the drowned man's teeth had bitten into his flesh. He was enduring this kind of sharp pricking when he got into the carriage and went to find Thérèse and take her to the town hall and the church.

On the way, he picked up an employee of the Orléans Railway and Old Michaud, who were to be his witnesses. When they got to the shop, everyone was ready: Grivet and Olivier were there as Thérèse's witnesses, and Suzanne, all three of them looking at the bride in the way that little girls look at the dolls they have just dressed. Mme Raquin, though she could no longer walk, wanted to go everywhere with her children. They lifted her into a carriage and set off.

Everything went off decently at the town hall and the church. People noticed and approved of the couple's calm and modest demeanour. They spoke the sacramental 'yes' with such feeling that even Grivet was touched. They felt as though they were in a dream. While they stayed quietly sitting or kneeling side by side, wild thoughts were raging through them and tearing them apart. They avoided looking each other in the eye. When they got back into the carriage, they felt more like strangers towards one another than they had before.

It had been decided that the dinner would be a family affair, in a little restaurant on the hills of Belleville.[1] The Michauds and Grivet were the only guests. While waiting for six o'clock, the wedding party drove along the boulevards before getting into the eating-house, where a table with seven places had been laid in a yellow-painted room smelling of dust and wine.

The meal was not the jolliest of occasions. The couple were serious and thoughtful. Since that morning, they had been experiencing odd feelings, which they did not try to explain even to themselves. They had been stunned, from the beginning, by the speed of the formalities and of the service that had just united them for ever. Then the long drive along the boulevards had, as it were, rocked them to sleep. They felt that it had lasted for months on end. They had patiently let themselves be carried away by the monotony of the streets, looking at the shops and the passers-by with dead eyes, in the grip of a lethargy which dazed them, though they tried to shake it off with bursts of laughter. When they came into the restaurant, a crushing weariness weighed them down and they were overcome with a growing sense of torpor.

Seated opposite one another at table, they smiled awkwardly and kept sinking back into a state of pensive preoccupation. They ate, answered questions and moved like automata. The same succession of fleeting thoughts kept returning constantly to both their weary minds. They were married, but they were profoundly astonished to find that they had no awareness of anything new. They felt that a huge gulf still separated them and from time to time they wondered how they could cross this gulf. It seemed as though they were back before the murder, when a material obstacle stood between them. Then suddenly they remembered that they would sleep together that evening, in a few hours, and they looked at one another in amazement, not understanding they would be allowed to do that. They did not feel any union between them. On the contrary, they imagined that they had just been violently pulled apart and cast far away from each other.

The guests, giggling stupidly around them, wanted to hear them exchange intimacies, say 'tu' to each other, clear away any embarrassment; but they stammered and blushed and could not manage to behave as lovers towards one another in front of other people.

In the wait, their desires had worn out and all the past had vanished. They were losing their violent, lustful hunger and even forgetting their joy the same morning, the deep joy that had overtaken them both at the idea that from now on they would no longer be afraid. They were simply weary and stunned by everything that had happened; the events of the day were going round and round in their heads, monstrous and incomprehensible. There they were, silent, smiling, expecting nothing, hoping for nothing. A dull, anxious pain stirred in the depths of their despondency.

And Laurent, every time he moved his head, felt a sharp,

burning sensation eating into his flesh: his detachable collar was
pinching and cutting into Camille's bite. While the Mayor was
reading out the Code[2] and while the priest was speaking about
God, throughout this long day, he had felt the drowned man's
teeth digging into his flesh. At times, he felt as though a trail of
blood would run down on to his chest and stain his white
waistcoat red.

In herself, Mme Raquin felt grateful to the couple for their
solemnity: the poor mother would have been hurt by a loud
demonstration of happiness. To her mind, her son was there,
invisible, entrusting Thérèse to Laurent. Grivet did not feel the
same. He thought the wedding a bit sad and tried to cheer it up,
despite the looks he got from Michaud and Olivier, which
pinned him to his chair every time he made as though to get on
his feet and say something idiotic. However, he did manage to
get up once, to propose a toast.

'I drink to the children of the bride and groom,' he said, in a
suggestive tone of voice.

They had to clink their glasses. Thérèse and Laurent had gone
very pale when they heard Grivet's toast. It had not occurred to
them that they might have children. The idea shot through them
like an icy shiver. They touched their glasses nervously and
looked at one another in surprise, fearful at being there, face
to face.

The company left the table early. The guests wanted to accompany the couple as far as the bridal chamber. It was barely half
past nine when the wedding party came back to the shop in the
arcade. The woman who sold costume jewellery was still sitting
in her cubbyhole behind the tray lined with blue velvet. Out of
curiosity, she raised her head and looked at the newlyweds with
a smile. They caught the look and were terrified. What if the old
woman knew about their meetings, in the old days, and had
seen Laurent slipping into the little alleyway?

Thérèse went upstairs almost immediately, with Mme Raquin
and Suzanne. The men stayed in the dining room while the bride
got ready for bed. Laurent, limp and exhausted, felt not the
slightest impatience; he listened indulgently to the crude jokes
made by Old Michaud and Grivet, who told them without

restraint now that the ladies were no longer present. When Suzanne and Mme Raquin came out of the nuptial chamber and the old haberdasher told him, in a trembling voice, that his bride was waiting for him, he shuddered and stayed for a moment in a state of terror. Then he feverishly shook the hands that they held out to him and went in to Thérèse, supporting himself on the doorway, like a drunken man.

XXI

Laurent carefully closed the door behind him and remained for a moment leaning against it, looking into the room with an uneasy, embarrassed manner.

A bright fire was blazing in the grate, casting large patches of yellow light that danced on the ceiling and the walls, so that the room was lit by a bright, flickering light in which the lamp, standing on a table, paled by comparison. Mme Raquin had tried to arrange the room prettily, all white and perfumed, to make a nest for these fresh, young lovers. She had taken a particular pleasure in adding some bits of lace to the bedclothes and putting large bunches of roses in the vases on the mantelpiece. Gentle warmth and sweet fragrances hung about the room, where the atmosphere was serene and peaceful, bathed in a sort of drowsy voluptuousness. The simmering calm was broken only by the little dry crackling of the fire in the hearth. It was like a fortunate oasis, a forgotten corner, warm and sweet-smelling, shut off from all extraneous noise, one of those corners designed for sensuality and to satisfy the needs of the mystery of passionate love.

Thérèse was sitting on a low chair, to the right of the chimney. With her chin on her hand, she was staring hard at the flames. She did not look round when Laurent came in. In her lace-trimmed petticoat and bodice, she was a harsh white against the burning light of the fire. Her bodice had slipped and part of her shoulder was visible, pink and half hidden by a lock of black hair.

Laurent made a few steps into the room without speaking. He took off his coat and waistcoat. When he was in his shirt-sleeves, he looked again at Thérèse, who had not moved. He appeared to hesitate. Then he saw the shoulder and bent over, trembling, to put his lips against this piece of naked flesh. The young woman moved her shoulder away, turning around sharply. She gave Laurent such a strange look of repulsion and panic that he shrank back, worried and uneasy, as though overtaken himself by terror and disgust.

He sat down opposite Thérèse on the other side of the hearth. They stayed there in silence, not moving, for five long minutes. From time to time, a reddish flame would spurt out of the wood and reflections, the colour of blood, played over the murderers' faces.

It was almost two years since the lovers had found themselves alone in the same room, with no one watching, able to give themselves freely to one another. They had not had an amorous meeting since the day when Thérèse came to the Rue Saint-Victor, bringing Laurent the idea of murder with her. Caution had kept their flesh apart, and they had barely risked an occasional clasp of the hand or a furtive kiss. After Camille's murder, when they once more felt desire for one another, they had restrained themselves, waiting for the wedding night and the promise of wild passion when they were safe from punishment. And now, at last, the wedding night had arrived and they were left face to face, anxious and troubled by a sudden feeling of uncertainty. They had only to reach out and clasp one another in a passionate embrace; yet their arms were weak, as though already weary and satiated with love. They felt increasingly weighed down with the pressures of the day. They looked at one another without desire, with timid embarrassment, pained at their own silence and frigidity. Their ardent dreams were ending in a strange reality: it was enough for them to have succeeded in killing Camille and marrying one another, it was enough for Laurent's mouth to have brushed against Thérèse's shoulder, for their lust to be sated to the point of disgust and horror.

They began to search desperately in themselves for a little of the passion that had consumed them before. They felt as though their skin was empty of muscles and empty of nerves. Their anxiety and embarrassment grew; they felt ashamed of remaining silent and sad in each other's presence. They longed to find the strength to grasp one another in a crushing embrace, so that they would not have to consider themselves idiots. What! They belonged together! They had killed a man and acted out a frightful piece of play-acting so that they could wallow with impunity in constant gratification of their senses; yet here they were, on either side of the fireplace, rigid, exhausted, their minds troubled and their bodies dead. This outcome struck them as a horrid, cruel farce. So Laurent tried to speak about love, to evoke memories of former times, calling on his imagination to revive his feelings of desire.

'Thérèse,' he said, leaning towards her, 'do you remember our afternoons in this room? I would come through that door ... Today, I came through the other one. We are free, we can love one another in peace.'

His voice was weak and hesitant. The young woman, crouching on the low chair, kept looking at the flames, thoughtfully, without listening. Laurent went on:

'Do you remember? I had this dream: I wanted to spend a whole night with you, to fall asleep in your arms and to wake up the next morning to your kisses. I am going to accomplish that dream.'

Thérèse started, as though surprised to hear a voice muttering in her ear. She looked up at Laurent, whose face at that moment was lit up by a broad, reddish glow from the fire. She looked at this blood-stained face and shuddered.

The young man went on, more uneasy and more anxious:

'We've managed it, Thérèse, we've overcome all the obstacles and we belong to one another ... The future is ours, isn't it? A future of quiet happiness and satisfied love ... Camille is gone ...'

Laurent paused, his throat dry, choking, unable to continue. Camille's name had been like a blow in the stomach for Thérèse. The two murderers looked at each other, pale, haggard and shaking. The yellow light from the fire was still flickering on the walls and ceiling, the warm scent of roses hung in the air and the crackling of the firewood broke the silence with its dry little sounds.

Their memories were unleashed. Once Camille's ghost had been raised, he came to sit between the two newlyweds, opposite the blazing fire. Thérèse and Laurent could sense the cold, damp smell of the drowned man in the hot air that they breathed. They felt that there was a corpse beside them and they looked carefully at each other without daring to move. And now the whole dreadful story of their crime unfolded in their minds. The victim's name was enough to fill them with the past and force them to relive the horror of the killing. They looked at one another without opening their mouths, both having the same nightmare, at the same time, and both reading the same cruel story in each other's eyes. This terrified exchange of looks, and the silent account of the murder that they were about to give each other, caused them a feeling of acute, intolerable apprehension. Their fraught nerves threatened to break: they might easily cry out or even come to blows. To drive the memories away, Laurent violently subdued the horrified fascination that held him in the grasp of Thérèse's eyes and walked a few steps around the room. He took off his boots and put on some slippers. Then he came back and sat beside the fire, trying to talk about things of no importance.

Thérèse understood what he wanted. She made an effort to answer his questions. They chatted about this and that. They forced themselves to make idle conversation. Laurent said it was hot in the room; Thérèse replied that there was, however, a draught coming under the little door to the staircase. And they suddenly turned towards the little door with a shudder. The man quickly started to talk about the roses, the fire, anything he could see. The young woman made an effort, answering in monosyllables, so as not to let the conversation flag. They had drawn away from one another, trying to forget who they were and to treat each other as strangers brought together by chance.

Yet, despite themselves, by some strange phenomenon, even while they were speaking these empty words, each of them guessed the thoughts that the other was concealing beneath these commonplaces. They could not stop thinking about Camille. Their eyes carried on with the story of the past and their looks held a coherent, silent conversation beneath the aimlessly wandering one that they were speaking aloud. The words that they randomly uttered did not hang together, but contradicted themselves; their whole beings were concentrated on the silent exchange of memories. When Laurent spoke about the roses or the fire, of one thing or another, Thérèse perfectly well understood that he was reminding her of the struggle in the boat and the dull thud as Camille hit the water; and when Thérèse replied 'yes' or 'no' to some insignificant question, Laurent realized that she was telling him that she did, or did not, recall some detail of the crime. So they talked, unreservedly, without needing words, while speaking of something else. And since, in any case, they were not aware of the words that they were speaking, they followed their secret thoughts, sentence by sentence, and could easily have switched to telling their secret thoughts out loud, without ceasing to understand one another. Bit by bit, this sort of divination, and the persistence with which their memories constantly presented them with the image of Camille, started to drive them mad. They realized that they were following each other's thoughts, and that if they did not stop, the words would come of their own accord into their mouths and name the drowned man and describe the murder. So they clenched their teeth and ceased their conversation.

In the heavy silence that followed, the two murderers kept on discussing their victim. It seemed to them that their looks were penetrating each other's flesh and driving in sharp, clear statements. At times, they thought they could hear one another speaking aloud; their senses were distorted and sight became a kind of hearing, strange and fine; so clearly could they read their thoughts on the other's face, that these thoughts acquired a strange, resonant sound that shook their whole bodies. They could not have heard one another more clearly had they each screamed in a deafening voice: 'We killed Camille and his corpse is lying there between us, turning our limbs to ice.' And their frightful confession continued, ever more visible, ever more resounding, in the calm, damp air of the room.

Laurent and Thérèse had begun the silent story on the day of their first meeting in the shop. Then the memories came one by one, in chronological order: they told each other about the hours of pleasure, the moments of uncertainty and anger, and the dreadful instant of the murder. This is when they clenched their teeth and stopped talking about trivial matters, through fear of suddenly naming Camille without wanting to. But their thoughts did not stop, taking them afterwards into the anxiety and the fearful time of waiting that followed the murder. So it was that they came to think of the drowned man's body lying on a slab in the Morgue. In his look, Laurent told Thérèse about his horror and Thérèse, driven to the limit, forced by some iron hand to open her lips, suddenly continued the conversation aloud:

'Did you see him in the Morgue?' she asked Laurent, without naming Camille.

Laurent seemed to be expecting the question. He had read it a moment earlier on the young woman's white face.

'Yes,' he replied, in a choked voice.

The murderers shuddered. They drew closer to the fire and reached out their hands towards the flame, as though an icy draught had suddenly passed through the warm room. They stayed there for a moment in silence, crouching, curled up. Then Thérèse went on softly:

'Did he seem to have suffered a lot?'

Laurent could not reply. He made a horrified gesture, as though putting aside some ghastly vision. He got up, went over to the bed, them came back wildly, walking towards Thérèse with his arms open.

'Kiss me,' he said, offering her his neck.

Thérèse had got up, looking pale[1] in her nightclothes. She was leaning back, with one elbow resting on the marble mantelpiece. She looked at Laurent's neck. She had just noticed a pink patch on the white skin. A rush of blood to his head made the patch larger and coloured it a fiery red.

'Kiss me, kiss me,' Laurent repeated, his face and neck burning.

The young woman bent her head further back, to avoid his

kiss, and, putting the end of one finger on Camille's bite, asked her husband:

'What's this? I didn't know you had a scar there.'

Laurent felt as though Thérèse's finger was making a hole in his throat. As it touched him, he quickly started back, with a soft cry of pain.

'That . . .' he stammered. 'That . . .'

He hesitated, but could not lie and told her the truth in spite of himself.

'Camille bit me, you know, in the boat. It's nothing, it's healed . . . Kiss me, kiss me.'

The wretch held out his burning neck. He wanted Thérèse to kiss him on the scar, counting on the woman's kiss to calm the thousand stings piercing his flesh. With his chin up, advancing his neck, he offered himself. Thérèse, almost lying back on the mantelpiece, made a gesture of extreme distaste and exclaimed in a pleading voice:

'Oh, no! Not there! There's blood on it.'

She fell back into the low chair, trembling and holding her head in her hands. Laurent was stunned. He lowered his chin and looked vaguely at Thérèse. Then, suddenly, he grasped her head in his large hands with the ferocity of a wild animal and pressed her lips against his neck, on Camille's bite. For a moment, he kept the woman's head crushed against him. Thérèse did not struggle, but gave dull cries, stifling against Laurent's neck. When she could get away from his grip, she wiped her mouth savagely and spat into the fireplace. She had not spoken a word.

Ashamed at his brutality, Laurent began to walk slowly, between the bed and the window. Only the pain, the horrible smarting pain, had made him demand a kiss from Thérèse, and when Thérèse's lips had proved to be cold against his burning scar, he suffered even more. This kiss, obtained by violence, had broken him. The shock had been so painful that nothing in the world would have made him want another of the same. And he looked at the wife with whom he would have to live, who was shuddering, bent over the fire, with her back turned towards him. He kept thinking that he no longer loved this woman and that she no longer loved him. For almost an hour, Thérèse stayed slumped in her chair while Laurent walked backwards and forwards, in silence. Each of them was admitting, in terror, that their passion had died, that they had killed their desire for one another when they killed Camille. The fire gently died down and a great, pink mass of embers glowed in the grate. Little by little, the heat in the room had become suffocating and the flowers were fading, weighing on the thick air with their heavy scents.

Suddenly, Laurent thought he experienced a hallucination. As he was turning to go from the window back to the bed, he saw Camille, in a corner plunged in shadow between the fireplace and the wardrobe. His victim's face was greenish in colour and convulsed, as it had been on the slab in the Morgue. He stayed, rooted to the spot, faint and supporting himself on a piece of furniture. Hearing his dull moan, Thérèse looked up.

'There!' Laurent said in a terrified voice. 'There!'

He stretched out his hand, pointing to the dark corner in which he could see Camille's sinister face. Thérèse, seized with the same terror, came over and pressed herself to him.

'It's his portrait,' she muttered, in a whisper, as though the painted face of her husband could hear what she was saying.

'His portrait?' Laurent said, his hair standing on end.

'Yes, you know, the painting you did. My aunt was going to have it in her room from today. She must have forgotten to take it down.'

'Of course, his portrait . . .'

For a time, the murderer did not recognize the picture. He was so disturbed by it that he forgot that he had himself drawn the clumsy outlines of those features and filled in the dirty colours that now appalled him. Terror made him see the canvas as it really was: crude, badly composed and muddy, showing the grimacing face of a corpse against its black background. His work astonished him and crushed him with its atrocious ugliness. Worst of all were the two white eyes swimming in their soft, yellowish sockets, which precisely reminded him of the decaying eyes of the drowned man in the Morgue. For a moment, he could not catch his breath, thinking that Thérèse was lying to reassure him. Then he made out the frame and became a little calmer.

'Go and take him down,' he said softly to the young woman.

'No, no! I'm too afraid!' she replied, shuddering.

Laurent himself started to shake again. At times, the frame vanished and all he could see were the two white eyes staring hard at him.

'I beg you,' he said again, imploring her. 'Go and take him down.'

'No, no!'

'We'll turn him to the wall and then we won't be afraid.'

'No, I can't do it.'

The murderer, cowardly and grovelling, pushed the young woman towards the picture, hiding behind her so as to escape the drowned man's gaze. She dodged away and he decided to take the plunge: he went over to the painting and reached up, feeling for the nail. But the look of the portrait was so devastating, so foul and so unremitting, that Laurent, after trying to outstare it, had to admit defeat and shrank back, muttering: 'No, Thérèse, you're right. We can't do it . . . Your aunt will take it down tomorrow.'

He went back to walking up and down, hanging his head and feeling that the portrait was watching him, following him with its eyes. From time to time, he could not resist taking a look towards it, and then, in the depths of the shadow, he would still see the dead, flat stare of the drowned man. The thought that Camille was there, in a corner, keeping an eye on him, and present on his wedding night, examining the two of them, Thérèse and himself, made Laurent completely mad with terror and despair.

One event, which would have brought a smile to anyone else's lips, drove him entirely out of his mind. When he was in front of the fireplace, he heard a sort of scratching noise. The blood drained from his face: he thought that the scratching was coming from the portrait and that Camille was getting down out of his frame. Then he realized that the noise was coming from the little door leading to the staircase. He looked at Thérèse, who was again seized by fear.

'There's someone on the stairs,' he murmured. 'Who can be coming through there?'

The young woman said nothing. Both of them were thinking about the drowned man and an icy sweat broke out on their brows. They fled to the back of the room, expecting to see the door open suddenly and the corpse of Camille fall through it on to the floor. The noise continued, sharper and less regular, so that it seemed to them that their victim was scratching at the wood with his fingernails, trying to get in. For more than five minutes, they did not dare move. Finally, there was a miaow. Laurent went across and saw Mme Raquin's tabby cat, which had been shut into the bedroom by mistake and was trying to get out by scraping the little door with its claws. François was afraid of Laurent. In a bound, he leaped on to a chair, then, his hair on end and paws stiff, he gave his new master a hard, cruel stare. The young man did not like cats and François almost scared him. In this moment of fear and anguish, he thought the cat was going to leap at his face, to avenge Camille. The creature must know everything: there were thoughts behind those round, oddly dilated eyes. Laurent looked down, away from this animal's stare. He was about to give François a kick, when Thérèse shouted:

'Don't hurt him!'

Her cry gave him an odd feeling and a ridiculous idea came into his head:

'Camille has entered into the cat,' he thought. 'I must kill this animal. It looks human.'

He did not kick it, afraid that François would speak to him with Camille's voice. Then he remembered how Thérèse had joked, when they were lovers and the cat had seen them kissing; so it occurred to him that the cat knew too much and had to be thrown out of the window. But he did not have the courage to carry this through. François was still in an aggressive posture: with his claws out and his back arched by some vague annoyance, it was following its enemy's slightest movement with proud imperturbability. Laurent was upset by the metallic shine of its eyes. He hastily opened the dining-room door and the cat ran out with a sharp miaow.

Thérèse had sat down again in front of the dead fire. Laurent resumed his pacing from the bed to the window. And that is how they waited for daylight. They did not think to go to bed together: their flesh and their hearts were quite dead. They had only one desire: to get out of this room that was stifling them. They had a real sense of unease at being shut in together, breathing the same air. They would have liked to have someone else there, to interrupt their tête-à-tête and free them from the cruelly embarrassing situation of being together without speaking and unable to revive their passion for each other. The long silences tortured them, silences full of bitter, desperate sighs and unspoken accusations that they could clearly hear in the still air.

At last, day came, dirty, whitish, bringing a biting cold.

When the room was filled with pale light, Laurent shivered, but felt calmer. He looked straight at Camille's portrait and saw it for what it was, ordinary, childish. With a shrug, he took it down, calling himself an idiot. Thérèse had got up and was undoing the bed, to deceive her aunt and make her think they had spent a joyful night together.

'Now then,' Laurent said roughly. 'I hope we're going to get some sleep tonight. This childishness can't continue.'

Thérèse gave him a serious, penetrating look.

'You understand?' he went on. 'I didn't get married so that I would have sleepless nights. We're behaving like children. It was you who upset me, with your supernatural airs. Tonight, try to be jolly and not to put the wind up me.'

He forced a laugh, without knowing why he was laughing.

'I'll try,' Thérèse said, in a dull voice.

That is how Thérèse and Laurent spent their wedding night.

XXII

The following nights were even more anguished. The murderers had wanted to be together at night, to ward off the drowned man; yet, by some strange effect, since being together they had feared him even more. They exasperated one another, they got on each other's nerves, they suffered ghastly crises of terror and agony when they exchanged a simple word or a look. At the merest conversation, the slightest private exchange between them, they saw red, they flew into a rage.

Thérèse's dry, nervous character had reacted in an odd way with the stolid, sanguine character of Laurent. Previously, in the days of their passion, this contrast in temperament had made this man and woman into a powerfully linked couple by establishing a sort of balance between them and, so to speak, complementing their organisms. The lover contributed his blood and the mistress her nerves, and so they lived in one another, each needing the other's kisses to regulate the mechanism of their being. But the equilibrium had been disturbed and Thérèse's over-excited nerves had taken control. Suddenly, Laurent found himself plunged into a state of nervous erethism;[1] under the influence of her fervent nature, his own temperament had gradually become that of a girl suffering from an acute neurosis. It would be interesting to study the changes that are sometimes produced in certain organisms as a result of particular circumstances. These changes, which derive from the flesh, are rapidly communicated to the brain and to the entire being.

Before knowing Thérèse, Laurent had the ponderousness, the prudent calm and sanguine outlook of a peasant's son. He slept, ate and drank like an animal. At every moment, in every circumstance of his daily life, he breathed easily and placidly, content with himself and somewhat dulled by his own bulk. Hardly at all did he feel the occasional stirring in the depths of his stolid flesh. But Thérèse had developed those stirrings into frightful shudders. In this great body, soft and flabby, she had nurtured a nervous system of astonishing sensibility. Laurent had formerly enjoyed life through his blood rather than his nerves; now his senses became less crude. At his mistress's first kiss, he had suddenly been made aware of a life of the emotions that was quite new and moving for him. This life increased his sensual pleasure tenfold and gave such an intense nature to his joy that at first he was made virtually mad by it, and abandoned himself wildly to extremes of intoxication that his sanguine

temperament had never given him. Then, he underwent a strange
internal process: his nerves developed and came to dominate
the sanguine element in him, this fact by itself changing his
character. He lost his calm and his heaviness, no longer living a
half-awake existence. A time came when the nerves and the
blood balanced each other out, and this was a profoundly
pleasurable moment, a time of perfect living.[2] Then the nerves
dominated and he fell into the paroxysms that rack unbalanced
minds and bodies.

That is why Laurent came to shudder at the sight of a dark
corner, like a timorous child. This new person, the shivering,
haggard being that had just emerged in him out of the thick,
brutish peasant, experienced the fears and anxieties of those of
nervous temperament. A whole series of events – Thérèse's
passionate caresses, the feverish drama of the murder and the
fearful expectation of sensual pleasure – had driven him more
or less insane, keying up his senses and striking his nerves with
sudden and repeated blows. Then, inevitably, insomnia had
come, bringing with it hallucinations. From then on, Laurent
had lapsed into the intolerable existence and endless horror in
which he was now entrapped.

His remorse was purely physical.[3] Only his body, his tense
nerves and his trembling flesh were afraid of the drowned man.
His conscience played no part in his terror: he did not in the
slightest regret having killed Camille. When he was feeling calm
and the ghost was not there, he would have committed the
murder all over again, if he had thought that his interests
demanded it. In the daytime, he recovered from his terror,
promised himself that he would be strong and upbraided
Thérèse, accusing her of upsetting him. In his view, Thérèse was
the one who was scared and it was Thérèse alone who caused
the dreadful scenes at night in the bedroom. As soon as night
fell, as soon as he was shut in with his wife, he came out in a
cold sweat and childish terrors assailed him. In this way, he
went through periodic crises, nervous attacks that returned
every evening and deranged his senses by showing him the
grotesque green face of his victim. It was like the onset of a
terrifying disease, a sort of hysteria[4] of murder: the words 'ill-

ness' and 'nervous affliction' were really the only ones that could properly describe Laurent's fears. His face became contorted and his limbs stiffened: you could see that his nerves were tensing inside. His physical suffering was frightful, but the soul remained absent. The wretch did not feel a shred of remorse. His passion for Thérèse had infected him with a dreadful malady, that's all.

Thérèse, too, was deeply disturbed, but in her it was simply that her original temperament had been greatly over-stimulated. Since the age of ten, she had suffered from nervous disorders, partly as a result of the manner in which she had grown up in the over-heated, nauseous air of little Camille's sick room. Stormy rages and powerful fluids accumulated within her and were later to erupt as uncontrollable tempests. Laurent had been for her what she was for Laurent: a kind of violent shock. From their first love-making, her dry, sensual temperament had developed with savage energy; from then on, she lived only for passion and, increasingly abandoning herself to the ardent fevers within her, she arrived at a state of unhealthy stupor. She was overwhelmed by events and driven towards madness. In her terror, she reacted in a more womanly way than her new husband. She had vague feelings of remorse and unadmitted regrets. At times, she felt like falling on her knees and pleading with Camille's ghost, imploring his pity and swearing to appease him with her repentance. Laurent may have noticed these moments of weakness in Thérèse. When they were seized with a common terror, he turned on her and treated her savagely.

For the first few nights, they could not go to bed. They waited for daylight, sitting in front of the fire or walking backwards and forwards, as on their wedding night. They felt a kind of terrified repugnance at the idea of lying side by side on the bed. By tacit agreement, they avoided kissing and did not even look at the bedclothes, which Thérèse undid in the morning. When tiredness overcame them, they fell asleep for an hour or two in armchairs, only to wake up with a start, aroused by the sinister unfolding of some nightmare. When they did wake up, their limbs stiff and aching, with livid blotches on their faces, shivering with discomfort and cold, they would look at one another with amazement, astonished to see the other there and suffering a strange embarrassment towards each other, ashamed to show their disgust and terror.

In any case, they struggled against sleep as much as they could. They sat on either side of the fireplace and chatted about this or that, being careful to avoid letting the conversation lapse. There was a wide space between them, opposite the fire. When they turned round, they imagined that Camille had drawn up a chair and was occupying this space, warming his feet with lugubrious derision. The vision that they had had on the wedding night returned every night from then on. This corpse, silent and mocking, who listened in on their discussions, this horribly disfigured corpse, ever present, overwhelmed them with continual feelings of anxiety. They dared not budge, they blinded themselves with staring into the blazing hearth and, when they could no longer resist casting a fearful glance to the side, their eyes, irritated by the burning coals, created the apparition and bathed it in a reddish light.

Eventually, Laurent refused to sit down, though he did not tell Thérèse why. She realized that this behaviour meant that Laurent must be seeing Camille, as she was, so she announced in her turn that the heat was painful and that she would be better off a short distance away from the fireplace. She pushed her chair over to the foot of the bed and slumped down in it there, while her husband resumed his marching up and down. At times, he would open the window and let the cold January night fill the room with its icy breath. It brought his fever down.

For a week, the newlyweds spent all night in this way. They dozed off, catching a bit of rest during the day, Thérèse behind the shop counter and Laurent at his desk. At night, they were a prey to pain and fear. And the oddest thing yet was their attitude towards one another. They did not speak a single loving word, they pretended to have forgotten the past, appearing to accept and tolerate each other, like sick people feeling a secret pity for their shared miseries. Both of them hoped to hide their disgust and fear, and neither of the pair seemed to find anything strange in the way they spent their nights, which should have enlightened them about the true state of their minds. When they stayed up until morning, barely speaking to each other and blanching at the slightest sound, they acted as though they imagined this was how all newlyweds behaved in the first days of marriage: it was the clumsy hypocrisy of a couple of mad people.

Soon tiredness overcame them to such an extent that, one evening, they decided to lie down on the bed. They did not get undressed, but threw themselves fully clothed on the quilt, fearful that they might touch one another's bare skin. It seemed to them that they would get a painful shock from the slightest contact. Then, when they had dozed off like that for two nights in a restless sleep, they risked taking off their clothes and slipping between the sheets. But they stayed far away from one another and were careful not to touch by mistake. Thérèse went to bed first and got into the far side, against the wall. Laurent waited until she was settled down, then carefully stretched himself out on the front of the bed, right on the edge. There was a wide gap between them. This was where the body of Camille lay.

When the two murderers were under the same sheet and shut their eyes, they would imagine they could feel the damp corpse of their victim spread out in the middle of the bed, sending a chill through their flesh. It was like some grotesque barrier between them. They were seized by feverish delirium and the barrier would become an actual one for them; they would touch the body, they would see it lying like a greenish, rotten lump of meat and they would breathe in the repulsive odour of this heap of human decay. All their senses shared in the hallucination, making their sensations unbearably acute. The presence of this foul bedfellow would keep them motionless, silent and rigid with fear. At times, Laurent would consider violently grasping Thérèse in his arms, but he dared not move, telling himself that if he were to reach out an arm he would surely grasp a handful of Camille's soft flesh. At that, he would imagine that the drowned man had just lain down between them, to prevent them from touching one another. Eventually, he realized that Camille was jealous.

Occasionally, however, they would try to exchange a timid kiss to see what happened. The young man would tease his wife, demanding that she kiss him. But their lips were so cold that death appeared to have come between their mouths. They would feel nausea; Thérèse shuddered in horror and Laurent, who could hear her teeth chatter, would lose his temper with her.

'Why are you trembling?' he would shout. 'Are you afraid of Camille, then? Come on, the poor fellow can't feel his bones any longer.'

The pair of them avoided admitting the cause of their anxieties. When either of them imagined seeing the drowned man's pallid face before them, they would shut their eyes and enclose themselves in terror, not daring to talk to the other about the vision, for fear of inducing a still more frightful attack. When Laurent, driven to the end of his tether, accused Thérèse in a desperate fury of being afraid of Camille, the name, spoken aloud, would make the horror more intense. The murderer would lose his head.

'Yes, yes,' he spluttered, speaking to her. 'You're afraid of Camille ... I can see that, for God's sake! You're crazy, you don't have an ounce of courage. Huh! You can sleep easy. Do you think your first husband will come and pull your feet because I'm in bed with you?'

This idea, the suggestion that the drowned man might come and pull their feet, made Laurent's hair stand on end. He went on, still more savagely, tearing into himself.

'I'll have to take you to the cemetery one night. We'll open Camille's coffin and you'll see what a heap of rotten meat he is! Then perhaps you won't be afraid of him any more ... Come on, he doesn't know we pushed him in the water.'

Thérèse was moaning softly, with her head under the sheet.

'We pushed him in the water because he was in our way,' her husband went on. 'And we'd do it again, wouldn't we? Don't be such a baby. Be strong. It's silly to let this get in the way of our happiness. Don't you see, dear, when we're dead ourselves, we won't be any more or less happy under the ground because we chucked an idiot into the Seine, and will have been free to enjoy our love, which is to our benefit ... Come on, give me a kiss.'

The young woman kissed him, icy cold and frantic, and he was shivering as much as she was.

For more than a fortnight, Laurent wondered what he could do to kill Camille off again. He had thrown the man in the water and still he was not sufficiently dead, but came back every night to lie at Thérèse's side. Even when the murderers thought they had completed the killing and could indulge the sweet pleasures of their love, the victim would return to chill their marriage bed. Thérèse was not a widow: Laurent found himself married to a wife who already had a drowned man as her husband.

XXIII

Little by little, Laurent lapsed into raging madness. He determined to drive Camille out of his bed. At first, he had gone to sleep fully clothed, then he avoided touching Thérèse. Finally, in a desperate fury, he tried to clasp his wife to his breast and crush her rather than abandon her to his victim's ghost. It was a supreme gesture of brutal defiance.

In short, only the hope that Thérèse's kisses would cure his insomnia had induced him to share a bed with the young woman. And when he found himself in her bedroom, as the master, his flesh, rent by still more frightful agonies, did not even consider trying the cure. For three weeks, he remained in a state of apparent devastation, forgetting that he had done everything to possess Thérèse and, now that he did possess her, being unable to touch her without increasing his agony.

The excess of his suffering brought him out of this numbness. In the first moment of stupor, in the strange desperation of the wedding night, he had managed to overlook the reasons that had driven him to marry. But with the repeated attacks of his bad dreams, he was invaded by a dull irritation that overcame his cowardice and restored his memory. He recalled that he had married to drive away his nightmares by clasping his wife tightly to him. So he seized Thérèse in his arms, one night, taking the risk of crossing over the drowned man's corpse, and dragged her violently towards him.

The young woman, too, was at the end of her tether. She

would have flung herself into the flames if she had thought that the flames would purify her flesh and deliver her from her distress. She responded to Laurent's grasp, deciding to burn in the caresses of this man or else to find solace in them.

They locked into a frightful embrace. Pain and terror took the place of desire. When their limbs touched, it seemed to them that they had fallen against burning coals. They gave a cry and pressed more tightly together, so as to leave no place between their bodies for the drowned man. Yet they could still feel Camille's shredded flesh, foully squeezed between them, freezing their skin in places, even while the rest of their bodies was burning.

Their kisses were fearfully cruel. Thérèse's lips sought out Camille's bite on Laurent's stiff, swollen neck and she fixed her mouth on it with savage passion. Here was the open wound; once this was healed, the murderers could sleep easy. The young woman knew this, trying to cauterize the place with the fire of her kisses. But her lips burned and Laurent pushed her away harshly, with a dull moan: it felt to him as though a red-hot iron had been placed on his neck. Crazed, Thérèse persisted: she wanted to kiss the scar again, feeling a bitter pleasure in putting her mouth against this skin in which Camille's teeth had sunk. For a moment, she thought of biting her husband on the spot, removing a large piece of flesh and making a new, deeper wound which would take away the mark of the old one. Then, she thought, she would no longer go pale if she saw the mark of her own teeth. But Laurent protected his neck against her kisses. The wound smarted too much; he pushed her back each time as she reached out her lips. And so they fought, groaning and struggling in the horror of their embrace.

They realized that they were only increasing their own suffering. However much they exhausted themselves, frightfully grasping one another, they cried out with pain, they burned and bruised each other, but they could not calm their shattered nerves. Every embrace served only to sharpen their disgust. Even as they were exchanging these dreadful kisses, they were prey to a variety of hallucinations: they imagined that the drowned man was pulling on their feet and violently shaking the bed.

For a moment, they let go of one another. They were feeling insurmountable disgust and nervous repulsion. Then, they were not willing to give in, so they clasped one another again in a further embrace and were obliged once more to let go, as though red-hot pins had been stuck into their limbs. In this way, they tried again and again to overcome their disgust and to forget everything by tiring themselves out and exhausting their nerves. Yet every time their nerves were so on edge and so tense, causing them such feelings of exasperation that they might perhaps have died of nervous exhaustion if they had stayed in one another's arms. This struggle against their own bodies had driven them to the point of madness: they persisted obstinately, determined to overcome. Finally, a sharper crisis broke them with a shock of unimagined violence, and they thought that they were about to collapse in an epileptic fit.

Thrown back to the two sides of the bed, seared and bruised, they began to sob.

And in their sobs, it seemed to them that they could hear the triumphant laugh of the drowned man, as he slid back beneath the sheets, sniggering. They had been unable to drive him out of the bed; they were beaten. Camille was lying quietly between them, while Laurent wept at his impotence and Thérèse shuddered to think that the corpse might get it into its mind to take advantage of its victory and, in its turn, squeeze her in its rotting arms, as her legitimate master. They had made one final effort and, faced with their defeat, they realized that from now on they would not dare to exchange a single kiss. The paroxysm of passionate love that they had tried to reach in order to kill their fear had now plunged them even more deeply into the pit of terror. As they felt the cold of the corpse that, henceforth, would keep them for ever divided, they wept tears of blood and agonizingly wondered what would become of them.

XXIV

As Old Michaud had hoped when he engineered Thérèse's marriage to Laurent, Thursday evenings resumed, merry as in the
old days, after the wedding. With Camille's death, these soirées
had been seriously at risk. The guests had visited this house in
mourning only with apprehension and every week were afraid
that they would finally be sent away for ever. Michaud and
Grivet, who stuck to their habits with the obstinacy of brutes,
were appalled at the idea that the door of the shop would
eventually close upon them. They told themselves that the old
mother and young widow would get up one fine morning and
take their grief back to Vernon or somewhere, with the result
that, on Thursday evenings, they would find themselves outside
on the pavement with nothing to do: they imagined themselves
in the arcade, wandering about in a pitiful manner, dreaming of
huge domino games. In expectation of these bad days, they took
themselves round to the shop with an anxious and conciliatory
air, constantly thinking that they might never come here again.
For more than a year, they knew this fear, not daring to let
themselves have a laugh when confronted by Mme Raquin's
tears and Thérèse's silence. They no longer felt at home, as they
had done in Camille's day: it was as though they were stealing
every evening that they spent round the dining-room table.
It was in these desperate circumstances that Old Michaud's
selfishness drove him to the master-stroke of marrying off the
drowned man's widow.

On the Thursday after the wedding, Grivet and Michaud
made a triumphal entry. They had won. The dining room
belonged to them once more; they no longer feared that someone
might drive them away from it. They came in joyfully, they let
themselves go, they told all their old jokes one after another.
You could see from their smug, confident manner that as far as
they were concerned there had just been a revolution. The
memory of Camille had gone; the dead husband, that spectre
who had chilled them, had been expelled by the living husband.
The past returned with all its pleasures. Laurent was taking the

place of Camille and there was no longer any reason to be sad: the guests could laugh without upsetting anyone – and, indeed, they should laugh in order to spread joy in this excellent family that was good enough to invite them. Henceforth, Grivet and Michaud, who had ostensibly been coming here over the past eighteen months to console Mme Raquin, could put aside this little hypocrisy and come openly so that they could fall asleep, one opposite the other, to the click of dominoes.

Every week brought its Thursday evening and every week once again reunited around the table these dead, grotesque heads that had once exasperated Thérèse. The young woman talked about showing them the door; they irritated her with their bursts of silly laughter and their idiotic remarks. But Laurent told her that it would be a mistake to do this. As far as possible, the present must seem like the past; and, most of all, they had to keep friends with the police, those imbeciles who were guarding them against suspicion. Thérèse capitulated, and the guests, welcomed in, were delighted to contemplate a long series of warm evenings ahead of them.

It was around this time that the young couple started to lead a kind of double life.

In the morning, when the daylight drove away the terrors of the night, Laurent hastened to get dressed. He did not feel at ease or recover his egotistical composure until he was sitting at the dining-room table in front of a huge bowl of milky coffee, which Thérèse made for him. Mme Raquin was now such an invalid that she could hardly get down into the shop, but she would watch him eat with a maternal smile on her face. He would gorge on toast, filling his stomach, and gradually regain his self-assurance. After his coffee, he would drink a little glass of cognac. This finally completed the process of restoration. He would say: 'See you this evening,' to Mme Raquin and Thérèse, without ever kissing them, then stroll off to his office. Spring came and the trees beside the Seine were covered with leaves – a light, pale-green lace. Down below the river ran with a caressing sound, and up above the first rays of the sun were gentle and warm. Laurent felt revived by the cool air. He took deep breaths of this young life in the skies of April and May. He looked up

at the sun, stopped to watch the silver reflections shimmering
on the surface of the water, listened to the noises of the quayside,
let the sharp scents of morning sink into him and appreciated
this clear, happy morning with all his senses. He definitely did
not think much about Camille, though sometimes he did happen
to glance mechanically across to the Morgue on the other side
of the river, and would then remember the drowned man in the
way that a courageous one considers some foolish fright that he
has had. With a full stomach and a fresh, cool head, he lapsed
back into his calmly stolid nature, reached his office and spent
the whole day there yawning, waiting for the time to leave. He
became just a clerk like the rest of them, dull and bored, with
his head empty. The only idea he had at such moments was to
hand in his resignation and rent a studio; he would have vague
dreams of a new life of idleness, which were enough to keep his
mind occupied until evening. Never was he troubled by any
thought of the shop in the arcade. In the evening, having waited
since morning for it to be time to leave, he would be reluctant
to go out, full of his private worries and anxieties on his way
along the embankment. However slowly he walked, he would
eventually have to return to the shop. And there terror awaited.

Thérèse had the same feelings. As long as Laurent was not
with her, she felt all right. She had dismissed the cleaning
woman, saying that everything was dirty and left lying around
in the shop and the flat. She felt an urge to tidy up. The truth
was that she needed to walk around, to do something, to exhaust
her stiffened limbs. She bustled around all morning, sweeping,
dusting and cleaning the bedrooms, washing the dishes and
carrying out tasks that would previously have disgusted her.
These domestic duties kept her on her feet until noon, active
and silent, leaving her no time to think of anything except the
cobwebs on the ceiling and the grease on the plates. Then she
went into the kitchen and prepared lunch. While they were
eating, it grieved Mme Raquin to see her constantly getting up
to go and fetch the courses. She was touched and annoyed by
her niece's constant activity; she would scold her and Thérèse
answered that they had to save money. After the meal, the young
woman would get dressed and finally resign herself to joining

her aunt behind the counter. There, she would become drowsy.
Exhausted by her sleepless nights, she would nod off, abandoning herself to the delicious lethargy that overcame her as
soon as she sat down. They were only light snoozes, imbued
with a kind of delight, which calmed her nerves. The thought of
Camille vanished and she experienced the deep rest of sick
people whose pain is suddenly taken away. Her body felt relaxed
and her mind free: she lapsed into a sort of warm, healing
oblivion. Without these few moments of peace, her organism
would have broken down under the pressure from her nervous
system, but she drew enough strength from them to suffer yet
again and feel terror on the following night. In any case, she did
not fall asleep, hardly lowering her eyelids, lost in a dream of
peace. When a customer came in she would open her eyes and
produce the few sous' worth of goods requested, then drift back
into her vague reverie. She would spend three or four hours in
this way, perfectly happy, replying to her aunt in monosyllables
and taking a real delight in letting herself lapse into this state of
unconsciousness that took away thought and drew her back
into herself. She would only very occasionally cast a glance into
the arcade, feeling most at ease when the weather was overcast,
when it was dark and when she hid her weariness in the shadows.
The damp, mean arcade, traversed by a population of poor, wet
devils whose umbrellas dripped on the paving, seemed to her
like the passage into some place of ill-repute, a kind of sinister,
dirty corridor where no one would come and look for her or
bother her. At times, seeing the murky glows around her and
smelling the acrid scent of damp, she imagined that she had
been buried alive and thought she was in the earth at the bottom
of a communal grave, with the dead milling around her. The
idea calmed her and consoled her. She told herself that she was
safe now, that she would die and not suffer any longer. At other
times, she had to keep her eyes open: Suzanne would visit and
stay sewing beside the counter all afternoon. Thérèse now liked
the company of Olivier's wife, with her soft face and slow
gestures; she felt a strange sense of relief looking at this poor,
disconnected creature. She had made a friend of her and liked
having her by her side, smiling a pale smile and only half alive,

bringing a faint graveyard odour into the shop. When Suzanne's blue eyes, with their glassy transparency, stared into hers, Thérèse felt a beneficial chill in the marrow of her bones. She would stay like that for four hours. Then she would go back to the kitchen and try to tire herself out again, making Laurent his dinner with feverish haste. And when her husband appeared in the doorway, her throat tightened and a feeling of anxiety once more wrenched her whole being.

Every day, the couple experienced more or less the same feelings. In the daytime, when they were not face to face with one another, they enjoyed delightful hours of rest, but in the evening, when they were together again, a piercing sense of disquiet swept through them.

Their evenings, however, were quiet. Thérèse and Laurent, who shuddered at the idea of going back to their room, delayed going to bed for as long as possible. Mme Raquin, half recumbent at the back of a wide armchair, sat between them and chatted in her placid tones. She would tell them about Vernon, always thinking about her son, but not naming him, out of a sense that it would somehow be indecent to do so. She would smile at her dear children and make plans for their future. The lamp cast a pale light over her white face and her words took on an extraordinary softness in the still, silent air. And, on either side of her, the two murderers, not speaking or moving, seemed to be listening to her devoutly. In fact, they would not seek to follow the meaning of the good old woman's prattling; they were just happy at this soft sound of words, which prevented them from hearing the roar of their own thoughts. They did not dare look at one another; they would look at Mme Raquin, so as to keep a good face. They never spoke about going to bed and would have stayed there until morning, caressed by the flow of chatter from the old haberdasher, in the tranquillity that she created around her, if she herself had not expressed a wish to retire. Only then would they leave the dining room and return to their room in despair, like people hurling themselves into a chasm.

They very soon came to prefer the Thursday sessions to these intimate evenings. When they were alone with Mme Raquin, they could not deafen themselves. The slender thread of their aunt's voice and her tender merriment did not stifle the cries tearing them apart. They felt bedtime approaching and shuddered when they happened to glance towards the door of their room. Waiting for the moment when they would be alone became more and more painful as the evening progressed. On Thursdays, on the other hand, they were intoxicated by idiocies and forgot about each other's presence, so they suffered less. Even Thérèse came eventually to long for these days when they had guests. If Michaud and Grivet had not come, she would have gone to look for them. When there were strangers in the dining room, between her and Laurent, she felt calmer; she would have liked there to be guests always; and noise: something that would stun and isolate her. With other people, she exhibited a sort of nervous merriment. Laurent, too, reverted to his coarse peasant jokes, his belly laughs and his art student's tricks. Never had their gatherings been so jolly or so noisy.

That is how, once a week, Laurent and Thérèse managed to remain in each other's company without a shudder.

Soon they had a new cause for anxiety. Mme Raquin was gradually being overtaken by paralysis and they could foresee the day when she would be tied to her chair, physically and mentally incapable. The poor old woman was starting to mutter phrases that were not connected to one another, her voice was growing weaker and her limbs were failing one by one. She was turning into a thing. Thérèse and Laurent were horrified to see the vanishing of this person who, for the time being, was keeping them apart and whose voice roused them from their nightmares. When the old haberdasher had lost all understanding, when she was left dumb and stiff in her chair, they would be alone. In the evening, they would no longer be able to escape from an intimacy that they dreaded. In that case, their terror would start at six o'clock, instead of starting at midnight. They would go mad.

They devoted themselves entirely to preserving the health of Mme Raquin, which was so precious to them. They called in doctors, they attended to her slightest need and they even found that the job of sick-nurse helped them to forget, bringing a sense of peace that encouraged them to double their efforts. They did not want to lose this third party who made their evenings bearable, they did not want the dining room and the whole house to become a tormenting and sinister place like their bedroom. Mme Raquin was extremely touched by the care that they lavished on her; she congratulated herself, with tears in her eyes, at having brought them together and having given them her forty or so thousand francs. Never since the death of her son had she expected to find such affection in her declining years and, old woman that she was, she felt warmed through by the kindness of her dear children. She did not feel the relentless paralysis that, despite it all, was making her a little less mobile every day.

Meanwhile, Thérèse and Laurent led their double life. It was as though in each one of them there were two quite distinct beings: a nervous, terrified creature who would shudder as soon as dusk came, and a numb, forgetful one who breathed freely as soon as the sun rose. They were living two lives, crying out in pain when they were alone with one another and smiling complacently when there were other people about. Never did their faces in public hint at the suffering that came to tear them apart when they were together; they seemed calm and happy, instinctively hiding their woes.

Seeing them so untroubled by day, no one would have suspected that they were tormented every night by hallucinations. Theirs might have been seen as a marriage blessed in heaven, a couple living in perfect harmony. Grivet called them (suggestively) the 'turtle-doves'. When they had bags under their eyes after a long period without sleep, he teased them and asked when the baptism was due. And all the guests laughed. Laurent and Thérèse went a little pale and managed a smile; they were getting used to Grivet's risqué jokes. Whenever they were in the dining room, they could control their fears. No one could have imagined the frightful change that came over them when they shut the bedroom door behind them. On Thursday evenings especially this change was so sudden and violent that it seemed to belong to some supernatural world. So strange was the drama of their nights, so savage in its excesses, that it exceeded all credibility and stayed hidden deep inside their tormented beings.

Had they spoken about it, they would have been considered insane.

'How happy they are, those love-birds!' Old Michaud often used to say. 'They don't have a lot to say for themselves, but that doesn't mean they don't think about it. I'll bet they are all over one another when we aren't here.'

This was what everyone thought: Thérèse and Laurent would even be cited as a model couple. The whole Passage du Pont-Neuf praised the affection, the tranquil happiness and the endless honeymoon enjoyed by the couple. They alone knew how the corpse of Camille would lie between them, they alone would feel the nervous contractions beneath the calm surface of their faces which at night would horribly distort their features and change their peaceful expressions to a ghastly, tormented and grimacing mask.

XXV

After four months, Laurent thought about reaping the benefits he had anticipated from his marriage. He would have abandoned his wife and fled before the spectre of Camille three days after the wedding if self-interest had not tied him to the shop in the arcade. He bore his nights of terror and stayed despite his suffocating fears, so as not to lose the profits of his crime. If he were to leave Thérèse, he would lapse back into poverty and be obliged to keep his job; if, on the contrary, he stayed with her, he could indulge his taste for idleness and do nothing, living well off the income from the money that Mme Raquin had invested in his wife's name. It seems likely that he would have made off with the forty thousand francs if he had been able to cash the money in, but the old haberdasher, on Michaud's advice, had been careful to protect her niece's interests in the contract. There was consequently a strong bond attaching Laurent to Thérèse. So, as a compensation for his dreadful nights, he wanted at least to have himself kept in idle contentment, well fed, warmly clothed and with enough money in his pocket to

satisfy his whims. Only at this price would he agree to sleep
with the drowned man's corpse.

One evening, he announced to Mme Raquin and his wife that
he had handed in his notice and would be leaving the office at
the end of a fortnight. Thérèse gave a sign of anxiety, so he
hastened to add that he was going to rent a little studio where
he would go back to painting. He discoursed at length on the
tedium of his job and the broad horizons that Art would open
up for him. Now that he had some money and could try for
success, he wanted to see if he might not be capable of doing
great things. His speech on the subject merely concealed the fact
that he urgently desired to go back to his former bohemian
existence. Thérèse pursed her lips, without answering; she did
not intend Laurent to waste the little fortune that guaranteed
her freedom. When her husband pressed her, in order to obtain
her consent, she replied with a few curt answers and gave him
to understand that if he left his office, he would earn nothing
more and would be entirely dependent on her. As she spoke,
Laurent looked at her intently, which disturbed her. The refusal
she was about to make stopped in her throat. She thought that
she could read this threat in her accomplice's eyes: 'If you don't
agree, I'll tell all.' She began to stammer. At this, Mme Raquin
exclaimed that her dear son's wish was only too proper and that
he must have the means to become a man of talent. The good
woman spoiled Laurent as she had once spoiled Camille. She
was entirely softened by the young man's marks of affection
towards her, she belonged to him and always took his side.

So it was decided that the artist would rent a studio and have
a hundred francs a month for the various expenses that might
arise. In that way the family budget was settled: the profits from
the haberdashery business would pay the rent of the shop and
the apartment, and almost cover the family's day-to-day expen-
diture; Laurent would deduct the rent of his studio and his
hundred francs a month out of the two thousand and a few
hundred francs of income from the capital; and the rest of that
income would go on whatever else they needed. In this way,
they would not break into the capital. This made Thérèse a little
easier, but she made her husband swear never to exceed the

amount that had been allocated to him. And she told herself that, in any case, Laurent would not be able to draw on the forty thousand francs without her signature, promising herself that she would never sign any paper.

The very next day, Laurent rented a little studio that he had had his eye on for a month, at the bottom of the Rue Mazarine. He did not want to leave his work until he had a bolt-hole where he could spend his days in peace, away from Thérèse. At the end of the fortnight, he said farewell to his colleagues. Grivet was amazed by his departure. A young man, he kept saying, who had such a bright future before him, a young man who, in four years, had risen to a salary that he, Grivet, had taken twenty years to attain! Laurent astonished him even more when he told him that he was going to devote himself to painting.

At length, the artist moved into his studio. This was a kind of square attic, about five or six metres long and wide. The ceiling sloped abruptly, at a steep angle, with a wide window in it that threw a harsh white light on the floor and the blackish walls. The noise of the street did not reach up to this level. The room, silent, murky, with its window on the sky, seemed like a hole or a burial vault dug into grey clay. Laurent furnished this tomb as best he could. He brought two chairs with tattered cane seats, a table that he had to prop against the wall to prevent it sliding to the floor, an old kitchen cupboard, his paintbox and his old easel. The one luxury item in the place was a huge divan, which he bought from a secondhand dealer for thirty francs.

He waited for a fortnight without even thinking of picking up a brush. He would arrive between eight and nine o'clock, have a smoke, lie down on the divan and wait for noon, happy that it was morning and he still had long hours of daylight ahead of him. At twelve, he went out for lunch, then hastened back so that he could be alone and not have to look at Thérèse's pale face any more. In this way he would digest his food, sleep and lounge around until evening. His studio was a haven of peace where he felt calm and unafraid. One day, his wife asked if she could visit this dear refuge. He refused and when, despite this, she came and knocked on the door, he did not open it. That evening, he told her that he had spent the day at the Louvre. He was afraid that Thérèse would bring Camille's ghost with her.

Eventually, he grew tired of idleness. He bought a canvas and some paints and set to work. Not having enough money to pay for models, he decided to paint whatever his imagination suggested, without copying from nature. He started a man's head.

In any case, he did not shut himself up for too long. He worked for two or three hours every morning and spent his afternoons wandering around Paris and its suburbs. It was when he was returning from one of these long walks that he met, opposite the Institut, a former schoolfriend who had had a fine success at the last Salon, thanks to knowing the right people.

'Why, it's you!' the painter exclaimed. 'Oh, dear, poor Laurent. I'd never have recognized you. You've lost weight.'

'I got married,' Laurent replied, slightly put out.

'Married! You! In that case, I'm not surprised to see you looking a bit odd . . . So what are you up to now?'

'I've rented a small studio. I paint a little, in the morning.'

Laurent briefly described his marriage, then outlined his future plans, in an enthusiastic voice. His friend looked at him with an astonishment that Laurent found quite upsetting. The truth was that the painter could not recognize the rough, ordinary lad that he had previously known in Thérèse's husband. He felt that Laurent was acquiring an air of distinction. His face had thinned down and had a tasteful pallor,[1] while the stance of the whole body was more dignified and more relaxed.

'Why, you're becoming quite an elegant fellow,' the artist couldn't help remarking. 'You look like an ambassador. It's all the latest style. What school are you with?'

Laurent found this examination quite painful, but he dared not just walk off abruptly.

'Would you like to come up to my studio for a moment?' he eventually asked his friend, who would not go away . . .

'Indeed, I would,' the other man replied.

The painter was unable to account for the changes he saw in his former friend, and was keen to see his studio. He definitely was not going up five floors in order to see Laurent's new work, which would undoubtedly make him feel sick; all he wanted was to satisfy his curiosity.

When he had climbed the five flights and taken a look at the canvases hanging on the walls, his astonishment increased. There were five studies there, two women's heads and three men's, painted with real energy. The technique was sound and solid, each piece standing out against a grey background with magnificent brushstrokes. The artist went over to them eagerly and, in amazement, not even trying to conceal his surprise, asked Laurent:

'Did you do this?'

'Yes,' he answered. 'They're oil sketches that I'm going to use in a large picture that I'm planning.'

'Come on, no kidding. Are you really the person who painted these things?'

'Yes, I am. Why shouldn't I be?'

The painter did not dare to answer: because these pictures were done by an artist, and you have always been just a base artisan. He stood for a long time in silence in front of them. Admittedly, they were naïve, but they had a strangeness about them and such power that they implied the most advanced aesthetic sense. You would have thought they were the product of experience. Never had Laurent's friend seen sketches exhibiting such high promise. When he had examined the pictures carefully, he turned towards their creator:

'Quite honestly,' he said, 'I should not have thought you capable of painting such work. Where did you pick up this talent? It's not normally something that can be learned.'

He looked at Laurent, whose voice seemed softer to him, whose every gesture had a sort of grace. He could not guess the catastrophic event that had changed this man, developing a woman's sensibility in him and giving him sharper, more delicate feelings. Some strange phenomenon had doubtless taken place in the organism of Camille's murderer. It is difficult for analysis to penetrate such depths. Perhaps Laurent had become an artist as he had become lazy, after the great disruption that had unbalanced his mind and his body. Previously, he had been stifled by the heavy weight of his blood and blinded by the thick vapour of health surrounding him. Now, thinner, quivering, he had the restless vitality, the quick, sharp sensations of persons of a nervous temperament. In the life of terror that he was leading, his thoughts became exaggerated and rose to the ecstasy of genius; the sickness of the spirit, as it were, the neurosis[2] that was afflicting his being, was also developing a strangely lucid artistic sensibility in him. Since he'd killed a man, it was as though his flesh had become lighter, his brain, distraught, seemed immense to him, and in this sudden expansion of his ideas he saw exquisite creations and poetic reveries. This is why his hand had suddenly acquired its distinction and his works their beauty, in a moment becoming personal and alive.

His friend gave up trying to explain the birth of this artist and left with his astonishment undiminished. Before he went, he looked at the pictures once again and told Laurent:

'I have only one criticism to make, which is that all your sketches look alike. Those five heads resemble one another. Even the women have a sort of violent look that makes them seem like men in disguise . . . Now, if you want to make a picture out of those studies, you'll have to change some of the faces: your figures can't all look like members of the same family. People would laugh.'

He went out and, on the landing, added with a laugh:

'It's true, my friend, I'm glad to have seen you. Now I can believe in miracles . . . Good Lord! You've really got it!'

He went down and Laurent returned to his studio, deeply disturbed. When his friend had remarked that all the heads looked alike, he had quickly turned away to hide the pallor of his face. The fact was that this inescapable resemblance had already struck him. He came back slowly and stood in front of the paintings; and as he looked at them, turning from one to the other, a cold sweat ran down his back.

'He's right,' he murmured. 'They are all alike . . . They look like Camille.'

He stepped back and sat down on the divan, unable to take his eyes off the heads in the sketches. The first was an old man with a long white beard, but underneath the beard, the artist could make out Camille's slender chin. The second showed a young blonde girl, and this girl was looking at him with his victim's blue eyes. Each of the three other faces had some features of the drowned man. It was like Camille made up as an old man, as a young girl, taking whatever disguise the painter chose to give him, but always keeping the general character of his physiognomy. There was another frightful similarity in the heads, too: they seemed to be suffering, terrified, as though they were all crushed by the same feeling of horror. Each one had a slight fold to the left of the mouth that pulled back the lips and made them grimace. This fold, which Laurent remembered having seen on the drowned man's convulsed features, marked them with the sign of a foul family bond.

Laurent realized that he had spent too long looking at Camille in the Morgue. The corpse's image had been deeply impressed on his mind. And now his hand, without his realizing it, was constantly drawing the lines of this frightful mask, the memory of which followed him around everywhere.

Gradually, as he lay back on the divan, the painter thought he could see the faces come to life. So there were five Camilles in front of him, five Camilles that his own fingers had endowed with such power and which, through some terrifying mystery, represented every age and every sex. He got up, cut through the canvases and threw them outside. He felt that he would die of fright in his studio if he were to people it himself with portraits of his victim.

He had just been seized by a feeling of anguish: he was afraid that he could never again draw a head without representing the drowned man. He wanted to find out at once if he was in control of his hand. He put a white canvas on the easel, then with a piece of charcoal, he drew a face with a few lines. The face was like Camille. Laurent quickly rubbed out that sketch and tried another. For more than an hour, he struggled against the inescapable urge that drove his fingers; but with each new attempt, he came back to the head of the drowned man. Much as he exerted his will, avoiding the lines that he knew so well, he would draw these lines despite himself, obeying his rebellious muscles and nerves. At first, he had quickly set down the sketches, then he tried to guide the charcoal slowly. The result was the same: Camille, screwing his face up in pain, kept coming back on the canvas. The artist drew the most varied kinds of head in quick succession – angels, young women with haloes, Roman warriors with their helmets on, blond, pink-cheeked children, or old bandits covered in scars ... Yet always the drowned man was resuscitated, by turns as angel, woman, warrior, child and bandit. So Laurent turned to caricature, exaggerating the features; he made monstrous heads, he invented grotesques ... and all he did was to make the striking portraits of his victim more frightful. Eventually, he tried drawing animals, cats and dogs. The cats and dogs looked vaguely like Camille ...

A dull fury had overtaken Laurent. He broke the canvas with his fist, thinking with despair of his great painting. Now, he could no longer even consider it. From now on, he knew, he would only draw heads of Camille and, as his friend had said, figures that all looked alike would just make people laugh. He imagined what his work would have been; he saw, on the shoulders of his figures, men and women, the drowned man's pallid, horrified features; and the strange spectacle that this brought into his head seemed to him so horribly ridiculous that it filled him with despair.

So he would no longer dare to work, for he would always be afraid of bringing his victim back to life with the slightest stroke of the brush. If he wanted to live in peace at his studio he must never paint there. This idea that his fingers had this unavoidable and unconscious ability to reproduce constantly the face of Camille, made him look with terror at his hand. It seemed to him that the hand no longer belonged to him.

XXVI

The stroke that had been threatening Mme Raquin's health arrived. Suddenly the paralysis, which for several months had been creeping along her limbs, constantly on the point of gripping her entirely, seized her by the throat and immobilized her body. One evening, while she was quietly talking to Laurent and Thérèse, she stopped in the middle of a sentence, open-mouthed; she felt as though someone were strangling her. When she tried to cry out, to call for help, she could make only harsh croaking noises. Her tongue had been turned to stone, her hands and feet had stiffened. She was rendered dumb and immobile.[1]

Thérèse and Laurent got up, terrified by this thunderclap that had struck the old haberdasher down in under five seconds. Seeing her stiff like that, looking at them appealingly, they asked her repeatedly to tell them what was wrong. She could not answer, but kept giving them a look of deep distress. At this, they realized that all that was left before them was a corpse, one that was half living, one that could see and hear them, but could not speak. The catastrophe drove them to despair. Underneath, they cared little about the paralysed woman's suffering, but wept for themselves, obliged from now on to live for ever alone with each other.

From that day, the couple's life became unbearable. They spent agonizing evenings beside the stricken old woman who no longer appeased their terrors with her gentle chattering. She lay in an armchair like a parcel, like a thing, and they were left alone at either end of the table, awkward and uneasy. This corpse no longer kept them apart; from time to time they forgot about it and treated it like part of the furniture. And then their terrors of the night gripped them and the dining room became, like the bedroom, a place of horror in which the spectre of Camille loomed. This meant that they suffered for four or five additional hours every day. As soon as evening came, they shuddered, lowering the shade on the lamp to avoid seeing one another and trying to believe that Mme Raquin would speak and so remind them of her presence. If they kept her, if they did not get rid of her, it was because her eyes still lived and at times they would feel some relief in looking at them moving and shining.

They always put the old cripple in the full light of the lamp so that her face would be fully lit and they would constantly have it in front of them. For other people, this soft, pale face would have been an unbearable sight, but they felt such a need for company that they rested their eyes on her with real joy. It was like the decayed mask of a dead woman, with two living eyes in it: the eyes alone moved, rapidly turning in their sockets, while the cheeks and mouth looked as though they were petri-fied, possessing a horrifying immobility. When Mme Raquin abandoned herself to sleep, lowering her eyelids, her face, now entirely white and silent, was truly that of a corpse. Thérèse and Laurent, feeling that there was no longer anyone with them, would make a noise until the paralysed woman opened her eyes and looked at them. In this way, they forced her to stay awake.

They used to consider her a distraction to bring them out of their bad dreams. Now that she was an invalid, she had to be looked after like a child. The care that they lavished on her took their minds off their obsessions. In the morning, Laurent would get her up, carry her to her chair; in the evening he would put her back into her bed. She was still heavy and it took all his strength to lift her carefully in his arms and carry her. He was also the one who pushed her chair around. Her other needs were looked after by Thérèse: she was the one who dressed the cripple, fed her and tried to understand her every wish. For a few days, Mme Raquin could still use her hands, so she was able to write on a slate and ask for what she needed; then her hands died and she was unable to lift up or hold a pencil. All that was left after that was the language of the eyes and her niece had to guess what she wanted. The young woman devoted herself to the cruel task of sick-nurse: it kept her body and mind occupied and did her a lot of good.

So that they would not have to stay alone together, the couple would push the poor old woman's chair into the dining room early in the morning. They brought her in with them, as though she were essential to their existence. She had to watch their meals and listen to all their conversations. They pretended not to understand when she showed that she wished to go back to her room. She was useful only in preventing them from having to endure each other's company; she had no right to live by herself. At eight o'clock, Laurent went to his studio and Thérèse down to the shop, so the paralysed woman stayed alone in the dining room until noon; then, after lunch, she was alone again until six o'clock. Often, during the day, her niece would come up and busy herself around her, making sure that she had everything she needed. Friends of the family could not praise the goodness of Thérèse and Laurent too highly.

The Thursday evening gatherings continued and the cripple was present, as in the past. Her chair was brought over to the table and from eight o'clock until eleven, she kept her eyes open, fixing each of the guests in turn with her penetrating gaze. For the first few days, Old Michaud and Grivet were a little put out by this corpse of their old friend. They were not sure how they ought to look; they were not very much grieved, but they wondered what was precisely the correct degree of sadness to be exhibited in the circumstances. Should they address themselves to this dead face, or should they rather take no notice of it? Little by little, they adopted the solution of treating Mme Raquin as though nothing had happened to her. Eventually, they came to pretend that they were quite unaware of her condition. They chatted with her, putting the questions and replying to them, laughing for her and for themselves and never allowing the rigid expression on her face to disconcert them. It was an odd sight: these men seemed to be talking sensibly to a statue, as little girls talk to their dolls. The paralysed woman sat stiff and silent in front of them while they talked on, with lots of gestures, having very animated conversations with her. Michaud and Grivet congratulated themselves on their excellent behaviour. In this way, they thought they were showing good manners while additionally avoiding the awkwardness of the conventional expressions of sympathy. Mme Raquin must be flattered to see that she was treated as a healthy person and, because of that, they could enjoy themselves in her presence without the slightest scruple.

Grivet had an obsession: he insisted that he had a perfect understanding with Mme Raquin and that she could not look at him without his at once knowing what she meant. That was another sign of how considerate he was – except that, each time, Grivet got it wrong. He would often interrupt the game of dominoes and examine the paralysed woman whose eyes had been calmly watching them play, and announce that she wanted this or that. When they looked into it, either Mme Raquin wanted nothing or she wanted something else entirely. This did not deter Grivet, who would exclaim victoriously: 'I told you so!', then start again a few minutes later. It was quite different when the cripple did openly express a wish. Thérèse, Laurent and the guests, one after another, would name the things that she might want. On such occasions. Grivet would distinguish himself by the inappropriateness of his suggestions. He named whatever came into his head, haphazardly, always choosing the opposite of what Mme Raquin wanted – which would not prevent him from repeating:

'I can read her eyes like a book. Look, there, she's telling me I'm right . . . Aren't you, dear lady? Yes, yes . . .'

In any event, it was no easy matter to grasp the poor old woman's wishes. Only Thérèse knew how. She would communicate quite easily with this immured mind, still living but buried in the depths of a dead body. What was going on in this unfortunate being who was just enough alive to observe life without taking part in it? She could see, hear and no doubt reason in a sharp and clear enough way, but she no longer had any movement or any voice to express outwardly the thoughts that arose in her. Perhaps her ideas were stifling her. She could not have raised a hand or opened her mouth even if a single movement or a single word might determine the fate of the world. Her spirit was like one of those living people who are accidentally buried and who awake in the darkness of the earth under two or three metres of soil.[2] They shout and thrash around while others walk above them without hearing their appalling cries for help. Laurent would often look at Mme Raquin, with her tight lips and hands resting on her knees, putting all her life into her bright, quick eyes, and he would think:

'Who knows what might be going on in her mind? Some cruel drama must be taking place in the depths of this corpse.'

Laurent was wrong. Mme Raquin was happy, happy in the dedication and affection of her dear children. She had always dreamed of ending her life like this, slowly, surrounded by care and caresses. Of course, she would have liked to be able to speak so that she could thank the friends who were helping her to die in peace. But she accepted her state with resignation. The quiet, retiring life that she had always led and the gentleness of her personality meant that she did not feel the loss of speech and mobility too deeply. She had become a child again and spent her days without boredom, staring in front of her and dreaming of the past. She even came to enjoy staying in her chair like a well-behaved little girl.

Every day, her eyes took on a more penetrating softness and clarity. She had reached the point where she used her eyes like a hand and a mouth, to ask for things and to say 'thank you'; and so, in some strange and endearing way, she made up for the faculties that she lacked. The looks that she gave had a celestial beauty, in the midst of a face on which the flesh hung soft and contorted. Since the time when her twisted, unmoving lips had lost the power to smile, she had smiled with her eyes, with delightful tenderness. Moist lights shone and dawn rays emerged from them. Nothing was more remarkable than these eyes laughing like lips in that dead face: the lower part of the face remained dreary and wan, while the upper part was divinely lit. It was for her dear children, especially, that she would put all her gratitude and all the feeling in her soul into a simple glance. When, morning and evening, Laurent took her in his arms to move her, she thanked him lovingly with looks full of tender affection.

So she lived for several weeks, awaiting death and thinking herself safe from any further disaster. She thought that she had paid her debt of suffering. She was wrong. One evening she was smitten by a dreadful blow.

Even though Thérèse and Laurent put her between them in the full light of day, she was no longer enough alive to keep them apart and protect them against their anguish. When they forgot that she was there, that she could see and hear, madness overcame them, Camille rose before them and they tried to drive him away. Then they would stammer, let slip confessions without meaning to, remarks that eventually revealed everything to Mme Raquin. Laurent had a sort of fit in which he spoke like a man in a trance. Suddenly, the paralysed woman understood.

A frightful grimace passed across her face and she experienced such a shock that Thérèse thought she was going to leap up and scream. Then she lapsed back into a state of complete rigidity.

This sort of shock was all the more terrifying since it seemed to have galvanized a corpse. For an instant feeling returned to her, then vanished, leaving the cripple more haggard and pallid than ever. Her eyes, which were usually so soft, had become hard and black like pieces of metal.

Never had despair struck any being so hard. The awful truth burned the crippled woman's eyes like a flash of lightning and entered into her with the finality of a thunderclap. If she could have got up, released the cry of horror that was rising in her throat and cursed the murderers of her son, she would have suffered less. But now that she had heard everything and understood everything, she was forced to remain motionless and silent, keeping the explosion of her pain inside her. It seemed to her that Thérèse and Laurent had tied her up and pinned her to her chair to prevent her from leaping out at them, and that they were taking a horrible delight in repeating: 'We killed Camille,' after putting a gag on her mouth to stifle her sobs. Terror and torment raged within her, but found no way out. She made superhuman efforts to lift the weight that was oppressing her, to unblock her throat and clear the way for the flood of her despair. But it was in vain that she struggled with the last of her energy: she felt her tongue cold against her palate and could not tear herself away from death. She was held rigid by the powerlessness of a corpse. Her feelings were like those of a man who has fallen into a lethargy and is being buried alive: gagged by the fetters of his own flesh, he hears the dull thud of spadefuls of sand above his head.

The ravages in her heart were still worse. She felt as though something inside her had collapsed. She was crushed. Her whole life was destroyed, all her charity, all her kindness, all her care had been brutally knocked over and trampled underfoot. She had led a life of affection and gentleness and now, in her last hours, when she was about to take her belief in the simple goodness of life into the grave with her, a voice was shouting that everything was a lie, everything was criminal. The veil had been torn apart, showing her, beyond the love and friendship that she imagined she saw, a frightful vision of blood and shame. She would have cursed God if she could have uttered a blasphemy. For more than sixty years, God had deceived her, treating her as a kind, gentle little child and amusing her with the sight of lying pictures of tranquil happiness. And she had remained a child, foolishly believing in a myriad of silly things, without seeing the reality of life as it was, mired in a bloody slough of passion. God was bad. He should have told her the truth earlier, or else allowed her to depart with her innocence and her blindness. Now all that was left was for her to die, denying love, denying friendship, denying charity. Nothing existed except murder and lust.

So! Camille had died at the hands of Thérèse and Laurent, and the two of them had plotted their crime in the throes of their shameful adultery! For Mme Raquin, this idea presented such an abyss that she could not adjust to it or grasp it clearly and in detail. She felt only one sensation: that of a dreadful fall. It seemed to her as though she were falling down a cold, black hole. And she thought: 'I am going to be crushed at the bottom.'

After the first shock, the enormity of the crime seemed unreal to her. Then she felt afraid that she might go mad, once she had become convinced of the adultery and the murder, as she remembered some little events that she had not previously been able to explain. Thérèse and Laurent were indeed Camille's murderers: Thérèse, whom she had brought up, and Laurent, whom she had loved like a gentle and devoted mother. This idea went round and round in her head like a huge wheel with a deafening noise. She guessed such repulsive details, she plumbed the depths of such profound hypocrisy, she witnessed in her mind such a cruel double game that she wanted to die to escape from the thoughts. One single idea, formulaic and inescapable, crushed her brain with the weight and persistency of a grindstone. She would repeat to herself: 'My child was killed by my children.' She could find nothing else to express her despair.

After this sudden change of heart, she looked frantically for a self that she could no longer recognize. She was overwhelmed by the sudden invasion of thoughts of revenge that drove all the goodness out of her life. When the transformation was complete, there was darkness inside her. She felt a new being, pitiless and cruel, being born in her dying flesh, a being that would like to bite into the killers of her son.

Now that she had succumbed to the devastating embrace of paralysis and had realized that she could not leap at the throats of Thérèse and Laurent, whom she dreamed of strangling, she resigned herself to silence and immobility, and large tears fell slowly from her eyes. Nothing was more distressing than this silent, unmoving despair. These tears, running one after another across this dead face, in which not a line moved, this inert, pallid face in which the muscles could not weep and only the eyes sobbed, was the most moving of sights.

Thérèse was overcome with terrified pity.

'We must put her to bed,' she said to Laurent, indicating her aunt.

Laurent hastily pushed the cripple into her room. Then he bent down to pick her up in his arms. At that moment, Mme Raquin hoped that some powerful spring would raise her to her feet; she made a supreme effort. God could not allow Laurent to clasp her to his breast; she was sure that thunder would strike him if he showed such monstrous impudence. But no spring drove her and the heavens kept their thunderbolts. She remained there, slumped in the chair, passive, like a bundle of washing. She was grasped, lifted and carried by the murderer. She experienced the horror of feeling herself soft and powerless in the arms of the man who had killed Camille. Her head rolled on to Laurent's shoulder and she looked at him with eyes made wider by terror and repulsion.

'Go on, then, have a good look at me,' he murmured. 'Your eyes won't eat me . . .'

And he threw her roughly on the bed. The cripple fainted away. Her last thought was one of fear and disgust. From now on, morning and evening, she would have to suffer the foul embrace of Laurent's arms.

XXVII

Only a fit of terror had induced the couple to speak and confess in front of Mme Raquin. Neither one of them was cruel; they would have avoided making such a revelation out of sheer humanity, even if their safety had not required them to keep silent.

The following Thursday, they were especially uneasy. In the morning, Thérèse asked Laurent if he thought it wise to bring the paralysed woman into the dining room that evening. She knew everything and could arouse suspicions.

'Huh!' said Laurent. 'She can't move her little finger. How do you expect her to talk?'

'She might find a way,' Thérèse replied. 'Since the other evening, I have seen an implacable resolve in her eyes.'

'No, don't you see, the doctor told me everything is really finished for her. If she does speak once more, it will be in the last gasp of her death agony . . . Come on, she won't be with us for long. It would be stupid to burden our consciences any further by stopping her from coming along this evening.'

Thérèse shuddered.

'You don't understand!' she exclaimed. 'Oh, you're right, there has been enough blood. What I meant was that we could shut my aunt in her room and pretend that she has got worse, that she's asleep.'

'That's great!' said Laurent. 'Then that idiot Michaud would march straight into the room to see his old friend even so. That would be the best way to destroy us.'

He hesitated, trying to look calm, but the anxiety made him stutter.

'Better to let things take their course,' he continued. 'Those people are as daft as geese, they'll definitely not understand anything of the old lady's silent miseries. They'll never guess the thing itself, because they're too far from thinking it. Once we've tested the water, we can rest easy about the result of our indiscretion. You'll see, everything will be all right.'

That evening, when the guests arrived, Mme Raquin was in
her usual place, between the stove and the table. Laurent and
Thérèse pretended to be in good spirits, hiding their fears and
anxiously waiting for the incident that was bound to happen.
They had lowered the lampshade a long way, so that only the
oiled tablecloth was lit.

The guests had that banal, noisy bit of a chat that always
preceded the first game of dominoes. Grivet and Michaud naturally asked Mme Raquin the usual questions about her health,
and provided some excellent replies to the questions themselves,
as they were accustomed to do. After that, without taking any
further notice of the poor old woman, they happily immersed
themselves in their game.

Since learning the dreadful secret, Mme Raquin had eagerly
been awaiting this evening. She had gathered her last strength
to denounce the guilty pair. Up to the last moment, she was
afraid that she would not be joining the party: she thought that
Laurent would spirit her away, perhaps kill her, or at least shut
her up in her room. When she saw that they were allowing her
to be there, and she was in the presence of the guests, she felt a
warm surge of joy at the thought that she was going to try to
avenge her son. Realizing that her tongue was quite dead, she
tried out a new language. By an incredible exercise of will, she
managed as it were to galvanize her right hand, lift it a little off
the knee where it always lay, inert, and after that to make it
crawl little by little up one of the table legs which was in front
of her, until she managed to place it on the oilcloth. There, she
moved her fingers feebly as though to attract attention.

The players were very surprised to find that dead hand, soft
and white, on the table in front of them. Grivet stopped, his arm
raised, just at the moment when he was going to put down a
victorious double six. Since her stroke, the cripple had not once
moved her hands.

'Well, I never! Look at that, Thérèse,' Michaud exclaimed.
'Mme Raquin is moving her fingers. She must want something.'

Thérèse was unable to reply. With Laurent, she had followed
the paralysed woman's efforts and was considering her aunt's
hand, pale beneath the harsh light of the lamp, as a vengeful

hand, about to speak. The two murderers waited with bated breath.

'By golly, yes!' said Grivet. 'She wants something. Oh, we understand one another, she and I. She wants to play dominoes. Huh? That's right, isn't it, dear lady?'

Mme Raquin made a violent attempt to deny it. She extended one finger and bent the others back, with infinite pains, and started with agonizing slowness to trace out letters on the table. She had only made a few lines when Grivet once more exclaimed triumphantly:

'I see it! She's saying that I'm right to play the double six.'

The cripple gave him a furious look and again started the word that she wanted to write. But Grivet kept on interrupting her, saying that it was not necessary, that he had understood; and he would then suggest some idiocy. Eventually, Michaud told him to be quiet.

'For heaven's sake!' he said. 'Let Mme Raquin talk. Tell us, my old friend.'

And he looked at the oilcloth as though listening to something. But the cripple's fingers were tiring: they had started one word more than ten times, and now they could not form it without wandering to the left and to the right. Michaud and Olivier leaned over, but could not read it, so they obliged the victim to keep on repeating the first letters.

'Ah! That's it!' Olivier suddenly exclaimed. 'I've read it this time. She has just written your name, Thérèse. Look: *Thérèse and* . . . Carry on, dear lady.'

Thérèse almost cried out in agony. She watched her aunt's fingers slide along the oilcloth and it seemed to her that those fingers were writing her name and the admission of her crime in letters of fire. Laurent had leaped to his feet, wondering if he ought to throw himself at the old woman and break her arm. He thought that all was lost and could feel the cold weight of retribution on him as he watched that hand come back to life to reveal Camille's murder.

Mme Raquin was still writing, in an increasingly unsteady way.

'That's perfect, I can read it very clearly,' said Olivier after a short while, looking at the young couple. 'Your aunt is writing your two names: *Thérèse and Laurent*.'

At once, the old lady made affirmative signs, casting devastating looks towards the murderers. Then she tried to complete the sentence. But her fingers had stiffened and she was losing the supreme effort of will that had galvanized them; she could feel the paralysis moving slowly along her arm and once more grasping her wrist. She hastened to write another word.

Old Michaud read aloud:

'Thérèse and Laurent are . . .'

And Olivier asked:

'What are they, your dear children?'

The murderers, wild with fear, were on the point of finishing the sentence aloud. They were staring at the vengeful hand with anxious eyes when, suddenly, the hand was seized with a convulsion and dropped flat on the table. It slipped and fell on the old woman's knee like a mass of inanimate flesh. The paralysis had returned and halted the punishment. Michaud and Olivier sat down, disappointed, while Thérèse and Laurent felt such a sharp flood of joy that they thought they were about to faint with the sudden rush of blood thumping in their chests.

Grivet was annoyed at not having been believed. He thought that the moment had come to retrieve his reputation for infallibility by completing Mme Raquin's unfinished sentence. While they were searching for the meaning of the words, he said:

'It's quite clear. I can guess the whole sentence in Madame's eyes. She doesn't have to write it on the table for me; just one look will suffice. What she wanted to say was: "Thérèse and Laurent are taking good care of me."'

Grivet could congratulate himself on his imagination, because everyone agreed. The guests started to praise the young couple who were being so kind to the old lady.

'It is certain,' said Old Michaud gravely, 'that Mme Raquin wanted to acknowledge the tender care that her children lavish upon her. It's a tribute to the whole family.

And, picking his dominoes up again, he added:

'Right, let's carry on. Where were we? I believe Grivet was about to put down the double six.'

Grivet did put down the double six. The game went on, stupid and monotonous.

The paralysed woman looked at her hand, sunk in the most frightful despair. Her hand had just betrayed her. It felt to her as heavy as lead now; never again would she be able to lift it. Heaven did not want Camille to be avenged, but had taken away from his mother the one means she had to let men know that he was the victim of a murder. The unhappy woman told herself that she was no good any longer for anything except to join her child in the ground. She lowered her eyes, feeling useless from now on and trying to believe that she was already in the darkness of the tomb.

XXVIII

For two months, Thérèse and Laurent struggled with the agony of their marriage. Each was the cause of the other's suffering. So, gradually, hatred rose up inside them and in the end they were giving one another looks of anger, full of dark threats.

Their hatred was inevitable. They had loved each other like animals with a hot passion of the blood; then, in the nervous agitation of crime, their love had become hatred and they felt a kind of physical dread of their kisses; and now, with the suffering that marriage and a common life imposed on them, they rebelled and raged against one another.

Their hatred was frightful, with fearsome outbursts. They knew very well that they were a burden to one another, and told themselves that they would have a quiet life if they were not constantly together. When they were in each other's presence, it was as though a huge weight was stifling them, a weight that they wanted to push aside, to abolish. Their lips would purse and thoughts of violence would light their clear eyes; they longed to destroy each other.

Underneath, one single thought plagued them: they were angry at their crime and in despair at having for ever ruined their lives. All their anger and hatred came from this. They felt that the disease was incurable and that they would suffer from Camille's murder until they died; and this idea of perpetual suffering drove them mad. Not knowing who else to strike, they hit out at one another, in detestation.

They did not want to admit aloud that their marriage was an inevitable punishment for the murder; they refused to listen to the voice inside them that shouted the truth, displaying the history of their lives for them. And yet, in the crises of rage that shook them, each read clearly the cause of their anger, perceiving the fury of their egotistical being which, having driven them to murder in order to satisfy its appetites, found nothing in murder except a desolate, intolerable existence. They remembered the past and knew that only their dashed hopes of ease and tranquil happiness made them feel any remorse; if they could have embraced one another in peace and lived a joyous existence, far from mourning Camille, they would have relished their crime. But their bodies had rebelled, rejecting the union between them, and in terror they asked themselves where their horror and disgust would take them. They could see nothing except a future made awful by pain, with a sinister and violent conclusion. So, like two enemies bound together, making vain efforts to release themselves from this forced embrace, they were tensing their muscles and their nerves, bracing themselves without managing to break free. Then, realizing that they never would break free, irritated by the ropes eating into their flesh, sickened by physical contact, feeling their distress grow hour by hour, forgetting that they had tied themselves to one another and unable to bear their bonds a moment longer, they heaped bitter reproaches on one another and tried to lessen their suffering, to bind their self-inflicted wounds, by cursing, by deafening themselves with cries and accusations.

Every evening, a row broke out. It was as though the murderers were each looking for opportunities to arouse the other's temper in order to relax their own tense nerves. They kept a close watch on each other, felt each other out, probed their wounds to find the most exposed part of every scar, and took a bitter pleasure in making the other cry out in pain. In this way, they lived in the midst of continual agitation, weary of themselves and unable to bear a word, a gesture or a look without its hurting and their raging against it. Their whole beings were ready for violence; the slightest impatience and the most ordinary annoyance were enlarged in their unhinged organisms in some strange way, suddenly becoming heavily charged with brutality. A mere trifle would raise a storm that would last until the next day. A dish that was too hot, an open window, a denial or some simple remark was enough to drive them to insane pitches of fury. And always, at some point in the argument, they would throw the drowned man in one another's faces: one thing leading to another, they would manage to accuse each other of the drowning at Saint-Ouen. Then they would see red and be aroused to hysterical rage. There were frightful scenes, breathtaking furies, blows, foul cries and shameful acts of brutality. Usually, Thérèse and Laurent would reach this pitch of exasperation after dinner, and shut themselves in the dining room so that no one could hear the noise of their anguish. There, they could savage one another at ease, in the depths of this damp room, this sort of cellar in which the lamp cast its yellowish light. In the silence and the stillness of the air, their voices became dry and shrill. And they would stop only when they were driven to exhaustion: only then could they enjoy a few hours of rest. Their arguments became a kind of drug for them, as a means to reach sleep by draining their nerves.

Mme Raquin listened to them. She was constantly there in her chair, her hands resting on her knees, her head upright and her face unspeaking. She could hear everything and her dead flesh did not even shudder. Her eyes stared sharply at the murderers. Her torment must have been appalling, because in this way she learned, in every little detail, the facts that had led up to Camille's murder and followed it, and she entered deeper and deeper, step by step, into the foul crimes of those whom she had called her 'dear children'.

The couple's arguments informed her of every circumstance of the frightful story, setting out the episodes one by one before her terrified mind. And as she entered into this bloody swamp, she would beg for mercy, thinking she had reached the depths of infamy, yet she would have to go further still. Every evening she learned something new. The horrible tale expanded constantly before her, and she felt as though she were lost in a nightmare without end. The first confession had been crushing and brutal, but she suffered more from these repeated blows, the little facts that the couple let slip out, carried away by their rows, which threw sinister lights into hidden aspects of the crime. Once every day, this mother had to hear the story of her son's murder, and every day this story became more horrifying and more detailed, and was shouted in her ears with more cruelty and clarity.

Sometimes Thérèse would be seized with remorse at the sight of this pallid mask with large tears silently running down it. She would indicate her aunt to Laurent and beg him with a look to be silent.

'Oh, let her be!' he would cry harshly. 'You know she can't turn us in. Am I any happier than she is? We've got her money, I don't need to worry about her.'

And the row went on, bitter, violent, killing Camille over and over again. Neither Thérèse nor Laurent dared to give in to the charitable thought that sometimes came over them: that they should shut the cripple up in her room when they were quarrelling, and thus spare her the description of the crime. They were afraid that they might bludgeon one another if they no longer had this half-living corpse between them. Their sense of pity gave way to their cowardice and they inflicted unspeakable suffering on Mme Raquin because they needed her presence to ward off their hallucinations.

All their quarrels were alike and led to the same accusations. As soon as Camille's name was mentioned, as soon as one of them accused the other of killing the man, there was a dreadful outcry.

One evening at dinner, Laurent, looking for an excuse to get annoyed, decided that the water in the jug was warm. He announced that warm water made him feel nauseous and that he wanted cold.

'I couldn't get any ice,' Thérèse replied, drily.

'Very well, I shan't drink it,' said Laurent.

'The water's perfectly good.'

'It's hot and tastes muddy. It's like river water.'

Thérèse repeated: 'River water,' then burst into tears. Her mind had just made a connection . . .

'What are you crying about?' Laurent asked, guessing the reply and going pale.

'I'm crying . . .' the young woman sobbed, 'because . . . you know very well . . . Oh, my God! My God! You were the one who killed him.'

'You liar!' the murderer shouted. 'Admit it: you're lying! I may have thrown him in the Seine, but you drove me to murder.'

'Me? Me!'

'Yes, you! Don't play the innocent or oblige me to get the truth out of you by force. I need you to confess the crime and accept your part in this killing. That takes a weight off my mind and lets me feel easier in my self.'

'But I'm not the one who drowned Camille.'

'Yes, you were! A thousand times yes! Oh, you can pretend to be amazed and to have forgotten. Wait, I'll polish up your memory.'

He got up from the table, leaned towards the young woman and, his face blazing, shouted at her:

'You were on the bank of the river, remember, and I whispered to you: "I'm going to throw him in." And you agreed, you got into the boat. So you can see that you killed him with me.'

'That's not true! I was mad, I don't know precisely what I did, but I never wanted to kill him. You committed the crime by yourself.'

These denials tormented Laurent. As he said, the idea of having an accomplice lifted some of the burden from him; if he had dared, he would have tried to prove to himself that the full horror of the murder fell on Thérèse. He sometimes felt like beating her to make her confess that she was the more guilty of them.

He started to walk backwards and forwards, shouting wildly, followed by Mme Raquin's unblinking stare.

'Oh, the bitch! The bitch!' he spluttered, in a choking voice. 'She's trying to drive me mad! Huh? Didn't you come up to my room one evening, like a whore, and drive me crazy with your caresses in order to persuade me to get rid of your husband? You found him repulsive, he smelled like a sick child: that's what you used to tell me when I came here to see you. Was I thinking of all this, three years ago? Was I a scoundrel then? I lived quietly, like a decent fellow, not doing any harm to anyone. I wouldn't have hurt a fly.'

'You're the one who killed Camille,' Thérèse would say, over and over, with a desperate obstinacy that drove Laurent to distraction.

'No, you are the one, I'm telling you, you are the one!' he went on, with a furious scream. 'Look here, don't get on my nerves, or I could turn nasty. What, you wretch, don't you remember anything? You gave yourself to me like a harlot, there, in your husband's bed; you knew how to drive me out of my mind with lust. Admit it: you planned the whole thing because you hated Camille and had wanted to kill him for a long time. Of course, you took me for your lover so that you could set me against him and destroy him.'

'It's not true! What you're saying is outrageous! You have no right to reproach me with my weakness. I can say, like you, that before knowing you I was a decent woman and had never harmed a soul. I may have driven you insane, but you made me even madder. Laurent, let's not argue; don't you see . . . I would have too many things to reproach you with.'

'So what would you have to reproach me with?'

'No, nothing . . . You didn't save me from myself, you took advantage of my frailty, you enjoyed wrecking my life . . . I forgive you all that. But for pity's sake, don't accuse me of killing Camille. Keep your crime to yourself, don't try to appal me even more.'

Laurent raised his hand to slap Thérèse's face.

'Hit me, I'd rather that,' she went on. 'It will hurt less.'

And she offered him her cheek. He restrained himself, took a chair and sat down beside the young woman.

'Listen,' he said in a voice that he forced himself to control. 'It's cowardly of you to deny your share in the crime. You know very well that we committed it together, you know that you are as guilty as I am. Why do you want to make me bear all the responsibility by pretending you are innocent? If you were innocent, you would never have agreed to marry me. Remember the two years after the murder. Do you want to try a test? I'll go and tell everything to the Imperial Prosecutor and you'll see if we are not both condemned for it.'

They shuddered and Thérèse said:

'Men might condemn me, perhaps, but Camille knows that you did everything . . . He doesn't torment me in the night as he does you.'

'Camille leaves me in peace,' Laurent said, pale and trembling. 'You're the one who sees him returning in your nightmares: I've heard you cry out.'

'Don't say that!' Thérèse cried, angrily. 'I didn't cry out. I don't want the ghost to come. Oh, yes, I understand! You're trying to send him away from you. I'm innocent, I'm innocent!'

They looked at one another in terror, exhausted and afraid of having summoned up the drowned man's corpse. Their arguments always finished like that: they would protest their innocence and attempt to deceive themselves in order to drive away their bad dreams. They made constant efforts to shrug off responsibility for the crime and to defend themselves as though they were in the dock, each off-loading the most serious charges on the other. The strangest thing was that they were unable to deceive themselves with their protestations, because both of them recalled the precise circumstances of the murder. Even as their lips denied it, they could each read a confession in the other's eyes. Their lies were childish, their assertions ridiculous: disputes of empty words between two wretches who lied for the sake of lying, yet were unable to conceal the fact of their lying from each other. Each in turn took the role of accuser and, although the indictment that they raised against one another would never reach a verdict, they resumed it evening after evening with cruel determination. They knew that they would never prove anything, that they would not succeed in wiping out the past, yet they continued to try, always coming back for more, spurred on by pain and terror, defeated from the start by the crushing weight of reality. The most obvious advantage that they derived from their arguments was to produce a storm of words and shouts, the noise of which deafened them, for a moment.

And all the time that their fury lasted, while they were accusing one another, the paralysed woman did not take her eyes off them. A bright spark of joy glowed in her eyes when Laurent raised his broad hand against Thérèse's head.

XXIX

A new phase began. Thérèse, driven to extremes by fear and not knowing where to look for consolation, started to mourn the drowned man openly in front of Laurent.

She suffered a sudden collapse. Her overstretched nerves snapped and her dry, violent nature softened. Already, in the first days of her marriage, she had experienced emotional outbursts, and these returned, like a necessary and inevitable reaction. After she had struggled with all her nervous energy against Camille's ghost and when she had lived for several months in a state of vague irritation, rebelling against her sufferings and trying to heal them by sheer effort of will, she suddenly felt such weariness that she was overcome and gave in. So, a woman once more, even a little girl, no longer feeling she had the strength to stiffen herself, stand up and furiously drive off her terrors, she relapsed into pity, tears and regrets, hoping that these would bring her some relief. She tried to take advantage of the weaknesses of the flesh and the spirit that took hold of her: perhaps the drowned man, who had not given way to her annoyance, would give in to her tears. She felt a self-interested remorse, telling herself that this was probably the best way to pacify and please Camille. Like certain pious women who think they can deceive God and gain a pardon by praying with their lips and adopting meek attitudes of penance, Thérèse humbled herself, smote her breast and spoke words of repentance, without having anything more in the depths of her heart but fear and cowardice. Apart from that, she felt a sort of physical pleasure in abandoning herself, feeling soft and broken and offering herself to pain without trying to resist.

She crushed Mme Raquin with the weight of her tearful despair. She subjected the paralysed woman to daily use, making her a kind of prayer-stool, a piece of furniture before which she could confess her sins without fear and ask for pardon. As soon as she felt the need to weep, or to relieve herself with sobs, she knelt before the cripple and there cried out, panting for breath, playing a scene of remorse all by herself and finding relief in weakness and exhaustion.

'I am a wretch,' she stammered. 'I don't deserve forgiveness. I deceived you, I pushed your son to his death. You will never forgive me ... Yet perhaps if you could see the remorse that is wrenching me apart, if you could know how much I am suffering, then perhaps you would take pity on me ... No, there is no pity for me. I would like to die here at your feet, crushed with shame and sorrow.'

She would talk in this way for hours on end, swinging from despair to hope, blaming herself, then forgiving herself. She would take on the voice of a sick little girl, now snapping, now pleading. She would lie down on the floor, then get up again, acting according to whatever idea of humility or pride, repentance or revolt came into her head. She would even at times forget that she was kneeling in front of Mme Raquin, and continue her monologue in a dreamlike state. When she had thoroughly numbed herself with her own words, she would stagger to her feet and go back downstairs to the shop, dazed but calm, no longer afraid of bursting into a fit of nervous weeping in front of the customers. When she felt the onset of a new bout of remorse, she hurried back up to kneel, once more, in front of the cripple. And so it went on, ten times a day.

It never occurred to Thérèse that her tears and the display of her remorse must be imposing the most unspeakable agony on her aunt. The truth is that, if you were to invent a torture to inflict on Mme Raquin, you could surely not find anything more appalling than the dramas of repentance that her niece played out in front of her. The paralysed woman could perceive the egotism behind these outpourings of pain. She suffered agonies listening to these long monologues, which she was obliged constantly to undergo and which repeatedly reminded her of Camille's murder. She could not forgive; she shut herself into a pitiless idea of vengeance, which her disability made more acute; yet all day she had to hear these pleas for forgiveness, these despicable, cowardly prayers. She would have liked to reply; some things that her niece said brought crushing responses to her lips, but she had to remain silent, allowing Thérèse to plead her case without ever interrupting her. Her inability to cry out or to stop her ears filled her with inexpressible torment. And, one by one, the young woman's slow, plaintive words sank into her mind, like an annoying tune. For a while, she thought that the murderers were inflicting this sort of torture on her out of sheer, diabolical cruelty. Her only means of defence was to close her eyes as soon as her niece knelt before her: if she could still hear, at least she could not see her.

Eventually, Thérèse grew bold enough to kiss her aunt. One day, in a fit of repentance, she pretended that she had seen a hint of mercy in the eyes of the paralysed woman. She crawled along on her knees, then got up and cried in a distraught voice: 'You forgive me! You forgive me!' After this, she kissed the forehead and cheeks of the poor old woman, who could not move her head away. Thérèse experienced a sharp feeling of disgust as her lips touched the cold flesh, but she decided that this disgust, like the tears and the remorse, would be a fine way to calm her nerves, so she continued to kiss the cripple every day, as a penance and to give herself relief.

'Oh, how good you are!' she would exclaim at times. 'I can see that my tears have moved you. Your look is full of pity. I am saved.'

She would smother her with caresses, put her head on the old woman's lap, kiss her hands, smile happily at her and care for her with all the signs of passionate affection. After a while, she came to believe in the reality of this play-acting. She imagined that she had received Mme Raquin's pardon and from then on talked to her only of her happiness at having her forgiveness.

This was too much for the paralysed woman. It almost killed

her. Her niece's kisses gave her the same bitter feeling of repugnance and fury that filled her every morning and evening when Laurent picked her up to get her out of bed or to lie her down. She was obliged to suffer the foul embraces of the wretched woman who had betrayed and killed her son. She could not even use her hand to wipe off the kisses that this creature left on her cheeks. For hours on end, she would feel these kisses burning her flesh. This is how she became the plaything of Camille's murderers, a doll whom they dressed, whom they turned to right or left, and used according to their needs and whims. She remained inert in their hands, as if she had only sawdust in her belly, when in fact her guts came to life, anguished and outraged, at the slightest touch of Thérèse or Laurent. What made her most angry was the frightful mockery of this young woman who claimed to be able to read feelings of mercy in her look, when she would have liked with a look to strike the criminal down. She often made immense efforts to give a cry of protest, and put all her hatred into her eyes. But Thérèse, whom it suited to repeat twenty times a day that she had been forgiven, refused to guess the truth and smothered her with more caresses. The paralysed woman had to accept effusive thanks that she rejected in her heart. From now on, she lived in a state of complete, bitter and powerless irritation, confronted with this pliant niece who kept trying to demonstrate new signs of affection to reward her aunt for what Thérèse called her 'celestial goodness'.

When Laurent was there and his wife knelt before Mme Raquin, he would lift her up roughly.

'Stop play-acting,' he would say. 'Am I crying? Am I down on my knees? You're doing all this to upset me.'

Thérèse's remorse disturbed him to a peculiar degree. He was more troubled, now that his accomplice was dragging herself around, her eyes red with tears and her lips full of pleading. The sight of this repentance made flesh and blood increased his uneasiness. It was like an eternal reproach walking around the house. Apart from that, he was afraid that repentance would one day incite his wife to reveal everything. He would have preferred it if she had stayed stiff and threatening, earnestly defending herself against his accusations. But she had changed her approach and now willingly acknowledged her share in the crime, accusing herself, becoming soft and fearful, and using this as a basis to beg for redemption with humble ardour. Laurent was irritated by this attitude. Every evening now, their arguments would take a more damning and sinister turn.

'Listen,' Thérèse told her husband, 'we are guilty of a terrible crime, we must repent if we want to have any peace ... Don't you see, since I started to cry, I have been calmer. Do as I do. Let's admit together that we are being rightly punished for committing a frightful crime.'

'Pooh!' Laurent would answer brusquely. 'Say what you like. I know how devilishly cunning and hypocritical you are. Weep, if that amuses you. But, please, don't go on at me with your tears.'

'You're wicked, you are refusing to feel any remorse. But you're a coward even so. You caught Camille off guard.'

'Are you saying I'm the only one who's guilty?'

'No, that's not what I'm saying. I'm guilty, more guilty than you. I should have saved my husband from your hands. Oh, I know the full horror of my sin! But I shall try to obtain forgiveness, Laurent, and I'll manage it, while you will go on living a life of desolation. You don't even have the goodness in your heart to spare my aunt the sight of your shameful anger, and you have never spoken a word of regret to her.'

And she would kiss Mme Raquin, who closed her eyes. Then she would fuss around her, plumping up the pillow behind her head and showering her with affection. This exasperated Laurent.

'Leave her alone,' he would say. 'Can't you see that she hates you caring for her; she hates the sight of you. If she could lift up her hand, she'd slap your face.'

His wife's slow, plaintive words, and her attitude of resignation, would gradually drive him into a blind rage. He could see plainly what she was about: she no longer wanted to make common cause with him, but was trying to separate herself in the depth of her remorse, so as to escape the clutches of the drowned man. At times, he would tell himself that she might have chosen the right course, that tears would cure him of his terrors, and he shuddered at the idea of being the only one to suffer and fear. He would like to repent, too, or at least to act out a scene of remorse, just to see. But he could not find the necessary words and sobs, so he would lapse into violence and shake Thérèse in order to irritate her and bring her back to join him in his raging madness. The young woman worked hard at remaining unexcited, responding to his cries of anger with tearful submission and becoming proportionately more humble and repentant as he became rougher. In this way Laurent would be driven to a fury. To put the final touch to his annoyance, Thérèse would start singing Camille's praises, listing the qualities of the victim.

'He was a good man,' she said, 'and we must have been very cruel to lift a hand against that gentle heart, which never had a bad impulse.'

'Oh, yes, he was certainly good,' Laurent scoffed. 'What you mean is that he was stupid, don't you? Have you forgotten? You used to claim that the slightest word from him got on your nerves and that he could not open his mouth without saying something ridiculous.'

'Don't mock. That's the last straw, insulting the man you killed. You don't know anything about a woman's heart, Laurent. Camille loved me and I loved him.'

'You loved him! Huh! Did you really? That's new! I suppose it was because you loved your husband that you took me as a lover. I remember the day when you were lying with your head on my chest and saying that Camille made you feel sick when your fingers sank into his flesh, like sinking into clay . . . Oh, I can tell you why you loved me. You needed some more sturdy arms than that poor devil had to hold you with.'

'I loved him like a sister. He was the son of my aunt and benefactress. He had all the gentleness of a delicate nature, and would always behave in a way that was noble and generous, helpful and affectionate. And we killed him! My God, my God!'

She would cry and swoon away. Mme Raquin shot piercing glances at her, indignant at hearing Camille's praises on such lips. Laurent, powerless against this flood of tears, walked back and forth feverishly, looking for some way of finally crushing Thérèse's remorse. In the end, all the good that he heard about his victim caused him sharp pangs of anxiety; occasionally, he would really come to believe in Camille's virtues and this would increase his terror. But what drove him out of his mind and caused him to become violent was the parallel that the drowned man's widow would inevitably draw between her first and second husbands, entirely to the advantage of the first.

'Why, yes!' she would exclaim. 'He was better than you. I would prefer it if he were still alive and you in his place under the ground.'

At first, Laurent would shrug his shoulders.

'Say what you like,' she went on, warming to the subject. 'Perhaps I didn't love him when he was alive, but now I remember him and I do love him. I love him and hate you, that's what. You're a murderer . . .'

'Will you be quiet!' Laurent shouted.

'And he is a victim, a decent man killed by a rogue. Oh, I'm not afraid of you. You know that you're a wretch, a brute with no heart or soul. How do you expect me to love you, now that you are bathed in Camille's blood? Camille lavished affection on me and I'd kill you, do you hear, if that could bring him back and restore his love.'

'Shut up, you bitch!'

'Why should I? I'm speaking the truth. I would buy forgiveness at the cost of your blood. Oh, how much I am weeping and suffering! It's my fault that this scoundrel murdered my husband. One night, I must go and kiss the earth where he lies. That will be the last joy of my flesh.'

Laurent, driven crazy by these frightful pictures that Thérèse conjured up, flew at her, knocked her down and knelt on her, his fist raised.

'That's right,' she cried. 'Hit me! Kill me! Camille never raised a hand against me, but you are a monster.'

And Laurent, spurred on by these words, would shake her in his rage, hit her and bruise her body with his clenched fist. On two occasions, he nearly strangled her. Thérèse went limp beneath his blows. She experienced a fierce, bitter pleasure at being struck. She would abandon herself, offer herself up, provoking her husband to hit her again and again. This was another cure for the misery of her life: she would sleep better at night when she had been well beaten in the evening. Mme Raquin experienced an exquisite sense of pleasure when Laurent pulled her niece across the floor in this way, kicking her.

The murderer's existence had become truly dreadful since the day when Thérèse had the hellish notion of feeling remorse and openly mourning Camille. From then on, the wretch lived constantly with his victim: at every moment, he had to listen to his wife extolling and bewailing her first husband. The slightest opportunity would set her off: Camille used to do this, Camille used to do that, Camille had this quality, Camille loved her in that way. Always Camille, always these sad remarks mourning the death of Camille. Thérèse used all her venom to intensify the cruelty of this torture that she was inflicting on Laurent in order to protect herself. She went into the most intimate details and described the trivial events of her youth with sighs of nostalgia, in this way mingling the memory of the drowned man with every act of her daily routine. The body, which was already haunting the house, was now brought into it openly. It sat on the chairs or at the table, lay down on the bed, and used the furniture or whatever else was lying around. Laurent could not pick up a fork, a brush or anything without Thérèse letting him know that Camille had touched it before him. Constantly running up against the man he had killed, the murderer came to feel an odd sensation that almost drove him mad: through being so often compared to Camille and using things that Camille had used, he came to think that he was Camille; he identified with his victim. His brain was bursting, so he would rush at his wife to make her be quiet, so as not to hear the words that were driving him insane. All their rows would end in blows.

XXX

The time came when it occurred to Mme Raquin to let herself die of hunger in order to escape the agony that she had to endure. Her resistance was at an end; she could no longer bear the torment imposed on her by the continual presence of the murderers and she dreamed of finding an end to all her suffering in death. Every day, when Thérèse kissed her, and when Laurent took her in his arms and carried her like a child, her pain intensified. She made up her mind to escape from these caresses and embraces which aroused such horrible repugnance in her. Since she was no longer fully enough alive to revenge her son, she preferred to be entirely dead and leave the killers with nothing except a body, devoid of feeling, which they could treat as they wished.

For two days, she refused all food, using the last of her strength to clench her teeth and spit out what they managed to get into her mouth. Thérèse was in despair. She wondered where she could kneel and weep in repentance when her aunt was no longer there. She talked endlessly to her, to convince her that she should live; she wept, she even grew angry, as she had done in the past, opening the paralysed woman's jaws as one does the jaws of an animal that does not want to be fed. Mme Raquin held firm. The struggle was appalling.

Laurent maintained an attitude of perfect neutrality and indifference. He was amazed by the violent efforts that Thérèse put into preventing the cripple's suicide. Now that the old woman's presence was no longer useful to them, he wanted her to die. He would not have killed her himself, but since she wished for death, he saw no need to deny her the means to achieve her goal.

'Oh, leave her!' he would shout at his wife. 'Good riddance. Perhaps we will be happier when she is not here any more.'

This last remark, which he often repeated in front of her, aroused strange emotions in Mme Raquin. She was afraid that Laurent's hopes would be fulfilled, and that after her death the couple would enjoy tranquil, happy days. She told herself that it was cowardly to die and that she had no right to go before she had seen the sinister adventure through to its end. Only then could she go down into the shades and tell Camille: 'You are avenged.' The thought of suicide began to weigh on her when she suddenly considered the unknowns that she would take into the tomb: there, amid the cold and silence of the earth she would sleep, eternally racked by doubts about the punishment of her tormentors. To sleep properly the sleep of death, she had to lapse into insensibility feeling the sharp joy of revenge; she had to take with her a dream of hatred satisfied, one that she would dream throughout eternity. She took the food that her niece brought her and agreed to carry on living.

In any case, she saw that the end could not be far away. Every day the couple's situation became more tense and more unbearable. They were heading quickly towards a crisis that would destroy them both. Day by day, Thérèse and Laurent took up ever more threatening positions towards one another. It was not only at night that their intimacy tortured them: their whole days were spent in crises of self-destructive agony. Everything brought terror and suffering to them. They lived in a hell, wounding one another, making whatever they did and said bitter and cruel, each hoping to drive the other towards the gulf that they could feel before their feet, and falling into it together.

Both of them had had the idea of separating. Each in turn had dreamed of running away to enjoy some rest far from this Passage du Pont-Neuf where the damp and dirt seemed to have been designed especially for their desolate existence. But they did not dare, they could not escape. The thought of not rending each other apart, of not staying there to suffer and inflict suffering, seemed impossible to them. They were obstinate in their hatred and cruelty. A sort of attraction and repulsion drove them asunder and kept them together at the same time. They felt that peculiar sensation of two people who, after an argument, want to separate, yet keep on coming back to shout fresh insults at one another. Then there were material obstacles to flight: they did not know what to do with the cripple, or what to say to their Thursday guests. If they fled, people might suspect something: they imagined being hunted down and guillotined. So they stayed, out of cowardice; they stayed and grovelled in the horror of their existence.

When Laurent was not there, during the mornings and afternoons, Thérèse would go from the dining room to the shop, gnawed by anxiety, not knowing how to fill the void that every day sank deeper in her. She was at a loose end when not weeping at Mme Raquin's feet or being beaten and insulted by her husband. As soon as she was alone in the shop, a sense of despondency overcame her: she would look out numbly at the people going up and down the dirty, black arcade, and become mortally depressed in the depths of this dark tomb stinking of the graveyard. Eventually, she asked Suzanne to come and spend whole days with her, hoping that the presence of this sad creature, all soft and pale, would calm her nerves.

Suzanne gleefully accepted the offer. She still felt a kind of respectful friendship towards Thérèse, and had long wanted to come and work with her while Olivier was in his office. She brought along her embroidery and took up Mme Raquin's empty place behind the counter.

From that day on, Thérèse left her aunt more alone. She went up less often to weep on her knees and kiss her dead cheeks. She had something else to occupy her. She made an effort to listen to Suzanne's slow chattering on about her family and the trivialities of her monotonous life. It took Thérèse out of herself. She was sometimes surprised to find herself getting interested in some nonsense and would later smile bitterly to herself over it.

Little by little, she lost all the customers who used to come to the shop. Since her aunt had become immobilized upstairs in her chair, she let the shop go to the dogs, abandoning the goods to dust and damp. There was a smell of mould about the place, cobwebs hung from the ceiling and the floor was hardly ever brushed. Apart from that, what drove the customers away was the strange manner in which Thérèse would sometimes greet them. When she was upstairs, being beaten by Laurent or seized by a fit of terror, and the bell on the shop door tinkled imperiously, she would have to go down, almost without taking the time to tie up her hair and wipe away her tears. On such occasions she would serve the waiting customer brusquely and often not even take the trouble to serve her, shouting down from the top of the wooden staircase that she no longer had whatever the customer wanted. This offhand treatment was not calculated to retain the clientele. The little girls who worked in the district were used to the gentle manners of Mme Raquin and took themselves elsewhere when they got Thérèse's rough treatment and mad looks. And when Thérèse took Suzanne in with her, the exodus was complete: the two young women did not want to be disturbed in their gossiping and made sure they drove off the last few customers who were still bothering to turn up. From then on the haberdashery business no longer contributed a single sou to the household budget and they had to break into the capital of forty or so thousand francs.

Sometimes, Thérèse would go out for a whole afternoon at a time. No one knew where she went. She must have taken on Suzanne not only to keep her company but also to keep shop while she was away. In the evening, when she came back exhausted, her eyelids black with fatigue, she would find Olivier's little wife hunched behind the counter, smiling a vague smile and sitting exactly as she had left her five hours earlier.

Five months after her wedding, Thérèse had a scare. She became convinced that she was pregnant. The idea of having a child by Laurent appalled her, though she could not explain why. She was vaguely afraid that she might give birth to a drowned baby. She thought she could feel the cold of a soft, rotting corpse in her womb. She wanted at any cost to get rid of this child that was chilling her and which she could not carry any longer. She said nothing to her husband, but one day, after she had severely provoked him, he began to kick her and she offered him her belly. She let him kick her almost to death and the next day she had a miscarriage.

Laurent, for his part, was leading a dreadful existence. The days seemed unbearably long to him, each one bringing the same anxieties, the same heavy tedium, which would settle on him at particular moments with a deadening monotony and punctuality. He dragged himself through life, horrified every evening by the memory of the last day and anticipation of the next. He knew that from now on all his days would be alike and each would bring the same suffering. He could see the weeks, months and years awaiting him, dark and pitiless, coming one after another to settle on him and stifle him. When there is no hope for the future, the present acquires a vile, bitter taste. There was no rebellion left in Laurent; he slumped and gave himself up to the void that was already starting to possess his being. The idleness was killing him. First thing in the morning, he would go out, wandering aimlessly, sickened by the thought of doing the same thing as he had done the day before, and forced despite himself to repeat it. He would go to his studio, from force of habit, obsessively. This grey-walled room, out of which you could see only an empty square of sky, filled him with melancholy sadness. He would fling himself down on the divan, his arms dangling and his thoughts leaden. In any case, he did not dare to touch a brush now. He had made some fresh attempts and Camille's face had always sniggered at him from the canvas. To avoid lapsing into insanity, he eventually threw his box of paints into a corner and abandoned himself to the most utter laziness. He found this imposed idleness incredibly hard to bear.

In the afternoon, he would rack his brains to think of something to do. He would spend half an hour on the pavement in the Rue Mazarine wondering about it, hesitating between the various forms of entertainment that he might choose. He rejected the idea of going back to his studio and would always decide to go down the Rue Guénégaud, then walk along the banks of the Seine. So until evening he would carry straight on, in a daze, shivering suddenly from time to time when he looked at the river. Whether he was in his studio or in the street, he felt the same oppression. The next day, he would start all over again, spending the morning on his divan and, in the afternoon, wandering along the river bank. This had lasted for months and could go on for years.

Sometimes it occurred to Laurent that he had killed Camille in order to enjoy a life of leisure, and he was quite astonished, now that he did have nothing to do, to be enduring such misery. He would have liked to oblige himself to be happy. He would prove to himself that he had no reason to suffer, that he had just achieved the height of happiness, which consists in folding one's arms, and that he was an idiot not to indulge tranquilly in such bliss. But his arguments collapsed in the face of reality. Inside, he was forced to admit that idleness made his sufferings even worse, leaving him every moment of his life to think about his despair and experience its incurable bitterness. Laziness, the animal existence that he had dreamed of, was his punishment. There were times when he eagerly longed for some occupation that would take him out of himself. Then he would let himself go and abandon himself to the dull fate that bound his limbs, all the better to crush him.

In truth, he felt some release only when he was beating Thérèse in the evenings. This gave him relief from the dull ache inside.

His worst suffering, one that was both mental and physical, came from the bite that Camille had inflicted on his neck. There were times when he imagined that this scar covered his whole body. If he did manage to forget the past, he would seem to feel a sharp pricking, which brought the murder back to his flesh and into his mind. He could not stand in front of a mirror without seeing the phenomenon that he had so often noticed, one that never failed to terrify him: the emotion that he felt would have the effect of bringing the blood up to his neck, making the scar purple and causing it to eat into his flesh. This sort of living wound that he had on him, which would awake, redden and gnaw at the slightest hint of anxiety, terrified and tortured him. He came to believe that the drowned man's teeth had buried some creature there that was devouring him. He felt that the piece of his neck with the scar on it no longer belonged to his body; it was like some alien flesh that had been stuck on in that place, like poisoned meat rotting his own muscles away. In this way he carried the living, devouring memory of his crime everywhere with him. When he used to beat Thérèse, she would try to scratch him on that spot; sometimes her nails would dig into it, making him scream with pain. Usually, she would sob when she saw the bite, to make it even more unbearable for Laurent. Her whole revenge for his brutality towards her was to torment him with the help of that bite.

Often when he was shaving he had been tempted to cut into

his neck in order to remove the marks of the drowned man's teeth. Looking into the mirror, when he lifted up his chin and saw the red mark under the white shaving soap, he would be seized with sudden fury and bring the razor quickly across, ready to cut into the living flesh. But the cold of the instrument on his neck[1] always brought him back to his senses. He would feel faint and have to sit down and wait until his cowardice had been appeased enough for him to continue shaving.

In the evening, he would emerge from his lethargy only to launch into an outburst of blind, puerile anger. When he was tired of quarrelling with Thérèse and beating her, he would kick out at the wall, like a child, looking for something to break. This would relieve his feelings. He had a particular loathing of François, the tabby cat, who as soon as he came in would take refuge on the paralysed woman's lap. If Laurent had not yet killed it, this was only because he did not dare to pick it up. The cat would look at him with large, round eyes, staring diabolically. It was these eyes, constantly settled on him, that drove the young man mad: he wondered what they meant, these eyes, forever looking in his direction, and in the end he really got the wind up and imagined some ridiculous things. When he was sitting at the table he would abruptly turn round at any time, in the midst of a quarrel or a long silence, to see François's look examining him in this serious, implacable manner, then he would go pale and lose his head. He was on the point of yelling: 'Hey! Say something! Tell me what you want, for once.' When he managed to tread on a paw or on the cat's tail, he did so with savage joy, but then the poor creature's miaowing filled him with a vague sense of horror, as though he had heard a person cry out in pain. Laurent was literally afraid of François, especially since the cat had taken to living on the old woman's knees, as though inside an impregnable fortress from which he could fix his green eyes with impunity on his enemy, Camille's murderer, who found some resemblance between the cat and the paralysed woman. He told himself that the cat, like Mme Raquin, knew about the crime and would denounce him some day if he were ever to speak.

Finally, one evening, François was staring so hard at Laurent that the latter, driven to exasperation, decided that enough was enough. He opened wide the dining-room window and went over to grasp the cat by the skin of its neck. Mme Raquin understood, and two large tears ran down her cheeks. The cat started to snarl and hiss, stiffening itself and trying to turn round to bite Laurent's hand. But he did not let go. He whirled the cat around his head a couple of times, then smashed it as hard as he could against the great black wall opposite. François struck it and, his back broken, fell on to the glass roof of the arcade. Throughout the whole of that night, the wretched animal dragged itself along the gutter, its spine fractured, making harsh miaowing noises. That night, Mme Raquin mourned François almost as much as she had done Camille, and Thérèse had a dreadful nervous crisis. The cat's moans in the darkness under their windows were quite sinister.

Soon Laurent had new things to worry him. He was disturbed by certain changes that he noted in his wife's attitude.

Thérèse became sombre and taciturn. She no longer smothered Mme Raquin with her repentance and her grateful kisses, but instead resumed her old attitude of cold cruelty and self-centred indifference towards the paralysed woman. It was as though she had tried remorse and, when that failed to relieve her pain, had turned towards other remedies. No doubt her sadness came from her inability to find peace in her life. She looked at the cripple with a sort of contempt, like some useless object that could not even serve to console her any longer. She attended to her as little as possible, short of letting her die of hunger. From that moment on, she dragged herself around the house, silent and depressed; and she started to go out more often, staying away as many as four or five times a week.

These changes surprised and alarmed Laurent. He thought that remorse was taking a new form in Thérèse and coming out as this bored melancholy that he noticed in her. This boredom seemed to him far more disquieting than the despairing chatter that she had previously heaped on him. She no longer said anything, she did not argue with him, she seemed to keep everything locked up deep inside her. He would have preferred to hear her exhausting her suffering than to see her turned in on herself in this way. He was afraid that the anxiety would one day be too much for her and that, to relieve her feelings, she would go and tell everything to a priest or a magistrate.

At this, Thérèse's frequent excursions took on a disturbing meaning for him. He thought that she must be looking for a confidant outside and was preparing to betray him. Twice, he tried to follow her, but lost her in the street. He began to keep watch on her once again. An obsession took hold of him: Thérèse was going to reveal everything, pushed to extremes by her suffering, and he had to gag her, to stifle the confession in her throat.

XXXI

One morning, Laurent, instead of going up to his studio, settled down at a wine shop, which occupied one of the corners of the Rue Guénégaud, opposite the arcade. From there he began to study the people who were coming out on to the pavement of the Rue Mazarine. He was looking out for Thérèse. The evening before, the young woman had said that she would be going out early and that she would probably not be back until evening.

Laurent waited a full half-hour. He knew that his wife always took the Rue Mazarine, but for a moment he was afraid that she had evaded him by going down the Rue de Seine. He thought of going back to the arcade and hiding in the alleyway right beside the house. Just as he was getting impatient, he saw Thérèse quickly emerging from the arcade. She was dressed in light colours and, for the first time, he noticed that she was done up like a street-walker, with a long train. She was mincing along the pavement in a provocative manner, looking at the men and lifting up the front of her skirt, taking it in her hands, so that she was showing the front of her legs, her laced boots and her white stockings. She went up the Rue Mazarine. Laurent followed.

The weather was mild and the young woman walked slowly, her head a little thrown back, her hair hanging down her back.

Men who had looked at her as she came towards them turned round to see her from behind. She went down the Rue de l'École-de-Médecine.[1] Laurent was terrified: he knew that there was a police station somewhere around here and thought to himself that there was no longer any doubt about it, his wife was definitely going to turn him in. So he vowed to rush over and grab her if she went through the door of the police station, to beg her, beat her and force her to keep silent. At one street corner, she looked at a constable going past, and Laurent dreaded seeing her go up to the man, so he hid in a doorway, fearful suddenly that he would be arrested on the spot if he showed himself. For him, the walk was a real torment: while his wife was sauntering along the pavement in the sunshine, carefree and shameless, her skirts trailing, here he was following her, pale and trembling, thinking that it was all over, there was no escape, he was for the guillotine. Every step she took seemed to him a step nearer his punishment. Fear gave him a sort of blind certainty, which every one of the young woman's actions only served to increase. He followed her, going where she went, as a man goes to the scaffold.

Suddenly, coming out on to the former Place Saint-Michel, Thérèse headed towards a café that was then on the corner of the Rue Monsieur-le-Prince.[2] She sat down in the middle of a group of women and students at one of the tables on the street. She greeted all these people as friends, shaking their hands. Then she ordered an absinthe.

She appeared to be at her ease, talking to a young, fair-haired man who had probably been waiting there some time for her. Two girls came and leaned over the table where she was sitting, and started to talk familiarly to her in their husky voices. Around her were women smoking cigarettes and men kissing women openly on the street, in front of passers-by who did not even bother to turn round. Laurent, standing motionless under a doorway on the far side of the street, could hear their coarse laughs and swear words.

When Thérèse had finished her absinthe, she got up, took the arm of the fair-haired man and set off down the Rue de la Harpe. Laurent followed them to the Rue Saint-André-des-Arts.

There, he saw them go into a lodging-house. He stayed there in the middle of the street looking up towards the front of the house. His wife appeared for a moment at an open window on the second floor; then he thought he could see the fair-haired young man's hands taking her around the waist. The window clanged shut.

Laurent understood. Without waiting any longer, he set off calmly, happy and reassured.

'Huh!' he said, as he walked back towards the Seine. 'That's better. This way at least she has something to do and won't get up to mischief. She's a lot smarter than I am.'

What astonished him was that he had not been the first to have the idea of relapsing into vice. He could have found a cure there for his terrors. He had not thought of it, because his flesh was dead and he no longer felt the slightest desire for debauchery. His wife's infidelity left him entirely unmoved; he experienced no revulsion of the blood or the nerves at the idea of her in the arms of another man. On the contrary, it amused him: he felt as though he had been following the wife of some acquaintance and chuckled at the trick that she was playing on her husband. Thérèse had become so much a stranger to him that she no longer had any place in his heart; he would have sold and delivered her to another man a hundred times for the sake of an hour's peace.

He started to stroll along, enjoying the sudden, pleasant feeling of having switched from anxiety to calm. He was almost grateful to his wife for going to join a lover when he had thought she was on her way to the police. He was pleasantly surprised by the unexpected outcome of this adventure. What was most clear to him in all this was that he had been wrong to worry, and that he ought to indulge in a little vice himself to see if it might not relieve him by drowning out his thoughts.

That evening when he got back to the shop, Laurent decided that he would ask his wife for a few thousand francs and go to any length to get them out of her. It occurred to him that vice is expensive for a man, and he felt vaguely envious of women, who can sell themselves. He waited patiently for Thérèse, who was not yet back. When she did come in, he tackled her gently and said nothing of spying on her that morning. She was a little drunk and her clothes, carelessly buttoned, gave off the rancid smell of tobacco and liquor that hangs around bars. Tired out, her face blotchy, she could hardly stand on her feet, heavy with the shameful exhaustion of her day.

There was silence at the table; Thérèse did not eat. At dessert, Laurent put his elbows up and asked point blank for five thousand francs.

'No,' she answered drily. 'If I gave you a chance, you'd ruin us . . . Don't you know how things stand? We're heading straight for penury as it is.'

'Perhaps we are,' he replied calmly. 'I don't care. I want money.'

'No, a thousand times no! You've left your job, we're not making anything from the haberdashery, and we're not going to be able to live off the income from my dowry. Every day, I have to break into the savings to feed you and give you the hundred francs a month that you squeezed out of me. You won't have anything more, do you understand? There's no point in asking.'

'Just think a moment, and don't refuse me like that. I'm telling you, I want five thousand francs, and I'll have them. You'll give them to me, whatever you say.'

This placid obstinacy infuriated Thérèse and completed her intoxication.

'Oh, now I understand!' she yelled. 'You want to finish as you started. We've been keeping you for four years. You only came here to eat and drink and since then you've been living off us. His Highness does nothing, his Highness has contrived to live at my expense, with his arms folded. No, you won't have anything, not a penny. Do you want me to tell you what you are? Well, I will. You're a . . .'[3]

She said it. Laurent shrugged his shoulders and began to laugh, replying merely:

'You've picked up some nice words from the company you're keeping nowadays.'

This was the only reference he chose to make to Thérèse's adultery. She looked up sharply and said, in a bitter voice:

'In any case, I'm not mixing with murderers.'

Laurent went very pale. For a moment he stayed silent, staring at his wife, then he said, in a trembling voice:

'Listen here, my girl, let's not row with each other. It won't do either of us any good. I'm at the end of my tether. It would be a good idea if we made a deal, if we don't want something dreadful to happen. I asked you for five thousand francs because I need it. I might even tell you that I'm thinking of using the money to make sure we have a quiet life.'

He gave an odd smile and went on:

'Now, think and give me your final word.'

'I've thought it all through,' the young woman replied. 'As I told you, you won't get a sou.'

Her husband jumped to his feet. She was afraid he would beat her and hunched up, determined not to give way to his blows. But Laurent did not even go near her; he just said coldly that he was tired of life and that he was going to the local police station to tell them all about the murder.

'You're driving me to the limit,' he said. 'You're making my life unbearable. I'd rather have done with it. We'll both be tried and condemned. That's it.'

'Do you think you're frightening me?' his wife shouted. 'I'm as sick of it as you are. I'm the one who's going to the police, if you don't. Oh, yes! I'm ready to follow you to the scaffold, I won't be such a coward as you. Come on, let's go to the police station.'

She had got up and was already walking towards the stairs.

'That's right,' Laurent stammered. 'We'll go together.'

When they were down in the shop, they looked at one another, anxious and afraid. It felt as though someone had just pinned them to the ground. The few seconds that it had taken to come down the wooden staircase had been enough to show them, in a flash, what would happen if they confessed. At one and the same time, they saw the gendarmes, prison, the assizes and the guillotine – all at once and clearly. In their hearts, they felt weak, they were tempted to fall on their knees and beg each other to stay, not to reveal anything. Fear and confusion kept them there, motionless and silent for two or three minutes. Thérèse was the first to speak and give way.

'After all,' she said, 'it's very silly of me to argue over the money. You'll manage to squander it all for me one day or another. I might as well give it to you straight away.'

She made no further attempt to disguise her defeat. She sat down at the counter and signed an order for five thousand francs, which Laurent could cash at a bank. There was no further talk of police commissioners that evening.

As soon as Laurent had the money in his pocket, he got drunk, went out with girls and embarked on a noisy, riotous existence. He spent nights away from home, slept during the day and stayed up late, looking for excitement and trying to escape from reality. All he managed to do was to make himself more depressed. When people were yelling and shouting all around, he could hear the great silence inside him; when a woman was kissing him or when he emptied his glass, he found nothing in his intoxication but melancholy and sadness. He was no longer able to indulge in lust and gluttony: his being had cooled and, as it were, gone hard inside; food and kisses only irritated him. Sickened before he began, he could not manage to arouse his imagination, to excite his senses and his stomach. The more he drove himself to debauchery, the more he suffered, and that was that. Then, when he got home and saw Mme Raquin and Thérèse, his lassitude gave way to frightful attacks of terror. He swore that he would not go out any more, but stick with his suffering, get used to it and overcome it.

Thérèse for her part went out less and less often. For a month, she lived as Laurent did, on the pavements and in cafés. She would come back for a moment in the evening, give Mme Raquin something to eat, put her to bed, then go out again until morning. On one occasion, she and her husband went for four days without seeing one another. Then she felt a profound sense of repulsion and realized that vice was not doing her any more good than the pretence of remorse. In vain had she visited all the lodging-houses of the Latin Quarter, in vain had she led an indecent and dissolute life. Her nerves were shattered; debauchery and physical pleasure no longer gave her a strong enough shock to bring oblivion. She was like one of those drunkards whose palate is burned out and who remains indifferent even to the fire of the strongest liquors. Lust left her unmoved and she no longer sought anything from her lovers except boredom and exhaustion. So she would leave them, telling them that she had no further use for them. She was seized with a desperate laziness that kept her in the house, in a stained petticoat, her hair undone, her face and hands unwashed. She found forgetfulness in filth.

When the two murderers were face to face like this, tired out, having exhausted all means to save themselves from each other, they realized that they no longer had the strength to fight. Debauchery had rejected them and cast them back on their anguish. They found themselves once more in the dark, damp house in the arcade, where from now on they were more or less imprisoned, because, often though they had tried for salvation, they had never managed to break the bloody chain that bound them together. They no longer even dreamed of achieving this impossible feat. They felt so driven, crushed and linked by circumstances that they realized any attempt at rebellion would be ridiculous. They resumed their life together, but their hatred became fury.

The evening rows began again. In fact, the blows and shouts lasted throughout the day. Mistrust was added to hatred and this mistrust finally drove them mad.

They were afraid of one another. The scene that followed Laurent's demand for five thousand francs was soon being replayed morning and evening. They had an obsession with betraying one another. They could not escape from it. When one of them spoke a word or made a movement, the other imagined that he or she was planning to go to the commissioner of police. At that they would fight or plead with one another. In their anger, they would shout that they were going to reveal all and terrified one another to death; then they trembled, humiliated themselves and promised, with bitter tears, to keep silent. They suffered terribly, but did not feel brave enough to cure their ills by putting a hot iron on the wound. When they threatened to confess to the crime, it was only to scare each other and to drive the thought away, because they would never have found the strength to speak and to look for peace in punishment.

More than twenty times, they went as far as the door of the police station, one following the other. Sometimes it was Laurent who wanted to confess to the murder, sometimes it was Thérèse who would hurry to give herself up. And they always met again in the street, deciding to wait a little longer, after exchanging insults and earnest entreaties.

Each new crisis would leave them more suspicious and afraid. They spied on one another, from morning to evening. Laurent no longer left the house in the arcade and Thérèse would not let him go out alone. Their mutual suspicion and their terror of admitting their guilt brought them together in an awful union. Never since they were married had they lived so closely together and never had they suffered so much. But despite the pain that they inflicted, they never took their eyes off one another, preferring to put up with the most agonizing torments rather than be apart for an hour. If Thérèse went down to the shop, Laurent would follow her, afraid that she might talk to a customer. If Laurent was standing at the door, watching the people going up and down the arcade, Thérèse would stand next to him to make sure that he did not speak to anyone. On Thursday evening, when the guests were there, the murderers would exchange pleading looks, and listen with terror to what the other was saying, each expecting a confession from his or her accomplice and discovering compromising meanings in every new sentence the other began.

This state of war could not go on for much longer.

It got to the point where both Thérèse and Laurent, separately, dreamed of escaping by means of a new crime from the consequences of their first one. It was essential for one of them to disappear for the other to enjoy a measure of peace. This idea occurred to them both at the same time: both felt the pressing need for separation and both wanted that separation to be eternal. The murder that they were each thinking about seemed natural to them, inevitable, a necessary consequence of the murder of Camille. They did not even discuss it, they just accepted the scheme as their only salvation. Laurent decided that he would kill Thérèse, because Thérèse was getting in his way, because she could destroy him with a word and because she caused him unbearable misery. Thérèse made up her mind to kill Laurent for the same reasons.

This firm decision to murder calmed them a little. They made their plans. As it happens, they were acting impulsively, without taking many precautions; they were only vaguely thinking about the probable consequences of a murder committed without taking into consideration the need for flight and protection against repercussions. They felt an imperious need to kill one another and obeyed this need like wild animals. They would not have given themselves up for their first crime, which they had so skilfully concealed, yet they were risking the guillotine by committing a second one and not even considering how to hide it. They were not even aware of this contradiction in their behaviour. They told themselves simply that if they did manage to escape, they would go and live abroad after taking all the money. Over a period of a fortnight to three weeks, Thérèse had withdrawn the few thousand francs that remained of her dowry and was keeping them locked up in a drawer, which Laurent knew about. They did not for an instant consider what would happen to Mme Raquin.

A few weeks earlier, Laurent had met one of his old school-friends, who was now an assistant to a famous chemist much concerned with toxicology. This friend had shown him round the laboratory where he worked, pointing out the equipment and identifying the drugs. One evening, when he had made up his mind to murder and Thérèse was drinking a glass of sugar water in front of him, Laurent remembered having seen a little stone flask in the laboratory containing prussic acid. Recalling what the young assistant had told him about the terrible effects of this poison, which strikes its victims down, leaving few traces, he decided that this was the poison he needed. The next day, he managed to get away, went to see his friend and, while his back was turned, stole the little stone flask.

The same day, Thérèse took advantage of Laurent's absence to sharpen a large kitchen knife that they used to crush sugar and which was quite blunt. She hid the knife in a corner of the sideboard.

XXXII

The following Thursday, the evening at the Raquins' (as their guests continued to call the family), was an especially merry one. It went on until half past eleven. As he was leaving, Grivet said that he had never spent such an agreeable few hours.

Suzanne, who was pregnant, spoke constantly to Thérèse about her pains and joys. Thérèse appeared to be listening with much interest; with staring eyes and tight lips, she would bend her head forward from time to time and her lowered eyelids cast a shadow across her whole face. Laurent for his part was paying close attention to the stories of Old Michaud and Olivier. These gentlemen had an unfailing fund of anecdotes and Grivet managed only with difficulty to get a word in between two sentences from the father and son. In any case, he had some respect for them and considered them good talkers. That evening, talk had replaced games and he gauchely announced that he found the former police commissioner's conversation almost as amusing as a game of dominoes.

In the more than four years that the Michauds and Grivet had spent Thursday evenings at the Raquins', they had not once grown tired of these monotonous evenings, which returned with infuriating regularity. As they entered, they had never for a moment suspected the drama that was being played out in this house, so peaceful and so mild. Olivier would commonly remark, in a policeman's joke, that the dining room had 'a whiff of honesty' about it. Grivet, not to be outdone, called it the Temple of Peace. Recently, on two or three occasions, Thérèse had explained the bruises on her face by telling her guests that she had fallen over. In any case, none of them would have recognized the signs of Laurent's fist. They were convinced that their hosts' family was a model one, all sweetness and love.

The paralysed woman no longer attempted to reveal the infamous truth behind the dreary tranquillity of their Thursday evenings. Watching the murderers tearing into one another and guessing the crisis that was bound to erupt one day or another, as the inevitable result of the chain of events, she soon realized that the situation would resolve itself without her help. From then on, she remained calm and allowed the consequences of Camille's murder, which would kill the murderers in their turn, to take their natural course. She merely begged heaven to leave her enough life to witness the violent outcome that she foresaw. Her last wish was to feast her eyes on the spectacle of the ultimate suffering that would destroy Thérèse and Laurent.

That evening, Grivet sat down beside her and talked at length, filling in the questions and answers as he usually did. But he could not even get a glance out of her. When half past eleven struck, the guests got up briskly.

'We're so happy here,' Grivet said, 'that we never consider leaving.'

'The fact is,' Michaud added, 'that I'm never sleepy here, though my usual bedtime is half past nine.'

Olivier thought it was time for his little joke.

'You see,' he said, exhibiting his yellow teeth, 'there's a whiff of honesty hereabouts, that's why we're so happy.'

Grivet, annoyed that Olivier had got in first, declaimed with an expansive gesture: 'This room is the Temple of Peace.'

Meanwhile, knotting the ribbons on her bonnet, Suzanne said to Thérèse: 'I'll be here tomorrow at nine.'

'No,' the young woman replied, quickly. 'Don't come until the afternoon. I'll probably go out in the morning.'

She spoke in an odd, anxious voice. She accompanied her guests into the passage; Laurent came down, too, with a lamp in his hand. When they were alone, the couple gave a sigh of relief; they must have been suffering a vague feeling of impatience the whole evening. Since the previous day, they had been in a more sombre mood and were behaving more anxiously. They avoided looking at one another and went back upstairs in silence. Their hands were twitching convulsively and Laurent had to put the lamp down on the table to avoid dropping it.

Before putting Mme Raquin to bed, they were in the habit of tidying up the dining room, getting a glass of sugar water for the night and coming and going around the cripple, until everything was prepared. But that evening, when they came back up, they sat down for a moment, staring into space and pale-lipped. After a moment's silence, Laurent seemed to start, as though coming out of a dream, and asked: 'Well, then! Aren't we going to bed?'

'Yes, yes, we're going to bed,' Thérèse replied shivering, as though feeling very cold.

She got up and took the water jug.

'Leave it!' her husband shouted, trying to control his voice. 'I'll make the sugar water. You look after your aunt.'

He took the jug out of his wife's hands and filled a glass with water. Then, half turning away, he emptied the little stone flask into it and added a piece of sugar. While this was going on, Thérèse was crouching in front of the sideboard. She had taken the kitchen knife and was trying to slip it into one of the large pockets hanging from her belt.

At that moment, the strange sensation that warns one of the approach of danger made the couple instinctively turn round. They looked at one another. Thérèse saw the flask in Laurent's hands and Laurent saw the silver flash of the knife shining in the folds of Thérèse's dress. For a few seconds, silently, coldly, they stared at one another, the husband beside the table, the wife crouching next to the sideboard. They understood. Each one felt a cold chill on discovering that they had both had the same thought. As they mutually read their secret plans on their devastated faces, they felt pity and horror for themselves and each other.

Mme Raquin, sensing that the end was nigh, was watching them with a keen stare.

And, suddenly, Thérèse and Laurent burst into tears. A supreme crisis overwhelmed them and drove them into each other's arms, as weak as children. They felt as though something soft and loving had awoken in their breasts. They wept, without speaking, thinking of the degraded life they had led, and that they would continue to lead, if they were cowards enough to go on living. So, remembering the past, they felt so weary and sickened by themselves, that they had a vast need for rest, for oblivion. They looked at each other one last time, with a look of gratitude, considering the knife and the glass of poison. Thérèse took the glass, half emptied it and handed it to Laurent, who finished it in a gulp. It was like a shaft of lightning. They fell, one on top of the other, struck down, finding consolation at last in death. The young woman's mouth fell against the scar on her husband's neck left by Camille's teeth.

The bodies stayed throughout the night on the dining-room floor, twisted, arched and lit by the streaks of yellowish light cast by the shade of the lamp. And for nearly twelve hours, until the following day around noon, Mme Raquin, silent and unmoving, stared at them where they lay at her feet, unable to have enough of the spectacle, crushing them with her merciless gaze.

Notes

PREFACE TO THE SECOND EDITION (1868)

1. *temperament, not character*: See Introduction, pp. xxvi–xxvii.
2. *compelled to call their 'remorse'*: See Introduction, p. xxix.
3. *the back stage*: The accusation of hypocrisy had been made in similar terms by the Goncourts in the Preface to *Germinie Lacerteux*: the public, they said, 'likes saucy little books, the memoirs of whores, bedroom confessions, erotic filth . . .'
4. *two or three men who can read, understand and judge a book*: Zola is thinking in particular of the critics Hippolyte Taine and Charles-Augustin Sainte-Beuve.
5. *to the background of a novel*: Taine, in a letter early in 1868, makes comparisons with Shakespeare, Dickens and Balzac, as well as criticisms which are very similar to the ones that Zola mentions: 'a book should always be, more or less, a portrait of the whole, a mirror to an entire society . . . You need to enlarge your framework and balance your effects.' (Quoted in the Petits Classiques Larousse edition of *Thérèse Raquin* (see Further Reading), p. 441.)
6. *'putrid literature'*: A reference to the review of *Thérèse Raquin* in *Le Figaro*, 23 January 1868, by Louis Ulbach (see Introduction, p. xiii).

CHAPTER I

1. *Passage du Pont-Neuf . . . Rue Mazarine . . . Rue de Seine*: 'You describe the Passage du Pont-Neuf,' Sainte-Beuve said in his letter to Zola (10 June 1868). 'I know this arcade as well as anyone . . . [it is] flat, banal, ugly and, above all, narrow, but it does not possess the deeply melancholy colour and the Rembrandtesque shades that you ascribe to it . . .' The arcade in question is on the Left Bank of the Seine, but in 1912 it was rebuilt and renamed Rue Jacques-Callot. The Rue Mazarine, a street leading towards

NOTES

the river, forms a junction with the eastern end of the Rue Saint-André-des-Arts. The Rue de Seine runs from the Quai Malaquais to the Boulevard Saint-Germain, at right angles to the Passage du Pont-Neuf.

2.   *fifteen sous*: The unit of currency was the franc, divided into a hundred centimes. A sou was worth five centimes, but in the plural the word was (and still is) commonly used to mean a small amount of money. Five francs was worth about one American dollar or four English shillings (one-fifth of a pound sterling).

CHAPTER II

1.   *Vernon*: A small town in Normandy on the Seine.
2.   *Algeria*: The French conquest of Algeria began in 1830 and was more or less complete by the time this novel was written, though, as one can see from the fate of Captain Degans, it was not an entirely safe posting for the army. The country became an important colony with a large population of settlers from around the Mediterranean, and was to remain French until the war of independence (1954–62). It forms the background to travel writings and novels, and is frequently mentioned in nineteenth-century literature.

CHAPTER III

1.   *the Orléans Railway Company*: One of five railway companies in France, set up in 1838, it had its headquarters in the Gare d'Orléans, now the Gare d'Austerlitz, which was rebuilt in 1867–8.
2.   *from the Institut to the Jardin des Plantes*: The Institut is the building housing the five former royal academies, including the Académie Française. It moved to this building on the Left Bank of the Seine in 1806. The Jardin des Plantes is the botanical garden founded in 1635, which had the great scientist Georges-Louis Buffon (see note 4, below) as superintendent during the eighteenth century, when it was known as the Jardin du Roi. In 1792 it acquired a menagerie and in the following year the Museum of Natural History was set up in the garden, close to the Gare d'Orléans.
3.   *Port aux Vins*: Situated on the Quai Saint-Bernard, where wine was offloaded on its way to the wine market, the Halle aux Vins, was in the area between the Rue Jussieu and the Quai Saint-Bernard, now occupied by the Faculty of Sciences of the Universities of Paris VI and VII.

4.   *Buffon*: Georges-Louis Leclerc, Comte de Buffon (1707–88) (see
     note 2, above), was also the author of a 36-volume natural history
     covering cosmology, geology, zoology and botany, which was
     virtually an encyclopaedia of the scientific knowledge of his time.
5.   *the History of the Consulate and the Empire by Thiers and
     Lamartine's History of the Girondins*: The historian Adolphe
     Thiers (1797–1877) was the author of authoritative works on
     both the Revolution and the period of Napoleon I's rule. The
     poet Alphonse de Lamartine (1790–1869) published his history
     of the revolutionary faction of the Girondins in 1847. Both men
     were opponents of the regime of Napoleon III.

CHAPTER V

1.   *Jeufosse*: A small town built around an island upriver from
     Vernon.
2.   *sanguine beauty*: From the start, Zola stresses that Laurent's tem-
     perament is sanguine (as opposed to bilious, nervous or lymphatic
     (see Introduction, p. xxvi)). The physical description of Laurent
     corresponds to a person of sanguine type and the association of the
     colour red with him reinforces it.

CHAPTER VI

1.   *Rue Saint-Victor*: The Rue Saint-Victor runs across the angle
     formed by the meeting of the Rue Monge and the Rue des Écoles.
     Zola had a room in the Rue Saint-Victor during his first years in
     Paris.
2.   *gloria*: A sugared coffee or tea with brandy or rum.

CHAPTER VII

1.   *called each other 'tu'*: Using the familiar second-person singular
     form of the verb.
2.   *a sort of diabolical trance*: For the first time, the cat François is
     given some of the sinister attributes that make him such a memor-
     able presence in the novel.

CHAPTER IX

1.   *La Pitié*: The Hospice de la Pitié in the Rue Lacépède was not far
     from the Rue Saint-Victor. It was built in 1612, originally as a
     hostel for the homeless, and was later used as an orphanage. In
     1809, it became a general hospital attached to the Hôtel-Dieu,
     staffed by the nuns of Sainte-Marthe. It was demolished in 1912.

CHAPTER XI

1. *Saint-Ouen or Asnières*: Two towns north of Paris on the Seine, which were popular sites for weekend/day excursions. A number of painters also worked or relaxed here, including Édouard Manet.

2. *fortifications*: Paris was surrounded by an inner city wall, which chiefly served for customs purposes and to mark the administrative boundary of the city. In 1840, under Louis-Philippe, the fortifications were rebuilt both as a protection for the city and to mark its boundary, along the line of the present *boulevards extérieurs*. Beyond them was a so-called military zone, which was wasteland that no one was allowed to build on.

3. *aspens and oaks*: François-Marie Mourad, in his edition of the novel (see Further Reading), points out the similarities between the landscape described here and Édouard Manet's painting *Le Déjeuner sur l'herbe*, as well as other paintings, including Claude Monet's study for a painting, also called *Le Déjeuner sur l'herbe* (pp. 376–8).

4. *the Tuileries*: The gardens in Paris laid out by Le Nôtre in 1649, a classic example of a French formal garden, usually opposed to the more 'natural' style favoured by the English. It is not clear why Camille should think of the Tuileries as an English garden (though a painting by Manet, *La Musique aux Tuileries* (1862), does show a crowded scene in a relatively informal, almost woodland setting).

CHAPTER XIII

1. *the Morgue*: Situated after 1863 at the eastern point of the Île Saint-Louis, where it was moved from the end of the Pont Saint-Michel, on the Île de la Cité, where it was to be found at the time when the novel is set. Here unidentified bodies were kept for three days, behind a glass screen, under cold running water, to delay the process of decay. The description in Adolphe Joanne's *Paris illustré en 1878* (Paris: Hachette, 1878), pp. 921–4, corresponds well to that given by Zola in the novel. Joanne concludes by saying

> despite the horror of the spectacle and the customary respect of the people of Paris for death, it is not unusual to find a more or less solid crowd in the Morgue of men, women and children from the lower ranks of society. When the newspapers announce the

discovery of some crime, curious people arrive in large numbers, making a queue from morning until evening that sometimes reaches the number of between 1,000 and 1,500 persons.

2. *like a necklace of shadow*: Several writers have commented on the similarity of this description of the hanged girl to Manet's painting *Olympia* (where the girl is wearing a black velvet choker around her neck).

CHAPTER XVI

1. *her temperament*: At the start, Thérèse appears to be passive by nature. Her affair with Laurent has brought out her repressed, passionate nature, while the aftermath of Camille's death is accentuating the nervous element in her.
2. *the Salon*: The official exhibition of painting and sculpture (see Introduction, p. xix).
3. *Bacchante*: A female follower of the god Bacchus, whose devotees were driven mad by wine. This theme from classical mythology would be a typical motif for a painting at the Salon.

CHAPTER XVIII

1. *her organism demanded Laurent's violent embrace*: Thérèse, with her nervous temperament, needs the complement of Laurent's animal and sanguine one.

CHAPTER XX

1. *Belleville*: A working-class district in the north-east of Paris.
2. *the Code*: Weddings in France may consist in a religious service, but must include a civil ceremony, conducted by the Mayor of the *commune* or *arrondissement* in which they take place. As part of the ceremony, the Mayor reads out the sections of the Civil Code relating to marriage.

CHAPTER XXI

1. *looking pale*: Zola continues to insist on Thérèse's pale colouring, characteristic of a person of nervous temperament.

CHAPTER XXII

1. *nervous erethism*: A medical term meaning a state of nervous hysteria or overexcitement. The use of such medical vocabulary shows Zola trying to back up his study of character with the latest scientific understanding of human psychology. As he shows here,

temperament was not thought to be fixed: after the shock of Camille's murder, Laurent's sanguine nature is becoming more nervous, like Thérèse's, while she is moving into a state of hysterical hyper-nervousness.

2. *a time of perfect living*: The ideal situation for an individual was to achieve a balance between the temperaments, especially between the nervous and sanguine elements in his or her nature.

3. *His remorse was purely physical*: Zola, who was a non-believer, was keen to emphasize that the Christian idea of conscience had no part to play in the story: the awful terrors experienced by Laurent and Thérèse are not a result of Christian remorse, but a physiological reaction to circumstances, including fear of the consequences of their crime.

4. *hysteria*: Another medical term, to describe an affliction that was particularly associated at the time with women. Thérèse has communicated her feminine disease to Laurent and he has become more of a 'woman' now that his sanguine temperament has been altered to a nervous one.

CHAPTER XXV

1. *a tasteful pallor*: Another sign of the change in Laurent's temperament is that he has lost his ruddy, sanguine complexion, as well as his fleshy face and coarse manner.

2. *neurosis*: Zola subscribed to the belief that art came from a kind of disorder of the nervous system.

CHAPTER XXVI

1. *dumb and immobile*: Mme Raquin recalls the paralysed M. Noirtier in Alexandre Dumas's *The Count of Monte Cristo* (1844–5), who also plays a key role in the mechanics of the plot of that novel, even though he cannot move or speak. In Noirtier's case, however, he has a willing and sensitive interpreter in the person of his niece, to whom he communicates by moving his eyebrow.

2. *buried ... under two or three metres of soil*: Edgar Allan Poe's *Tales of Mystery and Imagination*, including 'The Premature Burial', were translated into French by Charles Baudelaire between 1848 and 1865. The American writer became even more popular in France than in his own country. His interest in morbid psychological states provided a link between the Gothic novel of the Romantic period and the taste for the macabre in the 'decadent' later years of the century.

CHAPTER XXX

1. *cold of the instrument on his neck*: Reminding him of the blade of the guillotine.

CHAPTER XXXI

1. *Rue de l'École-de-Médecine*: The street that more or less continues the line of the Rue Mazarine on the far side of what is now the Boulevard Saint-Germain.
2. *Rue Monsieur-le-Prince*: The streets in this part of Paris were changing as a result of Haussmann's rebuilding programme, but it is clear that Thérèse has turned up the Boulevard Saint-Michel and headed towards the Luxembourg Gardens.
3. *'You're a . . .'*: The missing word presumably is 'pimp'.

THE STORY OF PENGUIN CLASSICS

Before 1946 ...'Classics' are mainly the domain of academics and students, without readable editions for everyone else. This all changes when a little-known classicist, E. V. Rieu, presents Penguin founder Allen Lane with the translation of Homer's *Odyssey* that he has been working on and reading to his wife Nelly in his spare time.

1946 *The Odyssey* becomes the first Penguin Classic published, and promptly sells three million copies. Suddenly, classic books are no longer for the privileged few.

1950s Rieu, now series editor, turns to professional writers for the best modern, readable translations, including Dorothy L. Sayers's *Inferno* and Robert Graves's *The Twelve Caesars*, which revives the salacious original.

1960s The Classics are given the distinctive black jackets that have remained a constant throughout the series's various looks. Rieu retires in 1964, hailing the Penguin Classics list as 'the greatest educative force of the 20th century'.

1970s A new generation of translators arrives to swell the Penguin Classics ranks, and the list grows to encompass more philosophy, religion, science, history and politics.

1980s The Penguin American Library joins the Classics stable, with titles such as *The Last of the Mohicans* safeguarded. Penguin Classics now offers the most comprehensive library of world literature available.

1990s The launch of Penguin Audiobooks brings the classics to a listening audience for the first time, and in 1999 the launch of the Penguin Classics website takes them online to a larger global readership than ever before.

The 21st Century Penguin Classics are rejacketed for the first time in nearly twenty years. This world famous series now consists of more than 1300 titles, making the widest range of the best books ever written available to millions – and constantly redefining the meaning of what makes a 'classic'.

The Odyssey continues ...

The best books ever written

PENGUIN 🐧 CLASSICS

SINCE 1946

Find out more at www.penguinclassics.com